He'd come to save her.

Caros pulled Pelonia into his arms. "Are you all right?" She buried her cheek against his chest.

He held her while she shivered and trembled. For timeless moments, he rubbed her back until the tremors subsided.

Caros cupped her face and tipped her head back to search for injuries. He ran the pad of his thumb over the shallow cut on her throat. Thankfully, the wound no longer bled. The image of a blade held so close to her jugular would never leave him.

He angled the torch for a better view of her ashen face. "It's over now. They won't find us. Can you walk or shall I carry you home?"

"Home?" Her eyes filled with fat tears. "I have no home."

Caros tugged her against him again, holding her close while she sobbed. A promise to free her and help find her family sprang to the tip of his tongue.

No. His arms tightened around her. She was his. He couldn't let her go….

CARLA CAPSHAW

Florida native Carla Capshaw is a preacher's kid who grew up grateful for her Christian home and loving family. Always dreaming of being a writer and world traveler, she followed her wanderlust around the globe, including a year spent in the People's Republic of China, before beginning work on her first novel.

A two-time RWA Golden Heart Award winner, Carla loves passionate stories with compelling, nearly impossible conflicts. She's found Inspirational Historical Romance is the perfect vehicle to combine lush settings, vivid characters and a Christian worldview. Currently at work on her next manuscript for Steeple Hill Love Inspired Historical, she still lives in Florida, but is always planning her next trip…and plotting her next story.

Carla loves to hear from readers. To contact her, visit www.carlacapshaw.com, or write to Carla@carlacapshaw.com.

Carla Capshaw
THE GLADIATOR

Steeple
Hill®

Published by Steeple Hill Books™

STEEPLE HILL BOOKS

Steeple
Hill®

Recycling programs
for this product may
not exist in your area.

ISBN-13: 978-0-373-82824-1

THE GLADIATOR

Copyright © 2009 by Carla Hughes

www.SteepleHill.com

Printed in U.S.A.

And we know that in all things God works for the good of those who love Him, who have been called according to His purpose.

—*Romans* 8:28

Dedicated to:

My son, Deverell—my best blessing.

My parents, for their constant love and
encouragement.

My sister, Nikki. A talented, savvy woman-of-all-
trades. You're the best friend a girl could have.

My critique partners, Sheila Raye,
Paisley Kirkpatrick, Stacey Kayne and Jean Mason.
What would I do without you? Thank you for
not only reading my stuff, but for being amazing
friends who also happen to be awesome writers.

My agent, Michelle Grajkowski of Three Seas
Literary, for believing in me even when I insisted
on writing "unpopular" time periods.

My editor, Melissa Endlich, for taking a chance on
a new author. Your patience with this newbie won't
be forgotten.

And last, but most, thank you, Lord. You never fail
me. Your inspiration is endless.

Chapter One

Less than a day's journey from Rome, 81 AD

"Look around you, Niece. The gods are punishing you."

Pelonia raised tear-swollen eyes from her beloved father's lifeless face. From where she sat on the ground, her uncle Marcus towered over her, his mouth twisted in a snarl of contempt. Blood oozed from a gash at his temple.

Dazed by his cruel words, she watched him limp toward the torched wagons and pillaged tents of their once wealthy camp. Black smoke stretched toward the heavens. Its sharp stench singed her nostrils, burning her lungs until the fetid air promised to choke her.

Her father's head in her lap, Pelonia stroked his weathered cheek with trembling fingers. Was Uncle Marcus right? Was she being punished? Had her father been wrong to reject the old ways and teach his household to embrace the Christ?

Everywhere she looked, destruction sweltered in the morning's rising heat. All of her family's accompanying servants lay massacred along both sides of the stone-paved road. Only she and Marcus survived.

Pelonia looked toward the cloudless sky. Birds of prey circled overhead. Their hungry cries echoed in the stillness, mocking her as though they sensed she would join the corpses before she had time to bury them.

On the horizon, a cloud of dust marked the direction of their attackers' retreat. The marauders had struck before first light. She'd heard their battle cry from downstream where she'd sneaked away to bathe in private. By the time she ran back to camp, they'd taken flight. The demon's spawn had stolen everything of value—animals, spices meant as a gift for her cousin's wedding in Rome, and chests packed with rare purple cloth.

Worst of all, they'd murdered her father.

A wail of anguish rose in her throat, but she bit her lip to keep from surrendering to her grief. Her father would want her to be strong. She couldn't bear to disappoint him. Instead, she bent over his precious body and buried her face in his tunic, begging her Lord to restore his life, just as He had once done for Lazarus.

Long moments passed. No miracle came from heaven, only silence.

She sat up and brushed the graying hair from his brow. Bowing her head, she rocked gently, clinging to her composure when pain threatened her sanity.

God, oh God, her heart cried out. *How could You allow this? Why have You forsaken me when I have served You from my earliest days?*

Her uncle's hulking shadow loomed above her. "Hurry up, girl. There's nothing more we can do here."

Pelonia's head snapped up. "We can't leave our dead exposed! Already the vultures circle above us. Soon the wolves will come. Will you have our loved ones ravaged by both fowl and beast?"

Marcus kicked a rock with his sandaled foot. "I care not. I didn't pretend death and elude our attackers to die of thirst in this glaring heat."

"You pretended death? How could you not aid my father or defend—"

"Cease," he growled so close to her nose his stale breath made her shudder. "Someone knocked me unconscious. When I awoke… Why should I have sacrificed my life for nothing?"

"Because it is your *duty* to defend your family. And to see the dead properly cared for."

"Don't lecture me, girl!" Color ran high across his cheekbones. "I won't suffer your guilt when all but your father have traveled to Paradise. They won't know if their flesh is left to rot, nor will they care."

Pelonia adjusted her father's tunic, wishing she had clean linen to shroud him and the others before placing them in the ground. "Father's spirit is in heaven, Uncle, as are the rest of those who've died here."

"Then their bodies are of no consequence." His upper lip curled with ill-concealed scorn. "According to your religion, your God will give them new ones."

Pelonia winced. Marcus clung to his pagan beliefs, despite her father's years of prayer and good example. She lifted her gaze and squinted at the sun glinting over his shoulder. "How can you be so cruel? Except for me, Father was your last remaining kin."

His hawkish eyes narrowed. "Pelonius is dead, but I continue to breathe. Soon scavengers will see the smoke. We won't be safe once they come to investigate. Unless you wish to join these unfortunate wretches, we must leave *now*."

"No!" She eased her father's head to the damp earth and stood, bristling with defiance. "I won't abandon him or our servants. It's indecent and disrespectful. I won't do it."

His hand jerked up to strike her, but she didn't flinch. Jaw flexing with unconcealed rage, he dropped his fist back to his side.

As though he couldn't bear the sight of her, Marcus glanced to a point down the road. Her instincts warned her to look, but she didn't dare take her eyes off her uncle. He'd proven on many occasions to be as crafty as the Evil One himself.

After a long moment, his mood shifted and much of his hostility seemed to evaporate. He gave her an odd smile. "Then you're a fool, but I'll help you bury them."

Surprised by his capitulation, she swayed on her feet, light-headed with relief. She glanced down the cypress-lined road. A single horse and rider traveled in their direction, but remained at a distance. He didn't look threatening, but wariness pricked her, instilling a new need for haste. She hoped the newcomer proved to be a friend, but after the events of the morning, strangers weren't to be trusted.

Her attention returned to Marcus. "Thank you, Uncle. I couldn't finish this sad task without you."

He grunted. "You speak the truth for certain. You're even smaller than your mother, and she was tiny as a fawn."

"I wish I'd known her." Pelonia hurried toward the charred remains of their camp. Her mother had died giving birth to her seventeen winters past. With her father taken from her, she was an orphan. The thought penetrated her mind like the point of a sword. Her head ached. Loneliness crushed her. She and her father had always been close. He'd treated her as well as any might treat a favored son, let alone a daughter.

Her steps slowed near a destroyed tent. Using a tree branch, she poked through the smoldering ruins, searching for anything that might aid with the burials.

Finally, she found the iron head of a spade, its wooden

handle nothing but ashes among the scorched stones and broken shards of pottery. With the end of the branch, she pushed the tool from the embers.

Once the metal cooled enough to touch, she picked it up and headed to the shade of an olive tree. She knelt and began to dig, breathing in the pungent aroma of rich, black earth. Here she would bury her father, her dearest friend and protector. Her chest constricted with the thought of leaving him all alone along this barren stretch of road. Silent tears streamed down her cheeks, despite her best efforts to contain them.

She licked the salty moisture from her lips and dabbed her eyes with the back of her hands. Knees sore, her lower back aching, she finished the shallow grave at last and returned to her father's body. She grasped him under his arms. He was so heavy. Her muscles strained to drag him toward the tree and place him in the grave.

As she straightened his limbs, she thanked God for blessing her with a loving parent, even as she questioned why he'd been ripped from her so brutally.

She caressed his cheek one last time, then tore away the cleanest piece of her tunic's hem. Covering his face with the linen, she choked back sobs. Her entire body shook with sorrow as she placed the dirt over his remains.

"Pelonia, are you not yet finished?"

She patted down the last handful of soil. "Yes, Uncle, I'm done."

Not far away, Marcus waited beside a shallow grave he'd dug with a second, larger shovelhead. She covered the short distance and joined him. "I'll try to be quicker and be of more help. Perhaps if you dig, I can move the bodies and cover them."

The jingle of metal and distant voices carried on the morning breeze. She glanced down the road, brushing her dark hair from her eyes to get a better view. Much closer than before, but still at a distance, the rider continued his path toward them. A large caravan followed several paces in his wake.

From her vantage point, she saw the wagons were too close for comfort. Some covered, some exposed, many were rolling cages filled with people or exotic beasts. Near-naked men, most bound in chains, walked listlessly in the glaring sun.

"A slave caravan, Uncle! We must hide until it passes."

"They won't pester me. I'm too old to be of value and my tunic verifies my rank. *You,* on the other hand, are a prize."

Pelonia blinked in disbelief. Her heart throbbed with fear. She knew slave traders legally bought and sold men, women and children at markets throughout the empire. Ravenous for profit, they often preyed on the weak, prowling the byways in search of free stock.

The morning's events had made her one of the weak. She was the daughter of a prosperous Roman citizen, but this far from home she held no proof of her status. None of her wealth remained to buy protection. Her household had been destroyed. Even her luxurious clothes had been stolen or burned, leaving her with nothing but the simple linen tunic she'd worn to the river.

The feral gleam in her uncle's eyes spread a chill across her skin. "You cannot mean to sell me."

"Why not? You're cursed. I have no wish to invoke the gods' displeasure by protecting you. Besides, I'm your guardian now that your father is gone. I have a legal right to do with you as I wish. After the robbery this morning, I need funds to see me home. You're a comely maiden and will fetch a fair price."

"You're mad!" She darted away, panic pumping through her veins.

His fingers curled around her long hair. He yanked her

back, almost snapping her neck and ripping out some of
the strands.

His thick arm banded about her throat, pressing the back
of her head against his shoulder and exerting enough pressure for her to hold still or choke. "The gods have sealed
your fate, Pelonia. I knew it the moment I saw the scout
riding this way. I only had to keep you here until he came
close enough to claim you."

Terror exploded in her chest. She kicked and twisted, realizing she should have suspected treachery when he agreed
to help her bury the dead. Reaching above and behind her,
she clawed at his face. Warm blood tainted her fingers. She
bit his arm.

Marcus howled and let go. She ran, but he grabbed her
elbow and spun her to face him, striking her hard across the
side of the head. Her ears rang. Her jaw stung with pain.

Another blow. White specks of light burst behind her
eyes. She tasted blood. He backhanded her left cheek. She
fell to the ground, jarring her bones. The back of her head
bounced against a rock. Agony lanced through her skull.
Marcus's enraged countenance blurred above her. The edges
of her vision dimmed, began to turn black.

"Please, Lord, help me," she whispered, just before the
life she'd known ceased to exist.

As the orange glow of early evening settled over Rome,
Caros Viriathos stood at the arched second story window of
his bedchamber. His battle-scarred fingers stroked the
smooth head of his pet tiger.

Torches lit the large walled yard below where a dozen of
his best gladiators trained with a variety of weapons, per-
fecting their skills with each other and several wild animals.

While Caros listened to the clang of clashing metal and

the roar of angry lions, his gaze traveled from one pair of opponents to another. He studied each fighter's footwork, his speed, every sword thrust and jab of a trident. At sunrise, he would speak with each man in private, point out his flaws and demand perfection. Death might be inevitable, but it could be postponed. And sending men into the arena un-trained was a waste of life and capital.

He knew from experience. For ten brutal years, he'd fought in the games, a slave ripped from his Iberian home and forced to serve a cruel master. As an unrivaled champion, he'd won the mob's fickle affections. They rewarded him three years ago by demanding his freedom as the prize of a particularly bloody competition. Since then, he'd begun his own training grounds, the Ludus Maximus, and amassed a fortune. Even his former master acknowledged no one pre-pared gladiators more suited for combat than he.

He should have been pleased with his life, or at least his comfortable situation, but deep inside, he yearned for peace.

By day, his work kept him occupied, his mind focused on the task of teaching his men the art of battle. But it would soon be dark and the silence of night allowed the Furies to torment him for his past.

Fists clenched, Caros leaned against the marble window-sill. The aroma of roasting meats signaled the dinner hour. His men had finished training for the day. Their teasing gibes and easy laughter replaced the clash of weapons as they disappeared into the cookhouse. After the evening meal, they'd seek out their beds in the barracks, exhausted and ready for slumber.

Wishing his sleep came as easily, Caros had given up hope of ever winning the battle that waged in his head. For years, he'd fought the riot inside him, arguing with his conscience that he'd been forced to kill in the ring or be killed. He'd sampled every diversion Rome offered in an effort to distract him from the guilt gnawing at his soul. Nothing soothed him. Everything he'd tried proved empty until he had more and more difficulty suppressing the cries of all those he'd slain.

The tiger's tail swished on the mosaic-tiled floor, the only sound in the evening's stillness. Footsteps approached in the corridor, drawing his attention and a low growl from Cat.

A fist pounded on the door. "Master," Gaius, his elderly steward, called through the heavy wooden portal, "a slave caravan has arrived. There are a few good prospects. Do you wish to have a look?"

Eager for a distraction from his thoughts, Caros left his post at the window. He'd lost four men in the ring the day before and needed to replace them. "I'll be down in a moment, Gaius. Tell them to wait."

Caros pulled on a fresh tunic and reached for a weighty bag of coins on his desk. Moments later, he joined Gaius in one of the long side yards that ran the length of the house. The stench of animal dung and unwashed bodies made him grimace.

The slave trader, a stout man, paced the straw-covered stones next to a swaying elephant.

In the torchlight, the newcomer came to an abrupt halt when he noticed Caros approaching. He flashed his rotten teeth and his eyes sparkled with the thrill of a probable sale. He stepped forward, sweeping his stubby arms wide to prove he carried no weapons.

"Sir, I am Aulus Menus. You are known as the Bone Grinder, no? It is an honor to meet you." The slave trader bent at the waist in a flamboyant bow. "I saw you fight once four years ago. You took down five gladiators without a single wound to yourself. I can still hear the crowd chanting your name. It is easy to understand why your reputation as Rome's greatest champion is hailed far and wide."

"I'm sure you exaggerate." Unimpressed by the trader's flattery or the odor wafting from his person, Caros hoped the man visited one of the city's baths at the first opportunity.

"I assure you I don't exaggerate. I've heard your name praised as far as Alexandria. Some even hint you're a son of Jupiter. They whisper your name in hallowed tones and—"

"Enough. If you seek to gain my favor with compliments, be warned, you will not. I'm in need of four able-bodied men, no more. The taller, stronger and healthier the better."

"No more than four?" Some of the gleam left the slave trader's eyes. "I have thirty such men."

Caros looked toward the row of ragged beggars on offer. Sitting in the dirt, most appeared too weak to stand. Others sat beside them, skinny, dejected, already defeated. A few slightly stronger ones leaned against the wall. None of them would do. "Are you trying to swindle me? I need men for gladiators, not lion fodder."

In the torchlight, Aulus's face grew red, as though he sensed a hefty profit slipping through his fingers. "This is not my best merchandise. Follow me and I'll show you a host of potential champions."

Unconvinced, Caros nodded and followed anyway. Aulus carried a torch as they walked past the wheeled cages filled with reeking animals and all manner of degraded humanity. The sight of dirty, hollow-eyed children clenched his stomach. A youth sitting beside them reminded him of his own capture and sale into slavery. His loving mother and sisters had been tortured that day, then crucified while he was forced to watch.

Caros pushed the nightmare away. Resigned to the ways of the world, he hardened his heart and continued after Aulus.

"Here we are." The trader halted beside a wagon. He held up the torch, giving Caros a better view into the small prison where a score of men stood packed like fish in a net.

With a practiced eye, Caros considered them. Swathed in loincloths, all were healthier than the wretches in the first lot, but only two or three had the makings of a fighter.

"I told you, no?" Aulus flashed a confident grin. "Any one of these men could be your next champion."

Caros snorted. "How many champions have you trained?"

Aulus's smile faded. "None, but—"

"Then let me be the judge." He pointed to the three best men. "I'll take them if you offer a decent price. Otherwise be on your way."

"Seven hundred denarii each," the trader said without a blink.

Caros laughed. "You *are* a swindler, Aulus. These slaves aren't worth two hundred. You'll have to do better."

"Five hundred, then."

"Two-fifty."

"Four-fifty."

"Two-sixty," he said, enjoying the barter and the slave trader's increasing dismay.

Aulus glanced at his wares, obviously weighing his costs. "Four hundred."

Caros walked away. Several wagons ahead, he saw Gaius inspecting a pair of giraffes.

"Wait!" Aulus sounded pained. "You didn't let me finish."

With a glance over his shoulder, Caros raised a brow and waited for the price.

"Three-fifty."

He sensed the other man's defeat. "Two-seventy."

"Three hundred," Aulus said in disgust. "My final offer."

"Done." Caros returned to the beaten man and opened the

pouch he held. Coins clinked into the trader's outstretched palm as he counted out the correct sum.

While they waited for the new slaves to be released from the cage and led around to the barracks at the back of the house, Aulus counted the coins for a second time. Satisfied, he dumped them into his own drawstring pouch as they started back to the house's side door.

"That's only three men, Bone Grinder. You said you need four. If you won't purchase the men or children I have on offer, would you consider a wench?"

"We have enough women to meet our needs."

"I have one you could train for the ring," the trader persisted. "The mob loves a woman who can draw blood. They'll froth at the mouth when they learn she's a Christian as well as a maiden. I can see it now—"

"How do you know she's pure?" Caros interrupted, impatient. "Have you touched her?"

"Her uncle made the claim, and she's remained unsullied while in my possession."

"Her uncle?" A frown pinched Caros's brows. "Her own kin sold her?"

The slave trader shrugged. "It happens often."

"Were they starving?"

"Far from it. On a better day, I imagine the old man is quite rich."

"How can you believe a swine who would sell his own family?" Caros asked, the question tinged with disgust.

"He swore it by the gods."

"And why should I believe *you*?"

Aulus laughed. "Do you think I would lie to you when you could crush me like an acorn? Besides, why would I allow anyone to touch her and ruin a chance for greater profits?"

"Because you're a swindler."

Aulus didn't deny the charge. A grin spread across his lips. He stopped beside an open wagon where three piteous women sat chained to the sideboards. He lifted his torch, pointing to a fourth female stretched out on the floor.

Caros's gaze flicked over the sleeping girl. Purple bruises marred her small face. Long dark hair fanned out around her head, shining in the torchlight. "You intend to pawn this child off as a woman I can train for the ring?"

"I assure you she's no child."

"Why was she beaten? I've no need for a troublesome wench."

"My scout said she disagreed with her uncle's plans to sell her and the fellow disciplined her for it."

"When?"

"Earlier this morning."

"She hasn't woken?"

"Once, not long after midday." Aulus waved a fly from the tip of his nose. "She'll come to, but there's a nasty bump on the back of her head."

Intent on the girl, Caros's heart beat with an unfamiliar pang of compassion. Having been the recipient of the emotion so little himself, he'd almost forgotten it existed.

"I planned to sell her to a brothel, but since she's a Christian, I'm weighing my options." A wicked gleam sparked in the trader's eyes. "I was told the authorities will pay…three thousand denarii for such criminals."

His eyes narrowed on the slave trader. The claim wasn't true. The authorities might send her to the arena if she didn't deny her illegal sect, but they wouldn't pay for the privilege. He knew what the other man was up to. Aulus thought he had designs on the girl's virtue and would pay any price to have her. "I'll give you fifteen hundred for her."

Aulus laughed. "Oh, no, you won't cheat me this time. I'll take three thousand, nothing less."

"*I* cheat you? It will cost me a fortune to fatten up those wretches you sold me. Fifteen hundred is an expected price for any female slave."

"Ha! This isn't just any female. Virtue is rare these days. Three thousand, nothing less."

"Seventeen hundred."

"Three thousand is my final offer, Bone Grinder. Take it or leave it, it matters not to me. I'll have my profit from you or the authorities. Either way, she'll end up in the ring."

The girl moaned, drawing a concerned glance from Caros. A voice in his head warned him not to let her go. "You know the authorities will pay you nothing."

"Perhaps." A triumphant smile tugged at the trader's lips as though he sensed Caros weakening. "If they won't, a brothel will. There are few uses for a woman, but something tells me I'm bound to make a profit off this one."

His pride chafing, Caros realized he'd fallen into the weasel's trap. If he paid the three thousand denarii, Aulus would walk away with the exorbitant amount he'd originally demanded for the slaves *and* a healthy profit from the girl.

After another glance at the pitiful creature in the wagon, he didn't even mind being bested. Why her plight touched him when he was surrounded by a sea of human tragedy confounded him, but he had to have her.

Calling for Gaius, he gave him instructions to fetch the necessary funds. Once Gaius ran to carry out the order, Caros took the torch from Aulus and returned to the wagon. Chains rattled as the other three women tried to scatter from his presence, but he ignored them. His newest slave consumed his concern.

He reached over the wagon's side and caressed the girl's

flowing dark hair before examining the egg-sized bump on the back of her skull. With great care, he lifted one of her hands in his, noticing the fine bones and the soil caked under her fingernails.

"Master?" Gaius said, out of breath when he returned with a large bag of coins. "Shall I tell Lucia to prepare a mat for the new slave?"

The slave's hand still in his grasp, Caros nodded. "Tell her to fix one of her herbal concoctions as well. When the girl awakes, she's going to need relief from her pain."

As soon as his steward walked away, Caros heard Aulus's knowing laughter erupt behind him. "You're already besotted with the wench, no? I wonder what she'll think of *you* when she learns the number of Christians you've slain."

Chapter Two

Angry, unfamiliar voices penetrated Pelonia's awareness. Floating between wakefulness and darkness, she couldn't budge her heavy limbs. Every muscle ached. A sharp pain drummed against her skull.

The voices died away, then a woman's words broke through the haze. "She wakes. Fetch the master."

Hurried footsteps trailed away, while someone moved close enough for Pelonia to sense a presence kneel beside her.

"My name is Lucia. Can you hear me?" The woman pressed a cup of water to Pelonia's cracked lips. "What shall I call you?"

Pelonia coughed and sputtered as the cool liquid trickled down her arid throat. Swallowing, she grimaced at the throbbing pressure in her jaw. "Pel…Pelonia."

"Do you remember what happened to you? You were struck on the head and injured. You have bruised ribs. From the swelling, one or more may be cracked, but I believe none are broken. I've been giving you opium to soothe you, but you're far from recovered."

Her eyelids too heavy to open, Pelonia licked her chapped

lips, hating the rotten taste in her mouth. Uncomfortable heat warmed the right side of her face.

Gradually, her mind began to make sense of her surroundings. The warmth must be sunshine because the scent of wood smoke hung in the air, yet she heard no crackle of a fire. Her pallet was a coarse blanket on the hard ground. Vermin crawled in her hair, making her itch. Dirt clung to her skin and each of her sore muscles longed for the tufted softness of her bed at home.

Home.

Her muddled brain latched on to the word. Where was she if not in the comfort of her father's Umbrian villa? Where was her maid, Helen? Who was this woman Lucia? She couldn't remember.

Icy fingers of fear gripped her heart as one by one her memories returned. First the attack, then her father's murder. Raw grief squeezed her chest.

Confusion surrounded her. Where was her uncle? She remembered the slave caravan, his threat to sell her, but nothing more. Had Marcus succeeded in his treachery, or had someone come to her aid?

Panic forced her eyes open. Light stabbed her head like a dagger. She squeezed her lids tight, then blinked rapidly until she managed to focus on the young woman's face above her.

"The master will be here soon." A smile tilted Lucia's thin lips, but didn't touch her honey-brown eyes. "He commanded me to call for him the moment you woke."

"Where…am I?" The words grated in her throat.

"You're in the home of Caros Viriathos."

The name meant nothing to Pelonia. She prayed God had heard her plea and delivered her into the hands of a kind man, someone willing to help her contact her cousin Tiberia.

The thought of Tiberia brought a glimmer of hope. Somehow, she must contact her cousin at the first opportunity.

Her eyes closed with fatigue. "How…how long have I…been here?"

Lucia laid her calloused palm to Pelonia's brow. "Four days and this morning. You've been in and out of sleep, but now it seems your fever has broken for good. I'll order you a bowl of broth. You should eat to bolster your strength."

Her stomach churned. Four days and she remembered nothing. Tiberia must be frantic wondering why she'd failed to attend the wedding.

As children, she and her cousin had been as close as sisters. They'd corresponded regularly and maintained their deep friendship ever since Tiberia's family moved to Rome eight years past. When Tiberia wrote of her betrothal to a senator, that the union was a love match, no one had been more pleased for her than Pelonia.

She opened her eyes. "I must—"

Lucia placed her fingers over Pelonia's lips. "Don't speak. Rest is what you need. Now that you've woken, Gaius, our master's steward, says you have one week to recover. Then your labor begins whether you're well or not."

"My cousin. I must…"

"You don't understand, Pelonia." Lucia hooked a lock of pitch-black hair behind her ear. "You're a slave in the Ludus Maximus now. A possession of the *lanista,* Caros Viriathos."

Lanista? A vile *gladiator* trainer?

"You have no family beyond these walls. You'd do well to accept your fate. Forget your past existence. Your new life here has begun."

"No!" She refused to believe all she knew could be stolen from her so easily.

Lucia frowned as though she were confronting a quarrelsome child. Tight-lipped, she crossed her arms over her buxom chest. "We will see."

Heavy footsteps crunched on the rushes strewn across the floor. The new arrival stopped out of Pelonia's view, but the force of the person's presence invaded the room.

The nauseating ache in her head increased without mercy. What had she done to make God despise her?

Focusing on Lucia, she saw the young woman's face light with pleasure.

"Master," Lucia greeted, jumping to her feet. "The new slave is finally awake. She calls herself Pelonia. She's weak and the medicine I gave her has run its course."

"Then give her more if she needs it."

The man's deep voice poured over Pelonia like the soothing water of a bath. Despite her indignation, some of her tension eased. Curious to see the man who had such a unique and unwelcome effect on her, she turned her head, ignoring the jab of pain that pierced her skull.

"Don't move," Lucia snapped. "You mustn't move your head or you might injure yourself further."

Pelonia stiffened. She wasn't accustomed to taking orders. Neither her father nor the tutors he'd hired to teach her had ever raised their voices.

Lucia glanced toward the door. "She's argumentative. I have a hunch she'll be difficult. She denies she's your slave."

Silence followed Lucia's remark. Pelonia's nerves stretched taut as she waited for a response. Would this man who claimed to own her kill or beat her? She'd heard of men committing atrocities against their slaves for little, sometimes no reason. Was he one of those cruel barbarians?

She sensed him move closer. Her skin tingled and her tension rose as if she were prey in the sights of a hungry lion. At last, the lion crossed to where she could see him.

Sunlight streaming through the window enveloped the giant. A crisp, light colored tunic draped across his shoulders and the expanse of his chest contrasted sharply with his black hair and the rich copper of his skin. Gold bands around his wrists emphasized the strength of his arms, the physical power he held in check.

Her breath hitched in her throat. She could only stare. Without a doubt, the man could crush her if he chose.

"So, you are called Pelonia," he said. "And my healer believes you wish to fight me."

Her gaze locked with the unusual blue of his forceful glare. For the first time, she understood how the Hebrew David must have suffered when he faced Goliath. Swallowing the lump of fear in her throat, she nodded. "If I must."

"If you must?" Caros eyed Pelonia with a mix of irritation and respect. He was used to grown men trembling before him. With her tunic filthy and torn, her dark hair rippling in disarray across the packed earthen floor and her bruises healing, his new slave looked like a wounded goddess. But she was just an ordinary woman. Flea-bitten and trodden upon. Why did she think she could defy him?

To her credit, she wasn't a simpering wench. Her resistance reminded him of his own the day he'd been forced into slavery. Beaten, chained by his Roman adversaries, he'd sworn no one would ever own him. He'd been mistaken, of course. This new slave would be proven wrong as well.

"Then let the games begin," he said, his voice thick with mockery.

"Games?" she asked faintly. "You think…this…this is a game?"

The roughness of her voice reminded him of her body's weakened condition—a frailty her spirit clearly didn't share. Crouching beside her, he ran his forefinger over the yellowed bruise on her cheek. She didn't flinch as he expected. Instead, she closed her eyes and sighed as though his touch somehow soothed her.

Her guileless response unnerved him. The need to protect her enveloped him, a sensation he hadn't known since the deaths of his mother and sisters. As a slave, he'd been beaten on many occasions in an effort to conquer his will. That no one ever succeeded was a matter of pride for him. Much to his surprise, he had no wish to see this girl broken, either.

"Of course it's a game." He lifted a strand of her dark hair and caressed it between his fingers. "And I will be the victor. I live to win."

"It's true." Lucia moved from the shadows. "Our master has never been defeated."

Defiance flamed in the depths of her large, doe-brown eyes. She didn't speak and he admired her restraint when he could see she wanted to flay him.

Challenged to draw a response from her, he trailed his fingers over her full bottom lip. "You might as well give in now, my prize. I have no wish to crush your spirit. I own you whether you will it or not."

She turned her head toward the stone wall, but he gripped her chin and forced her to look at him.

"Admit it," he said with no pity for her loss of pride. "Then you can return to your sleep."

She shook her head. "No. No one owns me…no one but my God."

He dropped his hand away as though she'd sprouted leprosy. "And who might your god be? Jupiter? Apollo? Or maybe you worship the god of the sea. Do you think Neptune will leave his watery throne and rescue you?"

"The Christ." For the first time, her voice didn't waver.

So, she admitted following the criminal sect. Caros studied her, wondering if she were a fool or had a wish for death. "Say that to the wrong person, Pelonia, and you'll find yourself facing the lions."

"I already am."

He laughed. "So you think of me as a ferocious beast?"

Her silence amused him all the more. "Good. It suits me well to know you realize I'm untamed and capable of tearing you limb from limb."

Her fingers clutched at the dirt floor. "Then do your worst. Death is better…than being owned."

Lucia scoffed under her breath, drawing Caros's attention to where the healer waited by the window, the noonday sun coursing through the open shutters.

"What foolishness." Lucia came to stand by a rough-hewn table littered with the bottles and bowls of her medicines. "I warned you the girl would argue, Master. I'd wager she deserved the thrashing she received if all she did was quarrel."

"The slave trader did mention she'd been beaten for a disagreement with her uncle." Caros's attention slipped back to Pelonia, who'd grown pale and weaker still.

Concerned by her pallor, he berated himself for baiting her, for depleting her meager strength when he should have been encouraging her to heal. Without pausing to examine his motives, he reached down and lifted her into his arms, prepared for her to protest.

When she sagged against his chest without a fight, her acquiescence alarmed him. She weighed no more than a laurel leaf and it occurred to him she'd eaten nothing more than tepid broth for the last several days. In her weakened state, had he shoved her to the brink of death?

Holding her tight against his chest, he whispered near her

ear. "Tell me, Pelonia. What can I do to aid you? What can I do to ease your plight?"

"Find…Tiberia," she whispered, the dregs of her strength draining away. "And free me."

Chapter Three

I will not weep.

Pelonia paused in weeding the kitchen's herb garden and wiped perspiration from her brow. Scents of basil and mint mingled with the sweetness of wild jasmine. A small fountain's splashing water and the aroma of fresh-baked bread reminded her of home.

The garden's rich black dirt stained her fingers, resurrecting painful reminders of her father's burial less than a fortnight ago. Fangs of betrayal bit deep. How could a loving God allow one of His most kind and humble servants to suffer so heinous a death?

Why had God delivered her to this gladiatorial training ground, this disgusting den of violence, to serve as a slave? How did He expect her to face Caros Viriathos on a daily basis when each sight of her captor filled her with resentment and simmering rage?

She ripped a weed from the dirt and flung it into a basket beside her. The *lanista* didn't have a right to imprison her here! In the week since Caros carried her from the slave quarters, he'd provided for her needs and seen her cared for, but his vow to rule over her kept him from finding Tiberia. His adamant refusal to contact her cousin, regardless of Tiberia's certain anxiety, stoked her frustration and her fury.

She sneered at the garden wall that marked the boundary of her prison. Caros Viriathos had stolen her life and she would see it returned. In a few days, her injuries would be completely healed and the occasional blurring of her vision would disappear the same as the knot on her head.

She would escape and find Tiberia, who wouldn't hesitate to buy her freedom. It didn't matter that a runaway slave faced the penalty of death. She couldn't abide the abysmal future she faced living as less than someone's chattel.

The weeds she'd discarded drew her attention. Bitterness bloomed until she tasted it. That's what God had done to her. Uprooted her from the flourishing soil of home and cast her aside as if she meant nothing. How could she trust a God who delivered her into such a deep chasm of despair?

The snap of a twig startled her out of her grim thoughts. A low growl directly behind her raised her hair on end. She froze, her breath lodged in her chest. Why hadn't she sensed the animal's approach? She'd heard the roar of big cats and sounds of various game in the training yard, but was the beast here?

Her heart stopped when warm, moist breath caressed her neck and a large wet nose sniffed her hair. From the corner of her eye, she saw the orange-and-black-striped head of a…*tiger.*

"Cat!" Caros's deep voice boomed across the garden. Pelonia's heart raced as though it meant to escape her chest.

"Cat!" he called again, his swift steps crunching dried leaves along the garden's path. "Come, before you terrify my new slave to death."

The tiger sniffed Pelonia's hair once more before he returned to his master. The animal's long, curved tail flicked her in the face as it sauntered off.

An eon seemed to pass before she took an even breath. Her muscles unlocked and she almost pitched forward into the herbs, her hands shaking with latent fear.

Caros's long shadow stretched across the herb bed in front of her. From her seat on the ground, he seemed as tall and formidable as a colossus.

He crouched beside her, his intense blue gaze riveted to her face. "Are you well or did my pet scare you speechless?"

Not wanting him to see her tremble, she tightened her fists and tried to ignore the tiger's golden eyes fixed upon her. "Your pet? Are you insane?"

He shrugged. "Some claim so."

"I agree with them." She pulled another weed. "Only a lunatic would allow a tiger to run loose in his garden."

"He wasn't actually free. He yanked his lead from my hand. It's your fault. You were in his domain and he wished to inspect you."

She gave him a level stare. "It's not my will that keeps me here. I'll gladly go to my cousin's home if I'm making the beast ill at ease."

"Beast?" Caros stroked the tiger's wide head and ignored her statement. "Hardly. He's as placid as a lamb with people he tolerates. He didn't kill you, so he must find you acceptable."

The powerful animal rolled to his side and Caros began to scratch his chin. Pelonia marveled at the sight of the huge contented cat. Sensing the affection between master and pet, she couldn't help but smile when Cat's eyelids began to droop and his body relaxed. Within moments he was stretched out in peaceful slumber.

"See? As placid as a lamb." Caros grinned. "His snoring will begin any moment."

As if on cue, a low rumble emanated from the sleeping

creature. She reached out her hand, then drew back. "Can I touch him?"

"Of course," he said. "Move closer so you don't stretch and hurt your ribs."

His thoughtfulness continued to perplex her. She brushed the excess dirt from her hands and did as he said. Hesitant at first, she stroked the top of the animal's head, surprised by the softness of its fur.

"Have you ever seen a Caspian tiger?"

She shook her head. "Sketches only. My father took me to a menagerie once. There were lions and a panther, but no tigers. Have you had this one long?"

Caros continued to watch her. "Three years, since he was a cub. He was the runt of his litter. My old *lanista,* Spurius, refused to feed him since Cat was sickly and he doubted he'd grow large enough for the ring. I fed him part of my rations and when I won my freedom a few months later I took Cat with me. As you can see, proper care has made him as healthy as any of his kind."

"You were freed? You were a slave once?"

He plucked a sprig of mint from a plant at the path's edge. "For ten years. From the age of fifteen, I fought as a gladiator."

She reached for a clump of basil to divide and replant. "Then you've lived the horror of having your freedom ripped from you and your life pitched on end?"

His face darkened. He nodded.

"Did you enjoy being a slave?"

"Why ask foolish questions? Who would *enjoy* being a slave?"

"Perhaps you liked killing for sport in the ring?"

His eyes narrowed. "I killed because I didn't wish to die."

Then how could he enslave others? The injustice of his

actions soured her stomach with disdain. She tossed the basil into the dirt and rose to her feet, wincing at the twinge of pain in her ribs.

The tiger opened his eyes, instantly alert. Wary of the predator, she stepped away, but her temper burned too strong to completely curb her tongue.

"You're a hypocrite, Caros Viriathos. How can you buy and sell flesh when you know firsthand of its brutality?"

Dropping the mint leaves, Caros stood, his stance suggesting he was ready for battle. "Think before you insult me, slave. Have I not been kind to you? Perhaps I've been *too* kind if you believe you can question me like an equal when you are not."

She chafed at the reminder of her degraded status.

"You're my property," he continued with confidence. "Remember your place."

Hot with indignation, she stared at him, silently defying his ownership. Eventually, she admitted, "I'm your prisoner, but once I find my cousin, I *will* buy back my freedom."

"You aren't for sale." His fists clenched at his side, his eyes turned the color of a stormy sea. "You are my *slave* and will be until I tire of you. Remember I hold your life in my hand. If I choose to see you dead, it will be so, but you won't be sold."

Inwardly, she trembled at the power he held over her. Tension crackled between them like a growing blaze. Cat sprang to his feet and began to pace with restlessness.

She took a step closer to Caros, a part of her wishing for death to end the misery she'd endured since leaving home. "My God alone can grant you the power to take my life. Should He do so, I will rejoice. Not only will I be free from you, but I will see my father in heaven and be face-to-face with my Savior."

"Your savior?" he scoffed. "You mean Jesus, the Jew the Romans crucified? He's dead. Even if He weren't, why would He want a shrew like you to pester Him for all eternity?"

The blood leeched from her face. His barb struck like the sting of a lash. Her father had taught her to live as an example of Christ's love to others. To trust that God held her in His hand and had a purpose for her life.

Since she'd buried her father, she'd refused to cry. She'd known he would want her to be strong. Shame replaced her anger. She'd tried so hard to please her earthly father, but what had she done thus far to please her *Heavenly* one?

The gate's creaking hinges sliced through the weighted silence. Pelonia glanced in the direction of the kitchen. Gaius, Caros's short, elderly steward approached, his face red from his hurried stride.

"Master." Gaius held up a roll of parchment. "I have word from Spurius concerning tomorrow's games."

Caros raked his hand through his thick, wavy hair. Releasing an exasperated sigh, he met the man halfway. While he and his steward discussed the news, Cat lay down in the shade of a lemon tree.

Pelonia watched the tall, arrogant man in front of her, a war waging within her heart and mind. Resentment battled with the knowledge that Caros was a man in need of God's love. A lifetime of teaching had impressed her to forgive, to be an example of compassion. But how could she be a light in this gladiator's brutal world when her own spirit felt cloaked in darkness?

Gaius retreated from the garden. Caros returned to her, his angular face an inscrutable mask. "Where were we?"

"At an impasse," she reminded him.

"Ah, an impasse." A devious smile formed about his lips. "Then I believe I have a solution to our dilemma. Apologize for your barbed tongue or I will take your silence to mean you understand your place here and have come to accept your fate."

Praying for patience, she took a deep breath to fortify herself, then slowly released it. "I've accepted nothing. However, I'm an honest woman, so I will be fair and tell you now my plans remain the same as they have been. As soon as I'm able, I will escape from you, find my cousin and see my freedom restored. Until then—"

"Say no more, slave. Perhaps you're unaware runaways are hunted like dogs and dispatched like rodents?"

"I'm aware of it," she said, refusing to be intimidated.

He shook his head, clearly bemused by his inability to cow her. "You're a unique woman, Pelonia. I've never met your like."

She raised her chin. "My father used to say the same."

Caros moved a few steps to the fountain and dipped his hand into the sparkling water. "What happened to him?"

The question stung like vinegar in a festering cut. Renewed sadness lodged a ball of pain in her throat. "God saw fit to take him home."

"When?"

Pelonia crossed her arms over her chest. She tried to make her voice emotionless. "On the road to Rome eleven days past. We were attacked by marauders. My father and our servants were killed. Everything of value was stolen. Only my uncle and I were left alive."

His eyes brimmed with compassion, awakening a desperate need for comfort. "How did you survive?"

Her eyes burned with unshed tears. She turned her back on him, nearly tripping over the basket of weeds by her feet. "I'd snuck away before dawn to bathe in the river. My father had told me not to go. He said it was too dangerous, that I and the other women could seek out one of the bathhouses once we reached Rome."

Her voice cracked. "We were so close, you see. Less than a day's journey to my cousin's home on the Palatine. But I didn't listen. I hate feeling unclean. My maid would have come with me, but I didn't want her to face my father's displeasure if he discovered my absence, so I went alone. I was in the water when I heard distant screaming. I tried to return with all possible haste. I would have given my life to save any of them. I would have. Honestly, I would have."

In two steps he was beside her, his arms banding about her shoulders. "I believe you. How did you escape?"

Enveloped in his strength, she allowed herself to forget they were enemies for a moment. She pressed her face to his chest, accepting the comfort she craved. "The thieves were gone by the time I arrived. They struck like lightning, unexpected and gone like a fast-moving storm."

"Why did your uncle beat you?"

Her eyes slipped closed. She inhaled the hint of spice on his skin. "I insisted he help bury the dead. He agreed because he'd seen a scout for the slave caravan approaching. When he told me of his plan to sell me, we argued and I tried to flee."

Caros's arms tightened around her. "I'm sorry, *mea carissima*. No one deserves to know such tragedy. Accept your life here, and I promise you will be treated with nothing but kindness."

"Your kindness is no worthy replacement for my freedom." She pushed his arms away, untangling herself from his embrace. "I can't accept a life of slavery. I'd shrivel up and die if I did. For whatever reason, God has seen fit I serve you for now. I'll do my best for His sake, but I won't promise to stay here forever."

Caros's eyes glittered like chips of blue glass in the

sunlight. A nerve ticked in his jaw. "Then I make no assurance either, slave. You shall have neither my protection nor my sympathy and we shall see how well your God defends you."

Chapter Four

Caros snatched up a *gladius* and pointed the sword's sharp tip toward his best gladiator. "Alexius, join me on the field. I need to spill blood."

Alexius, a *Mirmillo* specifically trained to fight with a straight, Greek-styled sword, chose his favorite weapon and followed Caros across the sunbaked sand.

At the center of the elliptical field, Caros rolled his shoulders, loosening his muscles.

Alexius settled into a defensive posture, a hint of his usual humor dancing in his dark eyes. "To what do I owe this honor, Bone Grinder?"

Caros tensed, his encounter with Pelonia fresh in his mind. All senses fully alert, he could feel her presence in the garden, tugging at him. He almost returned to her until his temper flared. He was a fool. She'd repaid his kindness with constant rejection. His grip tightened on the sword hilt.

Alexius raised his shield. "Hail, Master. Greetings from one about to die," he said, mocking the adage gladiators chanted to the emperor before battle.

Caros swung his sword and lunged forward, slicing the

other man's upper arm. "Don't test me today, Alexius. I'm in no mood for your humor."

Gaping at the stream of blood on his arm, the Greek grew serious, a state he reserved for the ring. He kicked sand in Caros's face, then thrust his blade with the speed of a whip. "And I'm in no mood to perish."

Blinking the sand from his eyes, Caros sidestepped the blow and plowed forward, whirling his weapon with the swiftness and force of a storm. Alexius fell back.

The atmosphere erupted with excitement. The other gladiators stopped training and cast lots on the victor. Voices cheered from the sidelines. A few slaves poked their heads from the upstairs windows, eager to witness the entertainment.

Caros's *gladius* struck the other man's shield. "A gladiator is always prepared for death."

Alexius plowed forward. His face contorted, his muscles straining against the force of Caros's attack. "I have an appointment with one of my admirers tonight. If I must die in my prime, I'd rather it be tomorrow."

As his sword sparked against the Greek's blade, Caros shook his head, almost amused. Unlike him, Alexius had rejected freedom when offered it. The Greek preferred the life of a gladiator, unaffected by its lowly status when women of every social standing practically worshiped him as a god.

The thought of women revived thoughts of Pelonia. Her huge brown eyes and her mouth made his pulse race, even as her defiance enflamed his displeasure. Worse, he disliked how his heart leaped at each new sight of her.

How could so contrary a female wreak such havoc on his senses? Mystified, Caros thought he'd conquered his emotions years ago. A quick temper usually meant a speedy death in the arena. Only cold efficiency kept a fighting man alive.

Why, then, couldn't he control his reaction to one impudent, albeit beautiful, slave?

With renewed irritation, he focused his energies on the fight at hand. Up and down the training field, the two warriors matched each other blow for blow.

The sun beat down on Caros's shoulders. Bloodlust pumped through his veins, releasing the aggression Pelonia stoked in him.

His sword flashed in the sunlight and caught Alexius on the leg. He smiled at the other man's look of disgust and shrugged. "A wound for your lady to tend tonight."

"I best not mark *you,* then. One more scar and your horde of beauties will run for Campania. You're ugly enough as it is."

"Ha! One of these days, I'm going to tire of your witless tongue and cut it from your insolent mouth."

Grinning, Alexius swung his shield at Caros's head. "Then again, the new slave Lucia mentioned this morning has no choice except to serve you. Perhaps you can force her to meet your needs."

Caros ducked from the shield just before it struck him and rammed his shoulder into the other man's middle. Frowning, he fumed at Alexius's suggestive tone. Had Lucia told him of Pelonia's rebellion?

Caros landed a fist to Alexius's stomach, then another. The other man groaned as he broke away.

The Greek recovered quickly and jabbed with his sword, catching Caros in the ribs. The cut stunned the breath from his lungs.

A smug expression crossed Alexius's face. "You're growing slow, Master. Perhaps you're getting old for this sort of play?"

"Think again," he said, his side stinging, "and leave delusions to your women."

Caros's free hand shot out. He caught Alexius's sword hilt and yanked. Alexius stumbled forward and fell to his knees, astonishment etched on his features.

Had they been in the ring, Caros could have delivered a deathblow with ease and been done with the match. But he wasn't fighting to the death—at least not with Alexius. His instincts warned Pelonia was another matter and he was in danger of losing both his will and his heart.

Caros eyed his fallen champion, dissatisfied with the fight. His sparring with Pelonia had offered far more interesting sport. Her fearlessness impressed him. "I'm not slow or old. I'm bored. I'd hoped you'd provide more of a challenge."

"I doubt even Mars could have bested you today." Alexius massaged his jaw and laughed, his good humor returning with ease. "Tell me, Bone Grinder, has your temper been appeased or do you still feel a need for blood?"

Caros glanced over his shoulder toward the garden behind the cookhouse where he'd last seen Pelonia. "I fear what I need most can't be solved with weapons."

Alexius's face twisted with confusion. "What is there if not battle?"

Peace. The thought beckoned him, tempting him with the idea of a different way of life. A way of life he'd known in his youth, but abandoned hope of ever finding again.

His desire to see Pelonia too strong to ignore, he left the field without answering Alexius. Before another hour passed he planned to make amends for how he'd treated her. Why drive a wedge between them when he wanted to know her better?

Pushing through the circle of men offering praise for his victory, he handed his *gladius* to one of the guards. He swiped a fresh tunic off a bench and pulled it over his head as he walked toward the cookhouse.

Without examining his need for haste, Caros returned to the garden. A breeze rustled the fruit trees and water splashed in the fountain, but there was an unnatural stillness that made him ill at ease.

"Pelonia?" His steps echoed along the walkway. He noticed Pelonia had done a fine job completing her task. Not only were the weeds gone, but the herbs were trimmed and the paths swept clean.

"Pelonia," he called again, eager to see her face once more.

The gate swung open. A wave of relief died the moment he turned and saw Lucia.

"She's not here, Master." The healer shifted a basket from one hip to the other. "I was on my way to find you. I've looked everywhere, but she's gone."

Tiberia left her plate of uneaten fruit and paced the family quarters of her new husband's Palatine home. Her fingertips brushed the marble top of a writing desk as she walked from one end of the large room to the other. Even the fragrant scent of incense did little to soothe her.

Marcus entered the chamber from where he'd been relaxing in the courtyard. A breeze followed him, rustling the gossamer drapes at each side of the tall doorway.

Taking a seat on the silk covered couch, he picked up a dish of honeyed almonds from a nearby table and stuffed several into his mouth.

Tiberia pitied him. The horror he'd suffered on his way to Rome was too vile to contemplate. Marcus had arrived the day after her wedding, told her of the attack and his brother's murder. How Pelonia had been kidnapped.

Tears formed in her eyes when she thought of her cousin. Poor Marcus had reluctantly shared how he'd fought for Pelonia's freedom, done everything in his power to keep her from being stolen. If not for his injuries, he'd said, he could have saved her.

"Are you well, my dear?" Marcus asked.

"It's Pelonia. I can't believe she's lost to me forever."

Setting the almonds aside, he cast his gaze to the woven carpet. "We must accept what the gods will. It's not for us to question."

She folded into a chair, feeling weak and far from her usually tenacious self. "I know. I'm just grateful I've had Antonius to lean on. I don't think I could have endured this without him."

"Yes, Fortuna has blessed you." He knelt before her. "You must remember that and focus on your new life. You're a senator's wife now with many responsibilities."

"How can I when I feel as though a hole has been gouged in my heart?"

"I understand, my dear. Who feels the loss of Pelonia and her father more than I? You and your husband are all the family I have left in this world and even that connection is solely by marriage."

She chose a linen square from the table beside her and dabbed her eyes. "No, Marcus, you must think of yourself as our true family. I may have been related to Pelonia through her mother, while you claimed paternal ties, but if blood cannot bind us together, surely this shared misfortune makes us kin."

"You are most kind." Marcus lowered his head. "If only I'd been able to save my brother and precious niece."

Her heart broke for the grieving man. Guilt washed over her. Had it not been for her wedding, Pelonia and her household would still be alive.

Vowing to do all she could to help Pelonia's last paternal relative, she patted Marcus's shoulder. "I should never have invited our loved ones to see me wed. Iguvium is too far north and the journey is perilous. Had I not, they—"

"No, you mustn't blame yourself." Marcus's hand strayed to her knee. "It's tragic to be sure, but my brother and his household courted punishment. What other fate could they expect when they turned from our ancestors and forsook our gods? I believe I yet live because the gods protected me."

Discomfited by his familiar manner and harsh opinion of his brother and Pelonia, Tiberia left the chair and walked to the window where a kestrel balanced on the edge of the sill. For years Pelonia had written about her faith in the crucified Jew, Jesus. She'd often feared her cousin would be found out and sentenced to suffer some heinous punishment. Perhaps the gods *had* taken matters into their own hands after all.

Marcus came to stand close behind her. His knobby fingers clutched her shoulders. "I apologize if I upset you. Let us speak of it no more and remember my brother's house with nothing but fondness."

"Agreed," she said, oddly alarmed by his nearness.

"Good. You're very amiable." He fingered a curl by her temple before moving back to the bowl of almonds. "I can see you will make a fine senator's wife."

"Thank you." A glance over her shoulder revealed the old man's intense scrutiny. She tightened her shawl around her shoulders, willing her husband to return home quickly. "Excuse me, I must see to the evening's meal."

"By all means." He patted the seat beside him on the couch. "Then return soon and we shall reminisce for a time."

Hurrying from the chamber, Tiberia shuddered and hoped with all her heart she'd only imagined the lust flickering in the old man's eyes.

Chapter Five

Pelonia pulled open the door of the storage room she'd been ordered to clean. Dim light filtered through the slats in the closed shutters, exposing a mountain of dirt and clutter.

Stepping into the narrow cell, she leaned her broom against the wall and set down her bucket of water. She stretched the tight muscles of her back, her ribs burning from the day's strenuous labor. This room was her last. As soon as she finished, she planned to seek out her pallet before Lucia concocted more aimless chores for her to do.

With a fortifying breath, she adjusted her tunic, detesting the coarse brown material scratching her skin from her neck to her ankles. She longed for the soft linen and brightly colored silks she'd always worn at home. Hoping a breeze would alleviate the itching discomfort of her slave's garb, she went to the window and threw open the shutters.

Positioned on the upper story, the storage room provided a lofty view of the training field. Below, Caros shouted at the men gathered around him. His sharp hand motions and livid countenance testified to his fury though the distance between them kept her from discerning his words.

Had some calamitous misfortune befallen them or did Caros Viriathos entertain a perpetually black mood?

No, that wasn't fair. Over the previous week, he'd shown his capacity for kindness by having her cared for while she recuperated. He hadn't turned vicious until she'd refused to accept his ownership.

As the group of gladiators disbanded, she rejected all benevolent thoughts of the *lanista*. She couldn't afford to soften toward him. Caros had declared war against her in the garden. He'd threatened her, frightened her, ridiculed her.

Hate, an emotion she'd never sampled before coming to Rome, crept into her heart. In that moment, all the lessons she'd learned about faith and compassion rang hollow. How could anyone possibly follow all of Christ's commands? Would she ever be able to forgive and love her enemy?

She watched Caros return indoors. As though a violent tempest had passed, an atmosphere of calm descended. The gladiators returned their weapons to the guards and filed into their quarters.

She picked up a rag she'd brought with her and began to dust. A vision of Caros plagued her. No one had ever affected her quite like the gladiator. When she looked at him, she saw a compelling, world-weary man, too proud for his own good. Worse, the sense of helpless fascination she experienced in his presence mortified her.

If she were the righteous person she ought to be, she'd pray for him, but the faith to pray eluded her for the first time in her memory. Never before had God seemed so distant. The wrath marking Caros's face when he'd mocked God's ability to protect her filled her with fear. What if Caros were right? What if her heavenly Father could no longer protect her? What if He simply chose not to?

Exhausted from wrestling with unanswered questions,

she finished cleaning and headed downstairs. At the end of a long corridor, she came to a partially opened door. She knocked hard enough to push it wider. The room was empty, but something about the restful space drew her inside.

A wooden sword hung prominently on one wall. Small ancestral statues, three women and a man, sat atop a shelf beneath it. A couch and two chairs crafted of rich wood and the finest, deep blue coverings partially hid the mosaic masterworks of various animals and lush vegetation that covered the floor. On the wall opposite the sword, a fresco of mountains against the backdrop of a fiery setting sun, lent the space a haunting, solitary air.

Crossing to the window, she admired the house's inner atrium with its decorative columns and trio of fountains. Climbing red roses perfumed the air with a sweet scent that reminded her of her own flower garden at home.

An older man shuffled into the courtyard carrying a hoe and woven basket. When he saw her, she waved in greeting. A toothless grin flashed across his aged features before he tottered back the way he'd come.

How odd for him to retreat without a single word to her. She shrugged. What did she know of Caros's servants? Perhaps they were all as strange as their master.

She began to leave a moment before Lucia raced across the threshold. "Where have you been and what are you doing in the master's private room?" she demanded an octave higher than necessary. "If Servius hadn't seen you from the garden, the entire household would still be in an uproar searching for you."

"What game are you playing?" Pelonia asked. "You know I was cleaning the storage rooms as you ordered."

"You lie. I looked for you there. You were nowhere to be found."

"How dare you call me a liar? I…" Her words trailed away when Caros appeared in the doorway. The room seemed to shrink and her pulse began to race like a stallion set free.

"Master." Lucia looked to Caros with an eager smile. "I found her."

"So I see." His gaze scorched Pelonia from head to foot. "You may leave us, Lucia."

The young healer looked stricken, then resigned before she turned to go. "Beware of this one, Master. She has the face of Venus, but she's even more deceitful."

Caros didn't comment, leaving Pelonia with the uneasy feeling he agreed with Lucia's poison. Once they were alone, he stepped deeper into the room. "Where have you been?" he asked, his tone as emotionless as stone.

"Upstairs." Her gaze roamed over the large bruise on his cheek, the multiple gashes marring the sinew of his arms and exposed collarbone. How much more damage did his tunic conceal? He must be in pain. She resisted a tug of concern and the desire to tend his injuries.

"What were you doing there?"

"Lucia sent me to clean."

"I don't believe you. She wouldn't assign hard labor when you've yet to fully heal."

"She said you meant to punish me."

"Now I'm certain you lie. I said nothing to Lucia about you."

She looked away from his icy blue stare, irritated enough at being called a liar again to dismiss her concern for his wounds. "Your thoughts are your own. Believe what you will. But if you meant to show me how harsh life here will be without your protection, consider your point well made."

"If you were cleaning upstairs why are you here in my private room? Did you plan to rob me before attempting the escape you threatened?"

"First I'm a liar, now I'm a *thief?*" she asked, unreasonably hurt by his low opinion of her. "If you knew me better, you'd realize you have no need to question my honesty. What have I done to give you the impression I'd steal from you?"

Caros contemplated the question while he steadied his breathing. How dare she stand before him acting as though she was in the right? By the gods, she'd given him the scare of his life. Once he'd discovered her gone, he'd turned the *domus* upside down looking for her. Visions of her fleeing into the wrong spot and encountering his men had him locking them up in the middle of the day.

Unwilling to examine the fear he'd experienced when he thought she'd run away, he hugged his anger to him like a protective coat of mail.

"Well?" she demanded. "What have I done?"

He stepped toward her.

She jumped back, her palms outstretched as though to ward off an attack. "Don't come any closer."

He moved forward, within easy reach of her. "Why should I not?"

She dashed away, positioning herself behind a piece of furniture.

"Do you think a chair will offer protection if I choose to lay my hands on you?"

"Some protection is better than none." She squared her shoulders and lifted her chin. "Even gladiators gird themselves before a match."

"True, but no amount of armor can compare with experience. I've fought for almost half my life. You're as battle hardened as a kitten."

She crossed her arms over her chest. "I admit you're a better fighter than I—"

"Yet I'm not the one who usually begins our skirmishes."

"You blame me for the difficulties between us? I've done nothing—"

"But argue." Most of the anxiety she'd caused him began to melt away now that the shock of her disappearance had begun to wear off.

"I've done no more than defended myself. You're just unreasonable. Your high-handedness begs to be brought down a peg."

"Is that so?" He shoved the chair out of his way and gripped her upper arms before she realized his intent to strike. "If we were equals you might be the woman to chastise me. As it is, you're a slave who'd be wise to keep her opinions to herself."

"And you're a pompous...*gladiator!*"

Caros almost congratulated her. She'd held her ground, though he could see fear lurked in the depths of her soulful brown eyes.

"Why are you smiling?" Her distrust was unconcealed. "Have you devised some new punishment for me?"

He caressed her arms, enjoying the smoothness of her skin. "I thought I might train you to fight in the arena. A woman in the games is a novelty. If this display of temper is any indication, you certainly have the mettle for it."

She escaped from his hold and fled to the window. "Your humor is misplaced, *lanista*. If you trained me with a weapon, you'd be wise to refrain from sleep."

He laughed outright. "So, you'd kill me, would you? Doesn't your *God* frown on murder?"

With a defiant toss of her head, she glared at him. Glad to see her bruises all but gone, he admired the way the window framed her beautiful face and delicate stature. Even the ragged tunic did nothing to hide her appeal.

"Blasphemy is a sin the same as murder," she said. "God

might not pardon you for mocking Him, but given your contrary nature, I'm sure He'd understand my actions and forgive me without reservation."

"Perhaps," he said flatly. "But you might be surprised to find how difficult it is to forgive yourself."

Mollified by the horror in her eyes, he turned to leave. "Be warned, slave. Disappear again and you won't like the consequences. If you think dusting storage rooms is punishment, you'll realize it's child's play compared to the tasks I'll drop at your feet."

Outside, the sun beat down on him. He sensed Pelonia was jesting when she spoke of murdering him and her God's forgiveness for such an act, but what if it were true? What if her God were powerful enough to forgive the vilest crime and erase the guilt crippling his soul?

Hope flickered like an elusive flame inside him, then burned out just as quickly. He'd done too much evil to think of receiving mercy. He'd killed countless men, many of them Christians. Why would their God embrace an enemy?

He shook his head, his spirit bleak. He was lost with no way to be found. He should accept his fate and stop longing for redemption. Deep in his heart he accepted he wasn't worthy.

Chapter Six

Pelonia couldn't sleep. She tossed and turned on her hard pallet, her body begging for slumber, her mind too conflicted to rest. She kept envisioning Caros's dejected face when she'd taunted him. How could she have suggested she'd murder him or that God would forgive her for the crime? Yes, she'd been angry, but such meanness wasn't her way.

She didn't feel like herself anymore. Her whole life had changed for the bitter. She closed her eyes and tried to pray, once again asking for forgiveness and direction. Afterward, her heart was lighter, but God seemed just as distant.

She gazed out the open window. It would be dawn soon, but for now an array of stars twinkled in the tar-black sky. As a child, she'd loved gazing into the night, memorizing the constellations her tutors had shown her. A smile curved her mouth as she remembered her father pointing out different celestial patterns and teaching her the wonders of God's creation. With true gratitude, she thanked the Lord for those sweet memories.

Giving up on sleep, she flipped away the light covering and stood. Stiff muscles protested as she crossed the tiny room she'd inhabited since Caros brought her here from the slave quarters eight days ago. She wondered when she would join the other slaves. Surely Caros had better use for the space than to allow her a private chamber.

She rested her palms on the windowsill. The first rose-colored streaks of dawn painted the horizon. A cool breeze ruffled her hair and a dog barked in the distance, the only sound amid the silence.

Steps shuffled in the hall. Someone pounded on the portal loud enough to wake the deepest sleeper.

"It's time to rise," Lucia commanded through the closed portal.

"I'm coming."

"Be quick about it. Find out what herbs Cook needs from the garden and fetch them for him."

Pelonia changed her tunic and wrapped the shawl around her shoulders before venturing into the corridor. A series of lanterns lit the way downstairs to the back of the house. A pair of guards waited at attention by the rear door. With a hurried greeting to the giant, dark-skinned Africans, she crossed outside into the fresh air. The smell of baking bread made her mouth water.

Following the brick path to the kitchen, she glimpsed Caros training with a sword in the peach orchard. A look of concentration etched his handsome face. He didn't see her. Free to watch him without the expectation of conversation, she halted, mesmerized by the power and grace of his movements. He reminded her of music come to life in human form. Even the scar that looked like the swipe of a lion's claw across his chest did nothing to detract from his appeal.

"Don't fall in love with him," Lucia said, slithering up beside her. "If any woman ever claims his heart, it will be me."

Pelonia turned to see the healer fixed on Caros with a

hungry gleam in her eyes. "You have nothing to fear from me. The man I choose to love will be the exact opposite of Caros Viriathos."

"How so?" Lucia's gaze never left her master.

"I want my husband to share my faith."

"Husband?" The healer snickered. "You're a slave. Why do you think you'll be permitted to marry?"

Pelonia frowned. "I won't always be a prisoner here. I refuse to believe I'll never have a family of my own."

Lucia snorted. "You should be thankful you're alive and give up your fanciful notions."

"It's not fanciful to have faith. Circumstances can change as quickly as an ocean current."

"Like your fortunes did the day you came here?"

"Yes," Pelonia admitted, stung by Lucia's harsh reminder.

"Then I can do without your faith. Why serve a deity who finds pleasure in making you a slave?"

For a moment, Pelonia grappled for an answer. Lucia's question echoed the very words she'd asked herself so often since coming here. She glanced away from Lucia's sneer to find Caros had finished his practice.

Her face flushed with pleasure when she noticed him watching her. Embarrassed by her reaction, she sought out Lucia's harsh features like a lifeline.

"My God's ways are a puzzle at times," she said, clinging to her beliefs when she had little else to offer. "But I believe He'll work all for my good if I'm patient and wait for Him to reveal His purpose."

"Then you're a fool. Why wait for your God to cause you more pain? Why not take matters into your own hands?"

A rooster crowed. Caros went off to the gladiators' barracks. Two other slaves finished feeding the animals and walked past them into the house.

"I could arrange for your freedom," Lucia said once they were alone.

Pelonia's heart quickened. A surge of hope welled inside her as did her suspicion. "Why take such a risk? If Caros found out, he'd punish us both."

Lucia flipped her long black braid over her shoulder. "Isn't it obvious? I want the master for myself. Somehow you've bewitched him. He hasn't been himself since you came here. He's only waiting for your body to heal before he claims you, but I'm certain he'd forget you if you'd just disappear."

Why shouldn't she listen to Lucia? Both of them would have what they wanted if she accepted the healer's help. "When could you arrange for me to leave?"

The morning light gave Lucia's face a reddish cast. She smiled. "As early as tonight if you're willing."

Caros added another ladle of water to the red-hot coals. The liquid sizzled and steam filled the circular chamber of the bathhouse. He leaned against the warm marble wall, sweat beading on his skin.

After the morning's sword practice and another taxing workout in the bath's gymnasium, he hurt all over. Little wonder. His fight with Alexius yesterday had left his ribs bruised and his jaw throbbing. He'd been mad to double his usual exercise. Even more foolish to believe the added work would hinder his thoughts from straying to the unwelcome emotions Pelonia stirred in him.

The steam room's door swung wide. He opened one eye and stifled a groan when he saw Spurius Albius swiping a path through the curling white vapor. As always, Caros's temper flared at the sight of his former master, the man who'd stolen ten years of his life.

"There you are, Caros." Spurius's jowls bobbled as he spoke. "Gaius informed me I might find you here."

"What do you want? I'm on my way to the *frigidarium*. I'm in need of a cold swim before I head home."

"Leaving already?" Spurius hefted himself onto one of the marble ledges, adjusting his loincloth to accommodate his massive girth and stubby legs. "Isn't it too soon in the day?"

Caros closed his eyes and leaned his head back against the wall. "Not since you arrived."

Spurius chuckled. "Then I'll go straight to the point. I want you to fight again."

Caros lifted his head, battling his annoyance. "Why do you insist on vexing me with your endless attempts to drag me back to the arena? I've told you no a hundred times."

"I'm persistent. Besides, it's been a fortnight since you last turned me down."

"And I believe I told you if you asked me again I'd feed you to Cat."

Spurius shrugged. "I'm tough as old leather. He'd just spit me out."

"But he might enjoy gnawing on you first."

"If we were in your home, I might be frightened. But here—" Spurius motioned to the rising steam "—I'm safe."

"Not with me in the chamber."

Spurius used the edge of a cloth to wipe the sweat from his brow. "I know you hate me, but we both know you won't harm me no matter how much you'd like to see me dead. You were a condemned man once. I doubt you'd allow yourself to return to that lowly state."

Caros grunted, unable to argue with the truth. Ending the worm's life would please him to no end, but it wasn't worth sacrificing all he'd achieved. "Exactly. Neither will I return to the games. Entering the arena requires me to place myself back in bondage. Rome itself will fall before I'll forfeit my freedom or be forced to acknowledge another master."

"You're too proud, Caros." Spurius sighed. "The truth is the mob is easily bored. Every day, it grows more difficult to arrange the grand events the crowd demands. The mob wants *you,* their champion, and the games' sponsors are willing to pay any price for the spectators' continued enjoyment."

Caros tossed another ladle of water on the coals. "I'm retired, old man. If you wish to do business with me, speak to Gaius about Alexius or one of my other champions. Otherwise, distance yourself from my presence. My patience with you is over."

"But think of the riches you'd win," Spurius cajoled one last time. "You're still the best gladiator alive."

"I'm already rich. On the other hand, Alexius's talents are for sale."

Taking the hint, Spurius's shoulders slumped in capitulation. "Since you've brought up Alexius, why can't you be more like him? There's a man who understands and enjoys his place in the world."

"He's a slave by choice. If he wanted his freedom I'd let him have it."

Spurius frowned. "You've condemned me as a villain because I refused to sell you your freedom when you demanded it. But I ask you, what man would happily give up a gold mine? I was a fool to give the mob its way the day they chanted for your release. In the last three years I've lost ten fortunes for my drunken error."

Caros stood and tightened the cloth around his hips. "You're a fool, old man, drunk or otherwise."

"True enough, but I'm also determined. One of these days I'll tempt you out of retirement. You can be sure of it."

* * *

Pelonia sensed Caros's arrival in the garden before she heard him. Perching on tiptoe, she craned her neck for a better view of the herb-lined path. Caros and another man approached. Both were dark, tall and broad shouldered, but Caros moved with a grace that rivaled his tiger's. Breathless, she couldn't take her eyes off him.

He caught her staring and without warning sent the other man away. Without breaking their gaze, he closed the distance between them. "Why are you out here in the heat of the day?"

"Your steward assigned me to garden duty. I understood I'm to work here every day."

"I'll speak with him. There are easier tasks in the house."

"No, this is fine." She didn't want to rile Gaius. The old man could make her life miserable if he chose. "I tended flowers and maintained a large vegetable garden for my father's household."

He crossed his arms over his chest. The gold wristbands he wore glinted in the sun. "If you came from a wealthy family, as you claim, why toil like a slave?"

Disliking the accusation in his question, Pelonia plucked a low-hanging leaf from the lemon tree and breathed in the citrus scent. "Simply because I enjoy planting something, caring for it and watching it grow."

"I see. And how is it you never married? I'd expect a woman of your advanced age to have children of her own to nurture."

"*Advanced* age? Are you trying to insult me?" she asked with mock severity.

"By the gods, *no.*" He shifted uncomfortably. "But most women wed by the age of twelve or thirteen summers. You've yet to wrinkle, but…how old are you?"

"Seventeen." She bit her lip to keep from laughing at his discomfort. "And you? You have enough wrinkles for both of us, so I'd guess you are…?"

"Twenty-eight." He fingered the faint lines around his right eye. "Are you saying you find me ugly and withered?"

She laughed for the first time since her father died. "Goodness, no, but all the scars were a bit off-putting at first."

He sighed with exaggerated relief and led her to a bench beside the fountain. "Were? Does that mean my scars no longer bother you?"

In truth, she no longer noticed them. Not when the uniqueness of his azure eyes and the male beauty of his sculpted lips claimed all of her attention. "No, they don't bother me."

"Good." His gaze dipped to the ground and she saw the beginnings of a smile curve his mouth. He brushed a thick curl of black hair from his forehead. "But you have yet to answer me. What's wrong with you that you never married?"

She rolled her eyes. "There's nothing *wrong* with me. My father was an unconventional man. He thought it best I wed the husband of my choosing. I've yet to make the fortunate man's acquaintance."

Caros's laughter filled the garden. "Aha! Another woman in search of a perfect man. I doubt you'll find him."

Pelonia fought her own grin. "I've no wish for a perfect man. Just one who's perfect for me."

"Perhaps you've met him, but don't realize it. What if he were…one of my men?"

"He isn't."

"How do you know?"

She weighed her words with care. "I mean no disrespect, but…but my father would never have condoned my marriage to a man of your occupation."

"I see." His lips firmed into a hard line. "I should have

known, but it's easy to forget we gladiators are the scum of the earth when most of the empire worships our every move."

"I didn't mean to offend you."

"You didn't. I know the status of my profession. So, what virtues must this god among mortals possess to win your favor?"

"I want no god other than the One I serve. As for a husband, I pray…"

A bird chirped, filling in the late afternoon's silence while she debated whether or not to share further. Being a pagan, and a man, she doubted he would understand.

"Yes?" Caros persisted.

"There was a man named Paul of Tarsus," she said before she lost her nerve.

"You wished to marry him?"

"No." She shook her head, disconcerted by the sudden malice in his expression. "Paul was the first Jew to teach Gentiles the ways of Jesus. In his letters to the various Christian communities, he taught many truths."

"And for this you admire him? I, for one, would reconsider elevating a teacher who led me down a road to persecution and slaughter."

"On marriage," she continued as though he'd said nothing, "Paul taught a husband should love his wife as much as Christ loves his followers. A man should love her so much he would die for her if necessary, just as Christ died for all of us."

"Little wonder you put such stock in love." He grimaced. "And what did this Paul say a wife must do in return for her husband?"

"She must respect him."

Caros frowned. "A man must die for a woman and all she has to do is *respect* him for it?"

Pelonia grinned.

"Are you certain this Paul wasn't a female in disguise? It seems he concocted the rules to lean in a woman's favor."

She swatted his arm. "Paul was a great man, blessed with vast wisdom."

"So were Aristotle, Plato and Seneca. Why should I believe your Paul over the natural order—that woman is born to serve her husband, wanting nothing more than to bear his children?"

"Little wonder we Christians are persecuted for our radical ideas. Men rule the Empire and few of them want to purchase a slave when they can wed one."

"I purchased you, did I not? Though at three thousand denarii you were less than a bargain."

"Three *thousand*…?" Her mouth dropped open. "Why would you pay such a high price?"

His face grew serious. His eyes warmed in the space of a blink. He engulfed her hand in his much larger one and leaned closer until their lips almost touched. "The slave trader threatened to sell you to a brothel, but I refused to allow it."

Shocked to learn of the degradation he'd saved her from, she grappled for something appropriate to say. She wanted to thank him for his generosity, but her enslavement stole all but the smallest portion of gratitude from her heart. "I…why?"

"I mean to have you for myself."

She eased away from his hold, instantly missing the warmth of his touch. "The slave trader robbed you. He sold you a woman who wasn't for sale."

"My receipt and your presence in my home say otherwise."

"You confuse me. I'm certain you'd find a more willing female if you applied yourself to the task of looking for one."

His lips twitched. "I want only you."

Lucia's cold warning rang in her ears. "Because I'm a challenge? Or because I'm an innocent?"

The crisp air hummed with tension between them. "Neither and both. Truthfully…because there's a peace I feel in your presence that I've felt with no one else."

Mystified, Pelonia studied his angular features. His sincerity touched a chord deep inside her, but she found it impossible to trust him. She stood, eager to find the calm that eluded her in his presence. "After these last weeks, Caros, if you sense any peace left in me it's Christ and Him alone."

"Nonsense. I'm drawn to *you,* Pelonia, no other. From the first moment I saw you I wanted you for my own." His long fingers locked around her wrist, preventing her flight. "I won't relent until I've made you mine."

The quiet declaration confirmed Lucia's warning. She shook off his hold and rushed from the garden, his command to return chasing her down the path toward the house. Once in her room upstairs, she shut the door and flung herself on her pallet. Her whole body trembled from the shock of his admission. Her thoughts whirled as she tried to sort out the revelations in the garden. One moment she and Caros had been conversing, the next…

Her skin crawled when she thought of how close she'd come to waking in a brothel. Her father had shielded her, but she wasn't unaware of the harsh realities a female faced on her own. Shorn of a man's protection, most women fell into prostitution, or like her, were sold into slavery.

Neither was an acceptable choice, but for the moment slavery seemed the lesser of both evils. Had she been sold to a brothel, she would still be a slave, shamed with no hope of returning to her family. As it was, at least she had her virtue and the dream of freedom.

She curled into a ball. Her mind raced. Caros planned to make her his paramour. What had she done to draw his attention? He couldn't possibly be drawn to her disheveled and filthy appearance. She'd fought him at every turn. Surely he wasn't attracted to her less-than-servile nature?

Clasping her knees, she lowered her head. "Lord, where *are* You?" Straining to hear even the faintest whisper of guidance, she almost wept when she met with more silence. She'd already lost her father and freedom, would God allow her virtue to be stolen as well?

Lucia's offer rang in her ears. Any hesitation she'd harbored about the timing of her escape vanished. She'd been given the opportunity to flee and she must seek out Tiberia. If Caros sought to claim her, she had no ability or legal right to stop him. Every moment she lingered in his domain brought her closer to ruin.

She had no choice. She must leave tonight.

Chapter Seven

Anxious, Pelonia paced the shadows of her moonlit room. Lucia should arrive any moment with further instructions. Through her room's small window she checked the lantern-lit yard for the slightest hint of movement. The trainees had been locked in the barracks at twilight. The guards were nowhere in sight, but her stomach clenched with trepidation. If she were caught, and Caros refused to show mercy, she might lose her life.

A dog howled, lending the blackness an eerie quality that stretched her nerves. A knock on the door made her jump.

Pelonia opened the door to her coconspirator. "I've brought you some vegetable broth," Lucia said once the door was secured. "It was childish of you to skip the evening meal. How do you expect to have strength for tonight if you don't eat?"

"I didn't consider—"

"No, I figured as much, but I used your stupidity to aid us. I spread the seed you're feeling ill. When you don't come down tomorrow, people will believe you're unwell and passing the day on your pallet."

"Who will believe such a tale?" Pelonia accepted the

fragrant bowl of stewed tomatoes. "Since when is a slave allowed to shirk labor because of sickness?"

The lamp's glow highlighted Lucia's severe features. "Who *won't* believe it? Everyone is aware you're the master's current favorite."

Pelonia's cheeks heated with embarrassment. "I hate being the subject of gossip."

"You've been nothing else since the moment the master plucked you from the slave quarters and insisted you stay here in the house."

She cringed with mortification. Thankfully, her father didn't have to witness her dishonor.

"The entire household has made wagers to see how long before he tires of you."

Humiliated, she turned away. "When do I go?"

"Soon. First, you must listen and heed everything I'm about to say. When you leave the house tonight follow the street toward the amphitheater. Just before you reach the city gates, you'll come to a large statue of Caesar driving a chariot with winged horses. Once there, look for a man with two lanterns. He's the butcher's son, Pales. I've arranged for him to lead you to your cousin's home."

"You're certain he can be trusted?"

Pausing at the door, Lucia nodded. "Watch for me below your window. I'll give a birdcall to signal when it's time."

Several oil lamps bathed Caros's study with a warm orange glow. His gaze soaked in the wall mural of the setting sun and Iberian mountains. After all these years, he missed his native land and grieved the loss of his cherished kin.

His father, mother, sisters. Each of them held a revered place in his heart. With a fond smile, he lifted the ancestral statue he'd had fashioned to represent his father. Wise, the epitome of fairness, his father was the best man he'd ever known.

He replaced the carving and chose the one of his mother, the heart of his family's home. When Caros closed his eyes, he saw her wide smile, heard her gentle voice instructing him to be a man of peace, of honor.

How disappointed she would be to see what he'd become.

He put back the statue with care, then eased into one of the blue padded seats facing the inner courtyard. The illuminated fountain returned his thoughts to Pelonia, a subject never far from his mind.

He winced thinking of the disaster he'd spawned in the garden. By the gods, she must think him a rapist the way she'd fled. The horror on her face when he'd tried to kiss her made him cringe. In the future, he'd master his lust and nurture her trust, not her resistance.

Seeing Lucia enter the courtyard, he sat forward. Why wasn't the healer abed? He surged to his feet when he saw her look of panic.

"Master!" She ran toward him. "You must hurry. Pelonia, that ungrateful sneak, has fled. I was in my room upstairs when I happened to look out my window. There she was, creeping down the road like a common thief. I told you she'd be nothing but trouble."

Fear gripped him. "Which way?"

"Toward the city gates."

Quick steps took him to the bowels of the house. He strapped on a *gladius* and grabbed up a torch, then raced to the side door and into the night.

The torch held high to guide him, he broke into a run. During the day, Rome was dangerous enough, but after dark the streets crawled with every sort of human vermin.

If anything happened to her… He had to find her.

He picked up his pace. Shouting and bawdy laughter echoed from the street up ahead, but it was the woman's scream that raised the hackles on the back of his neck.

A grimy hand covered Pelonia's mouth from behind and dragged her head back against a rock-hard shoulder. A knife blade pressed to her throat filled her with terror. "Be quiet, wench! Someone'll think you don't like us."

Raucous laughter rippled through the drunken gang surrounding her like rabid dogs. Paralyzed with fear, she felt a trickle of blood slide down her neck. The stench of sour mead made her gag. She frantically searched the darkness. Shiny, inebriated eyes leered at her from the shadows. How many men were there? Six? Seven?

Dear God, please help me!

"I want her first," a deep voice slurred somewhere to her left.

"You'll have to wait your turn," another said, the words thick and muddled. Jeering laughter combined with lewd suggestions echoed through the street.

The pack grew bolder. Groping hands snatched at her clothes, pinched her, yanked her braid. The cloth of her tunic ripped, exposing her shoulder to the damp night air.

She squeezed her eyes shut. Unable to move or defend herself, she begged God for mercy.

The giant tightened his hand on her mouth. The pressure against her teeth cut her lip. She tasted blood.

He reached forward with the knife, the metal flashing in the moonlight between her face and the other wolves.

"All of you stand back," the giant ordered. "The woman promised I could have her first. You'll have to wait 'til I've had my taste."

What woman?

A flurry of drunken curses and outraged complaints

littered the night, but the long knife aided the pack's decision to slink backward.

"Such beautiful skin," the giant slurred near her ear. His sour breath churned her stomach. She gagged until she thought she might retch. He moved his hand from her mouth and buried his wet lips against the pulse racing in her throat.

She screamed. Her heel stomped his foot. He loosed his hold and the blade clanked on the stone street. Wild with fear, she jerked free from the drunk and ran.

Threats from her pursuing attackers spurred her onward. Was someone calling her name? Without slacking her pace, she turned a corner, then another and another until she was lost. Too scared to stop running, she pressed on, her lungs burning, her heart pounding.

Rapid footsteps gained ground behind her. The glow of a torch grew larger, lighting the narrow alleyway.

"Pelonia!"

Caros? She faltered, tripped on an uneven stone, felt herself falling.

A strong arm swooped around her middle, hauling her up just as her palms brushed the road. In a seamless movement, Caros turned her around, then pulled her against him. "Are you all right?"

She locked her arms around his waist and buried her cheek against his chest. Like an angel sent from God, he'd come to save her.

The heat of his torch warmed her skin, but did nothing to ease her chilling terror. He held her while she shivered and shook against him. For timeless moments, he rubbed her back until the tremors subsided.

Caros cupped her face with his free hand and tipped her head back to search for injuries. He ran the pad of his thumb over the shallow cut on her throat. Thankfully, the blood had dried and the wound no longer bled. The image of his woman, a blade held against her jugular, would never leave him. If she hadn't escaped those mongrels, he would have slaughtered them all.

He angled the torch for a better view of her ashen face. His gaze roamed over her, accessed the shock stamped across her shattered expression. "It's over now. They won't find us. Can you walk or shall I carry you home?"

"Home?" Her bottom lip quivered, her eyes filled with tears. "I have no home."

His chest constricted with pity. He tugged her against him, holding her close while sobs ravaged her tiny form. A promise to free her and help find her cousin sprang to the tip of his tongue.

No. His arms tightened around her. She was his. He couldn't let her go.

Once she quieted, he took her hand and began to lead her from the alley. "Come, Pelonia, you'll catch a cold. We must get you indoors."

She tugged free. "Why? So you can finish what those jackals started?"

A brow arched in question, he faced her. Illuminated by a pool of torchlight, her creamy cheeks smudged with tears, her lower lip swollen, she held her head high, daring him to deny her suspicion.

He narrowed the gap between them. "Are you crazed, woman? Haven't you realized by now I'm not going to rape you?"

She lifted her chin. "How can I trust such a claim? You said you meant to have me no matter what and there are rumors—"

"Rumors never cease. This is Rome. There's as much gossip here as there is air to breathe."

"You're a man. And I am your slave, or so you keep informing me."

He frowned, disliking the bitter accusation in her eyes. "Pelonia, if I meant to abuse your body, I would have done so already. You've been in my house, tempting me since the first time I saw you in the slaver's wagon."

Confusion furrowed her brow. She crossed her arms over her chest, as though to protect herself. "And what of tonight? Do you plan to punish me for my escape?"

He clasped her hand, tightening his grip when she tried to break the contact. "I haven't had time to consider it, though the gods know you deserve to be whipped."

"No, I do not. What did you expect after today in the garden?"

"I tried to kiss you, nothing more."

"Where I'm from, a man doesn't kiss a woman unless she's his wife. I've heard—"

"Rumors. Yes, I know. Who is this liar who's filled your head with poison against me?"

She glanced away, feigning a sudden interest in the cracked concrete wall of the building beside them.

He switched the torch to his other hand and flexed his fist, working the stiffness from his forearm. "Was it Servius? I know you worked with him this afternoon."

"No! He's a kind old man. Other than telling me where to find compost, he's barely spoken three words to me."

He raked his fingers through his hair in frustration. The culprit couldn't be one of his other gladiators, not when he'd been careful to keep her separate from them. "Was it another slave? Was it Lucia?"

"I'm cold." She avoided his eyes. "Can we go back to the house?"

So, it *was* Lucia. He heard the guilt in her voice. It was

a harsh disappointment to find the person he relied on most among his servants had become a viper. "Tell me the truth. Was it Lucia?"

"She's in love with you," she admitted after a long pause.

"Her actions speak otherwise. How can a person claim to love someone, then turn around and spread lies about him?"

"She was afraid of losing her place."

"She's done a fine job of it." He took her hand and compelled her to follow. "She'll be sold tomorrow."

"No!" She grabbed hold of his arm. "She helped me and—"

He slowed his pace and stabbed her with a harsh glare. "You mean she helped you escape?"

"I didn't say that."

"She did, didn't she?"

"I—"

"Tell me, woman!"

"Yes, but—"

"Did she send you in this direction on purpose?"

She looked pained, but nodded.

"Then not only will I sell her, I'll have her whipped first."

"Please, Caros, don't." Pelonia refused to walk further. "Why must you always threaten violence?"

"I'm a gladiator, remember? Violence is what I do best."

"I find that hard to believe after the gentle way you held me while I cried and soothed away my fear tonight."

The pity in her eyes was more than he could stomach. "It would be wiser if you did."

"I believe you'd prefer to be a man of peace."

Laughter gurgled in his tight throat. "You believe in a dead God, too."

"Don't blaspheme just because you know I speak the truth. Christ has done nothing to earn your scorn."

Smarting from her rebuke, Caros fell silent. A part of him admired her tenacious faith. Even in what must be the bleakest time of her life, she spoke as though she truly believed her God cared for her.

He tried to pinpoint the moment when he'd stopped believing in anything more than his own abilities. Perhaps it was during the dark days after his family's murder or those first terrifying hours in the ring. It had been so long ago he couldn't remember a time when he relied on anyone but himself.

He cast off his introspection. "You're wrong, Pelonia. Peaceful men don't thrive when forced to live a life of violence as I have."

They walked along the empty alley in silence until Pelonia murmured, "Maybe they do if there's a plan for them."

Would the woman never admit defeat? "What kind of plan?"

"I don't know, but who can determine the purpose of a life or why God allows one man to rise and another to fall. We can only trust Him."

"Trust," he scoffed, "mingles in the same net with love and I've survived with little of either."

"That breaks my heart." She squeezed his hand. "What of your family? Did they not love you?"

Her question pierced his chest like a stake. He'd known a wealth of tender emotions with his family, had trusted no one more than his parents and sisters. Watching all of them perish in the space of day had almost broken him.

One of his men opened the gates in front of the school. Caros led her to the front door of his house. He curved a tendril of her hair behind her ear, touched by her concern more deeply than he'd thought possible. "Don't fret about me or my family. Perhaps one day I'll tell you of my past. For now, I wish to make a bargain in order to avoid another fiasco like tonight."

"What is your bargain?" A hint of wariness crept into her voice.

"I will keep my distance, if you give your word not to escape."

She shook her head. "No, I...I couldn't make such a promise and plan to keep it. I won't run off into the night again. I've learned my lesson on that score, but if another opportunity presents itself, I'll take it."

He didn't know whether to laugh at her honesty or march her upstairs and chain her to a wall to ensure she never left him. "What if I vow—"

"To allow me to tell you about Christ?"

"What?" He'd never dreamed she'd bargain with something ridiculous. "I've no interest in your sect."

"I've no interest in living as a slave, either, but I won't try to leave—for a time—if you agree to give me a hearing."

Intrigued, Caros studied her. Why would she endure a life she found despicable just to tell him the ramblings of a crucified Hebrew? On the other hand, her offer might be the perfect solution. His agreement would buy enough time to break down her barriers and win her capitulation. He would have his way and what would it cost him to listen? It wasn't as if she were asking for his soul.

He planted the torch in the holder beside the door and cupped her face with his hands. Aware this might be the last time he touched her for what would seem an eternity, he memorized the texture of her soft skin and searched the depths of her earnest gaze. "I'll agree to your terms, for a fortnight, Pelonia. But be warned, my beautiful slave, by the end of two weeks' time I will have won your surrender. You'll never want to leave me."

"You think too highly of yourself, *lanista*."

A wolfish grin curved his lips. "Possibly, but remember, I've never lost a battle and I have no intention of losing this one."

Chapter Eight

Caros stood on the edge of the training field. The early morning sun shone hot and bright, glinting on the golden sand. Amid the clang of metal and grunts of pain, a dozen of his newest acquisitions fought to prove their worth.

None of them impressed him enough to sway his thoughts from Pelonia's escape of the previous night. Unable to sleep, he'd woken Alexius and railed at him for nearly an hour. The Greek had been no help. He'd merely laughed and asked how it felt to be enamored.

He'd almost punched his champion until he remembered Pelonia's disdain for violence. He'd stormed back to his own rooms then, convinced she'd whispered incantations over him. By the gods, he was Caros Viriathos, champion of the ring. A *lanista* surrounded by a sea of brutality. Until she arrived, he'd accepted the carnage that defined his existence.

Forcing visions of her soft brown eyes from his mind, he watched one of his assistants divide the trainees into six pairs. He concentrated on his men, but the bargain he'd struck with his beautiful slave kept luring his attention. Winning her favor dangled in front of him like honey before a starving man. Their battle of wills excited him like nothing he'd ever tasted. Other than granting her freedom, which would ruin his chance to see her, he'd do anything to win her favor.

He wished he'd sought her out this morning to relieve his concerns and determine her state of mind. Instead, he'd given orders not to wake her. After last night's ordeal, he felt she needed rest and tender care. The special meal he'd ordered for her pleasure included the finest food and drink Rome had to offer.

His musings turned black when he considered Lucia and her evil tricks. Justice demanded she be punished. He could not allow a snake to thrive in his home.

Caros picked up a *gladius* and entered the field before approaching a pair of trainees. The moment his shadow touched them, the shorter slave dropped his wooden, practice sword and backed away in fright.

Ignoring the coward, he addressed the taller, better fighter. "You were among the men I bought from Aulus's caravan, were you not?"

The slave nodded. "He bought us from a prison guard in Amiternum just days before our execution."

Typical. Many gladiators began their career in a similar fashion. Either a trader like Aulus bought and sold them for profit or the condemned were carted directly to the gladiatorial schools. Who better to perish for the mob's entertainment than those already sentenced to die? "What is your name?"

The man lifted his chin. "Quintus Fabius Ambustus."

"Why were you sentenced to death?"

Quintus squared his shoulders. "I refuse to worship the emperor."

Another Christian? Was he being surrounded? Only Jews and Christians denied what everyone else in the empire accepted by law whether they believed it or not. "If not the emperor, who do you believe is divine?"

"Jesus, the Christ," Quintus answered with conviction.

Caros's thoughts shifted back to Pelonia. What if she discovered he had another of her kind beneath his roof? After a steady diet, Quintus no longer appeared bone-thin or hollow-eyed. Good food and fresh water had restored life to his face and strength to his body. A woman might even think his dark hair and green eyes were somewhat handsome.

He frowned. What if Pelonia found Quintus appealing? They shared the same religion, something she believed necessary for a happy union. Could that common ground breed a deeper bond between them? What if her heart became entangled with the slave's and he lost all chance to make her his?

Jealousy, an emotion he'd never felt before and one he instantly hated, sizzled through him. He scowled and the Christian wisely backed away. "Whatever brought you here, you're my property for the time being. When you're ready, you'll enter the ring and achieve death or glory. It's up to you, but considering the investment I've made in your scrawny hide, I hope you'll choose the glory."

Quintus began to reply, but one of the guards crossed the sand and interrupted him. "Master, forgive me, but you said to inform you when the woman left her room. I believe she's headed for the garden."

Mindful of the bargain she'd struck with Caros the night before, Pelonia dressed quickly. She hadn't fallen asleep until dawn. Waking moments ago, she'd leaped from her pallet; the angle of the sun telling her it was already midmorning.

Her thoughts consumed by Caros, she hurried down the corridor. How strange the very person she'd sought to escape had been the one whose arms she'd clung to. Now, thanks to her vow, she was bound for a fortnight to give up her goal of freedom.

Strangely at ease with her situation, she grabbed up a wash bucket and clean linen cloth from the pantry before making her way outside and into the herb garden. Perhaps her time here had a purpose after all. Unless the Lord chose otherwise, Caros might never have another chance to hear the Good News.

As she collected water from the fountain, smoke from the kitchen fires mingled with the smell of chicken roasting for the noonday meal. Her stomach grumbling, she cupped her hands under the fountain's flow and splashed her face before quickly cleaning her teeth with the cloth.

Behind her a twig snapped. She picked up the overflowing bucket and turned, expecting one of the house slaves had come to berate her tardiness.

Her heart tripped. Cat watched her from a short distance away. His bright golden eyes studied her, his long, striped tail twitched. With a low growl, the tiger prowled toward her.

The bucket slipped from her fingers. Cold water splashed on her sandaled feet, soaking the hem of her tunic. Her gaze darted to the path that led back to the house. Anxious for an escape route or any sign of Caros, she saw neither.

Frozen with fright, she reminded herself the predator was a pet. Caros was probably somewhere close behind him. Gathering her courage, she stretched out her trembling palm and prayed the huge tiger wasn't hungry. "Hello, Cat. Do…do you remember me?"

Cat sniffed her fingers, then licked her palm with his abrasive tongue. He bumped her hand with his nose and pressed against her, snuggling his large head to her chest. She braced herself against the fountain to keep from falling backward.

Taking the hint, she ran her fingers over his fur, paying

special attention to each of his silken ears. Delighted by the experience of being so close to the exotic animal, she combed her fingers through the thick ruff of fur around his studded, leather collar.

"You're as sweet as a babe, aren't you, Cat?" No longer fearful, she remained cautious and scratched his chin, delighted to hear his soft sounds of enjoyment.

Snide laughter drew Pelonia's attention toward the garden entrance. Lucia strolled up the path toward her. The empty bucket she held swayed by her side.

"You've conquered the master, now you seek to tame the tiger, as well?"

Cat's massive body tensed. Pelonia tried to soothe him by stroking his ears, but the tiger remained alert, watchful. "I see you're not surprised I'm here, Lucia. I imagine you were disappointed when you learned Caros brought me back."

"Are you accusing me of something? If so, don't mince words. Speak plainly."

Before she'd fallen asleep last night, she'd come to realize Lucia's true purpose had never been to help her. She felt foolish for not seeing through the woman's plans, but now realized her craving for freedom had blinded her to Lucia's true motives.

"Did you ever believe I had a chance for escape?"

A smirk curved the healer's mouth. Her dark eyes were as hard as chips of jet. "No."

"Then why did you lie?"

"I wanted you gone. But I've accepted you're like the stink of old fish, impossible to get rid of unless the master disposes of you himself."

"Not true!" Her outrage clamored for release. "I wanted to flee. I'd have succeeded if you'd done as you promised and arranged for someone to guide me to my cousin."

"Your plan would have proven worthless in the end."

Lucia moved toward the fountain. "Caros is bewitched by you. He would have hunted you down and brought you back unless he became disgusted by the sight of you."

"He might try, but he'd need a legion to drag me back here once I reached my family. My cousin's husband is a senator. Do you think he'd let me rot in degradation when he has the influence to see me freed?"

Her back to the garden, the healer plunged her bucket beneath the fountain's flow. "By law you're the property of our master. If he refuses to sell, you can't be bought. He told you so himself. Why didn't you believe him?"

Because a future with no end to her enslavement was no future at all. "I'm certain he can be brought to reason."

Lucia shook her head. "I've been a slave my entire life. The *lanista's* slave since he opened the doors of this school three years past. I've seen how a man gazes at the woman he craves and I can see how much Caros yearns for you."

"You blame *me* for this?"

"Somehow you've made yourself a challenge to him and he never gives up until he's won."

"I've given him no reason to pursue me."

Lucia's lip curled. "He's drawn to your innocence. I won't accept it's anything more. If I hadn't been ill-used since girlhood, I'm certain I'd tempt him just as you have. My plan would have succeeded if only I'd waited longer to tell him you were gone."

Pelonia gaped, mystified by the bizarre workings of the woman's brain. "You make no sense. If you wanted me gone, why tell him I'd fled at all?"

"If you simply disappeared, he might have become obsessed to find you. As it was, I wanted him to *see* your disgrace. I wished for him to find you in the arms of another man. To have the image seared into his mind so he would never look on you with tenderness again. If you were not so pure, I'm convinced he'd lose all interest and send you away."

Numbed by Lucia's venom, Pelonia watched Cat trot toward the gate. Her breath hitched when she saw Caros beneath one of the olive trees a short distance down the path. He lifted his index finger to his lips, warning her to silence.

Pelonia's gaze darted back to where Lucia stood tangled in her own thoughts, her fingers locked on the lip of the fountain as if her outburst had drained her of strength. "I've waited three years for Caros to love me. With all of my being, I've longed to know the gentleness he's shown you without reservation."

The quiet confession tugged at Pelonia's heart, but the brutality she'd endured was still too raw to forgive the other woman. A light breeze rustled the lemon trees. Caros moved forward. Her eyes downcast, the healer didn't seem to notice his approach.

"Lucia, a word with you." His icy calm made Pelonia squirm with dread.

Lucia spun toward him, banging the bucket of water she'd placed by her feet. "Master, I didn't see you."

"So I gathered from the conversation."

The color drained from Lucia's face. "I can explain."

"No, allow me," he said coldly. "I rescued you from cruelty and made you an important member of this household. I gave you responsibility and more liberty as a slave than most free women ever dream of. You repaid my generosity with lies, theft—"

"Master, I never—"

"*Don't* interrupt me." The entire garden seemed to cringe from the quiet force of his rage. "You repaid me with jealousy and petty envy. Envy that would have seen a blameless girl raped and possibly murdered without a qualm."

"But Caros," Lucia whispered, placing her hand on his forearm with inappropriate familiarity. "You must listen to me!"

The woman must be insane. Pelonia worried for her welfare. Couldn't she see Caros teetered on the edge of committing mayhem? Why didn't Lucia heed the warnings of his clenched fists or the nerve ticking in his jaw? Why did she just stand there and not run for safety?

Caros cast her hand from him as though it were diseased. "You will be punished for aiding the escape of a slave and for slandering your master. You'll be whipped, then sold. Never darken my door again."

"Noooo!" Lucia fell to her knees, tears coursing down her face. "Please don't do this, Master. I *love* you. Can't you see the truth? If not for her, you would have come to *me.*"

Unable to watch the piteous sight, Pelonia turned away. Lucia's broken spirit sparked her compassion. When she thought of her own failings, the transgressions that stained her soul, who was she to judge the other woman? Without Christ's boundless love and forgiveness she might be as hopeless.

Lucia's sobs rang through the garden. She called Caros's name, begging him to hear her, but he remained deaf to her pleas. With Cat beside him, he didn't stop except to speak with a set of guards outside the gate.

Once Caros disappeared beyond her sight, she approached the other woman as though Lucia were a wounded animal. Seeing the guards move closer, she knelt beside the healer, unsure of the welcome she'd receive. When Lucia continued to weep, Pelonia eased her into an embrace.

Lucia didn't fight. She cried harder. Her tears soaked Pelonia's shoulder. A hard lump formed in her throat as she stroked Lucia's hair, silent in her attempt at solace.

When the tears subsided, Lucia pulled away, her cheeks

blotchy, her eyes lifeless. She wiped the damp rivulets from her face. "Can you imagine the pain I've endured since you came here? I've had to tend your wounds, ensure you lived, while knowing every day the man I worship is falling deeper and deeper under your spell."

Before Pelonia could reply, the guards seized Lucia and shuffled her from the garden, ignoring Pelonia's entreaties to stop. Distressed by the woman's treatment, she tried to imagine the hardship of Lucia's life, the harshness of an existence without affection.

She recalled her own history, the blessing of being raised by a father who cared for her and taught her of Christ's love. Her strength came from the truth she'd learned, the certainty that came from being nurtured in faith even when circumstances made her question God's fairness.

But what of Lucia? A slave from birth, she'd been denied familial attachment and weaned on the uncertainty of their society's fear and superstition. Who could blame her for dreaming of a life with a man of Caros's strength or for fighting for her place when she felt threatened?

Pelonia filled the buckets and carried them to an untended corner of the garden. Somehow she would have to sway Caros from the punishment he'd chosen. But how did she ask for mercy from a man who'd never known compassion? Why would he listen to her when, despite what Lucia claimed, she was nothing more to him than a challenge?

A guard approached and gave orders for her to meet Caros in the house. Eager to speak with him, she washed her hands and made her way to the cool interior courtyard where the smell of fresh bread and a table laden with delicacies awaited her.

Caros wasn't to be found, but the tall stranger she'd seen with him yesterday entered the open air space from the direction of the living quarters. With his hair rumpled and his short tunic wrinkled, he looked as though he'd just risen from a deep sleep. Not wanting to disturb one of Caros's guests, she turned to leave.

"Wait," he said, a Greek accent edging his Latin, "I'm Alexius, Caros's champion. You must be Pelonia, his newest paramour."

"I'm no such thing," she denied hotly.

"Of course you're not." A grin parted his lips, creating a long dimple in each of his lean cheeks. "That's why Caros woke me in the middle of the night ranting about you. It seems you're more trouble than you're worth."

She crossed her arms over her chest. "Is that what he told you?"

He shook his head, the sunlight glinting off his dark hair. "No, my opinion only. Is it true Lucia's to be whipped and sold today?"

"Not if I can stop it."

He moved to the table and chose an oatcake glistening with honey. "You think you can change Caros's mind?"

"I have to try."

"By all means, do. I'd hate to see Lucia sent away. She's an intelligent woman and there are few enough of those."

Pelonia arched a brow. "Perhaps you think so because only dim women will tolerate you."

He laughed, clearly not offended. "Lucia's talented with herbs and other medicines. Whether Caros admits it or not, she'll be difficult to replace."

"Thank you, Alexius. I believe you've given me the solution I need."

"I have? How so?"

"I'll explain later. Do you know where Caros is? A guard told me to meet him here, but…"

"I imagine he's on the field. If you were told to wait here, do so. The sand is no place for a dainty woman like you."

"But I must find him. He may have Lucia whipped at any moment."

"No, the men are occupied. He won't interrupt them with frivolity. The punishment won't begin until after the midday meal when the men are resting and it can serve as both a warning and entertainment."

Pelonia's stomach flipped. "Is Caros always so cruel?"

The Greek chewed a bite of peach and swallowed. "Why do you think he's cruel?"

"Don't *you* think it's harsh to have Lucia whipped for the men's amusement?"

"No. She disobeyed and betrayed him. A cruel *lanista* would use her for target practice."

She shuddered. "I tried to escape. What punishment do you think he has in store for me?"

"Ask him yourself." Alexius tipped his head toward the corridor and stood to leave. "There he is now."

In a few brisk steps, Caros joined Pelonia beside the table. For several long moments before Alexius announced his arrival he'd taken the chance to watch her unhindered. Her tart replies to the Greek amused him as much as her concern for Lucia amazed him.

"Have you eaten?" he asked.

"No, but Alexius seemed to enjoy the fruit."

"Why didn't you sample it? I doubt you've eaten since last night."

"It's not mine and I'm neither a thief nor a guest."

"You can't steal this. It's all yours."

"For me?" She glanced at the arrangement of breads and sweet cream, fresh berries, peaches, and oatcakes glistening with honey. "I don't understand. Aren't you angry with me?"

Her pulse ticked beneath the red gash on her neck. The reminder of the rapist's knife held against her throat stoked his ire toward Lucia. "I'm furious, but not with you."

She wrung her hands, her deep brown eyes widened with uncertainty. "How can you not be? I tried to escape."

He shrugged. "Every slave runs for freedom at least once."

"Did you?"

"More than once," he admitted.

"What happened?"

"I was flogged."

Tears formed in her eyes. "I'm sorry."

Why the tears? Did she fear he'd have her disciplined in a similar manner? "As you should be. I'll be lenient with you this time, but don't test me again."

"I'm not apologizing for my attempted escape. I'm sorry you were ever abused."

His heart beat faster. It seemed eons since anyone bothered to care if he lived or died, let alone whether or not he'd endured a mere whipping.

He cupped her face, her cheeks smooth and soft beneath his calloused palms. Aware of their bargain, that he was breaking his promise not to touch her, he crushed the urge to gather her in his arms. "Then your apology is unnecessary, *mea carissima*. My back no longer pains me. Unlike my heart, if you seek to leave me again."

Her gaze softened. "Our bargain," she reminded him softly. "I've given my word not to leave for a fortnight."

He brushed his thumb along her full bottom lip, comparing its rich color to the ripe peaches on the table. "By then you'll be mine and leaving me will be the last thing you want."

She stepped away as if rejecting the worst sort of temptation. "I doubt it, Caros. You speak of making me yours, but I'll never willingly give myself to a man who's not my husband."

He smiled, aware he never failed to claim what he set his mind to. "We'll see."

"Yes, we will." She tucked a strand of hair behind her ear and moved a few paces deeper into the shade. "Now, about Lucia."

He dropped his arms to his side and his hands balled into fists. "What about the cursed wench? If I hadn't been looking for you in the garden, I might not have heard her confess her crimes. As it is, I've already arranged to have her punished after the noonday meal."

"Please don't," she said, her eyes pleading. "Alexius told me your plans. Consider what it will mean for you and your men if she's gone."

"How can you, of all people, not wish to see her punished? Have you forgotten the course of sorrow and disgrace she charted for you?"

"I haven't forgotten, but I have chosen to forgive."

Astounded, he grasped for words. "You've forgiven her? Why? How?"

"How can I not? None of us has lived a blameless life."

He'd never met anyone with half her generous nature. Forgiveness was foreign to him. In his world, a man lived and died by the sword where one mistake might forfeit his life. There were no second chances. Once again, her strange way of thinking intrigued him. "Tell me why I should forgive her when she's earned the severest punishment?"

Pelonia prayed for wisdom before she spoke. If she ever hoped to impart the heart of the Gospel to this warrior, now might be her last chance. "I can't truthfully say she doesn't deserve what you intend for her."

He snorted. "I knew it."

"But Christ has pardoned me for the wrongs I've committed. I owe it to Him to follow His example and forgive others when they wound me."

"You should have told me we were discussing religion." He waved his hand to dismiss the subject.

"No, Caros, we're not." She gripped his forearm to stop him from leaving. "We're talking about love and kindness, generosity of spirit. The act of extending mercy, because…because you understand how much you need it for yourself."

For one unguarded moment, she saw through his hardened exterior to the place deep inside him that was raw with need.

Her heart nearly burst with want of comforting him. She could barely refrain from throwing her arms around him and holding him until the torment in his eyes disappeared for good.

He glanced skyward. "Few people ever receive mercy, Pelonia. Fewer still deserve it."

"True, but Christ taught He has enough mercy and forgiveness for anyone who asks Him for it. You must only believe in Him."

"You can't fathom the things I've done," he said so quietly she strained to hear.

She could imagine. A man of his skill in the ring had probably killed countless people over the years. "It doesn't matter what you've done, Caros. Christ's forgiveness is a gift. One none of us deserves, but His grace is extended to all just the same."

"How much will this 'gift' cost me? I used to visit the temples until the priests kept demanding more coin to fatten their coffers."

"It's free. You can't buy it or earn it. You must only believe."

He closed his eyes. An expression of pain marred his features. He shook his head. "I can't believe in grace or forgiveness when everything in my life has taught me there is none."

Her heart sank with disappointment. "You don't have to believe in Him this moment, Caros, but I pray one day you will."

Chapter Nine

Marcus Valerius contemplated his nephew by marriage, Senator Antonius Tacitus, with a healthy dose of respect. Shrewd beyond his thirty years, the senator would be difficult to dupe. Antonius's young wife, Tiberia, might be a beauteous and spirited woman, but her brain rivaled the size of a lentil. Not so her husband.

"Why do you need such a large sum of money, Marcus?" The senator tossed a parchment onto his bronze-plated desk. "As I understand it, you inherited your brother's holdings when the marauders killed him a fortnight ago."

"Yes, but the property is far from the delights and advantages one can find here in the capital. Besides—" Marcus spread his hands and schooled his lips into a cajoling smile "—is it really so large a sum between family?"

The senator's lips thinned. "Five thousand denarii is a large amount between anyone—especially family. What assurance do I have you'll repay me?"

"I'm willing to use the Umbrian estate as collateral," Marcus said, determined to risk all if necessary in his goal of establishing himself as an influential man of Rome. "The vineyards alone are worth ten times as much as I'm asking to borrow. When you consider the additional orchards, wheat fields, livestock, the villa and outbuildings…do you think I'd be foolish enough to risk the place if I weren't convinced of my plans?"

"A good business strategy doesn't ensure success, Marcus. Importing wine from your own estate and selling it here in the city without the expense of an importer sounds profitable, but there are innumerable wine merchants in Rome." Antonius adjusted the lantern light. "According to my wife, your brother opted against this sort of venture, claiming it was too risky."

Marcus gritted his teeth. Opening the wine shop was the first step in a larger scheme to obtain the recognition he craved. Years spent in the shadow of his twice-blessed older brother had left him virtually forgotten, his talents dismissed and his life almost wasted. With Pelonius dead and his troublesome niece sold into slavery, he finally had the means to fulfill his ambitions.

"From what my wife tells me," Antonius continued, "Pelonius turned your father's small farm into a thriving enterprise within a short time of his inheritance. Tiberia's high regard for your late brother and his undisputed financial acumen make me hesitant to go against his judgment."

Marcus hid his contempt for the younger man's lack of vision beneath a placid smile. No man worth his salt let a woman sway his decisions, but whether he liked it or not, he needed Antonius's influence. Once he'd made his own connections, Tiberia and her myopic husband could rot for all the care he gave. Until then, he planned to smile and nod in agreement when necessary, and when the time came, collect apologies from those who'd doubted his talents and superior intellect.

"It's true, my brother was favored by Mercury with his gift of commerce, but I'm equally gifted. It isn't my fault Pelonius inherited before me. If I'd been the elder son and the land passed down to me who knows how great our family's fortune might be."

Elated to find he held the senator's full attention, Marcus pressed on. "You'd be a fool not to loan me the funds. I promise you there's no need to fear you'll lose a single piece of silver. I'll pay you back with interest, of course. If I'm unsuccessful, which I won't be, you'll have the estate. Either way you're bound to profit."

"By the gods, it's a tempting offer." The senator picked up the parchment and studied the proposal with renewed interest. He eyed Marcus over the top of the page like a cat about to pounce on a wounded squirrel. "Very tempting. In fact, maybe I *should* loan you the money, then devise a scheme to make you fail. What better place to escape Rome's summer heat than to my own estate in the Umbrian hills?"

Marcus laughed nervously. Perhaps he'd been *too* persuasive. "As we're kin of sorts, Senator, feel free to enjoy my hospitality whenever you wish."

"That's good of you, *kin,* considering you've been a guest in my home for how many weeks?"

Marcus folded his hands in his lap, irritated by his host's subtle gibe. Adopting a wounded air, he straightened in his seat. "I apologize, Senator, if I've overstayed my welcome. Your dear wife was the first to embrace me as a relative since mine were taken so tragically on the way to your wedding. If, in my gratitude toward her, I've somehow offended you by claiming your people as my own, I—"

"Enough, Marcus. If you'd offended me, you'd be out on the street, not here in my study trying to wheedle me out of five thousand denarii."

Reminding himself to bide his time, Marcus cloaked his scorn beneath a reverential manner. "I'm glad to hear I remain in your good graces."

Antonius left his desk and went to a cabinet painted with a lush scene of Venus rising from the sea's foam. He opened one of its front panels and removed a bottle of wine. "I'll have an agreement prepared for us to sign by tomorrow's dinner hour."

Marcus fidgeted with excitement. He was on his way. "What rate of interest will you charge me?"

"Only twenty percent. It's fair enough considering the money lenders' price." The senator lifted the bottle of red wine. "Shall I pour you a glass of your family's finest to celebrate?"

Marcus accepted with his first genuine smile in weeks. Without a doubt he'd been right to sell Pelonia and cleanse the family of her Christian defilement. The gods must be pleased with his loyalty to them, for they'd been smiling on him ever since that fateful day.

He stood and accepted the glass Antonius held out to him. "Indeed, Senator, I'm happy to drink with you. There is much to celebrate and I'm confident there is even more excitement to come."

Pelonia had just finished weeding the vegetable garden when Caros's steward found her in the courtyard and delivered new orders.

"Make haste for the kitchen," Gaius said. "The master has invited a special guest to dine with him this evening. You're needed to help with the preparations."

A ruckus outside the front of the house caught his attention before she could reply.

"She's here!" Gaius bumped into a large potted palm on his swift retreat to the main door. A handful of house slaves scurried after him. Pelonia followed to the edge of the atrium, curious to see who'd set the household on fire.

Positioning herself behind one of the tiled columns lining the covered porch, she had a clear view of the proceedings without being seen.

Near the door, Gaius lined up the slaves in a tight row. The steward took a deep breath, forced a smile and swept open the portal.

Pelonia gasped. The woman who breezed across the threshold was easily the most beautiful vision she'd ever seen. Her unblemished, alabaster skin provided an elegant contrast with her black hair and exotic, kohl-rimmed eyes. Perfectly dressed in a flowing tunic of rare blue silk, she wore a matching *palla* around her shoulders. The shawl, in the same blue as the tunic, was shot through with gold thread that shimmered in the light.

An elaborate gold headpiece held her fashionable, upswept curls in place. Bejeweled baubles, rings and necklaces adorned her slender form from her tiny ears to her rich, blue-dyed leather sandals.

As the guest moved deeper into the house, she gave Pelonia a glimpse of the expensively crafted litter she'd arrived on and the four muscular slaves who'd carried it.

Perhaps the lady was royalty.

"Where is my favorite *lanista?*" the woman asked, quizzing Gaius on Caros's whereabouts. "I rushed here from across the city as soon as I received his message late this morning. Is it too much to expect he greet me at the door?"

Pelonia's interest heightened. Why had Caros invited this stunning woman to meet with him?

"He's due from the baths at any moment, my lady." Gaius helped her remove the shawl, revealing the guest's gold, sapphire studded belt. "He told me to make you comfortable if you arrived before he returned."

The guest seemed unimpressed. "Typical man. Issue a summons, then expect a woman to wait. Normally, I wouldn't tolerate such rudeness. If it were anyone besides my dear Caros, I'd leave this instant."

Pelonia stifled a laugh. She liked the new arrival's spirited manner.

"I'm sure he appreciates your patience, my lady." Gaius handed the *palla* to the first slave before ushering the woman past Pelonia and into a sitting room. The other slaves trailed in their wake.

"May I fetch you a drink?" Pelonia heard the steward ask. "Or would you prefer something to eat? What can I do to provide for your comfort?"

Pelonia peered around the corner. The woman perched on the sofa. Her head tilted at a regal angle, she contemplated the offer. "I suppose a glass of new wine will do. And a selection of those special rolls your cook bakes would also please me. Just make certain he doesn't skimp on the honey."

Gaius clapped and two of the slaves ran to do the visitor's bidding. The remaining two slaves gathered large peacock feather fans from the corner and began to wave them over the woman. Bracelets jangling, the new arrival folded her hands in her lap and leaned forward slightly for Gaius to fluff her pillows.

"How long before Caros returns?" she asked, tapping her fingers on her knee. "You know I bore easily, Gaius. Perhaps I'll venture to the training yard and take stock of the newest men." She sprang to her feet.

"My lady…" Gaius threw up his hands in defeat as she disappeared down the corridor in the direction of the training field. The steward shook his head and slanted a glance at Pelonia. "That fireball is Adiona Leonia. She's one of the richest widows in Rome and was among the master's first admirers. She's loved him for years."

Her favor toward the widow dimmed and a twinge of jealousy unsettled her.

Gaius waved his hand as if to erase his last statement from the air. "Forget my rash words. I'm not one to spread gossip about our master and you're needed in the kitchen. Widow Leonia will expect her meal prepared on time and to perfection. The master will be furious if she's disappointed."

Pelonia headed to the cookhouse. Her brow pleated with troubling questions. What did Caros want with Adiona Leonia? Was the vivacious beauty really in love with him? Most likely, but how did he feel about his admirer in return? Worst of all, had Caros been toying with *her* emotions when his heart already belonged to the widow?

Pelonia entered the kitchen, drowning in uncertainty. Heat blasted her. The aroma of cooked meat enveloped her and she noticed a trio of pigs roasting on a spit above the flames.

Adjusting her coarse tunic, she remembered the fine silk of the widow's ensemble, garments similar to the ones she used to wear every day and took for granted. She washed her hands in a bucket of tepid water, ignoring a pang of envy. She joined the other four slaves kneading dough by the window. Deep in debate about which gladiator they found most handsome, the girls didn't acknowledge her greeting.

Pelonia's fingers worked the sticky, wheat-colored mass atop the table. The girls' chatter faded as her thoughts drifted back to Adiona. Little wonder Caros found the woman attractive. She was too beautiful by half. Not only was she stunning, but her vibrant energy infused the air around her. She smelled fresh, too, clean with a hint of cinnamon and other fragrant spices.

Pelonia wrinkled her nose, disgusted by the smell of

smoked pork clinging to her own body. She hoped Cat didn't mistake her in the dark for his evening snack. With the back of her hand, she brushed the sweat from her brow and, knowing it would make it worse, resisted the urge to scratch the chafed area on her shoulder beneath her tunic.

Her fingers grew idle in the dough as she stared out the window. In less than a month, her life had changed beyond recognition. Her chest ached from holding in her grief. A well of loneliness opened inside her, dragging her into its darkness. She missed her father, her home, her friends. She missed being herself.

With all her heart, she wished Caros had met her as she used to be, not the bedraggled slave she'd become. Perhaps then he would respect her and view winning her affections as something more than a game.

"Stop dawdling!" The girl beside her jabbed an elbow in Pelonia's ribs. "Word is more guests are coming tonight. We have to hurry and get more loaves of bread in the oven."

Rubbing her side, Pelonia bit back a retort and finished kneading her portion of dough, then several others. Heat from the fire made her perspire until the itchy cloth she wore stuck to her back and chest.

What she wouldn't do for a bath. She longed for the soothing comfort of the water, the cleansing ointments on her skin—

"Pelonia?" A male slave called from the doorway. "Are you in here?"

She brushed the flour and bits of dough from her hands before wiping them on a towel. "Yes, here I am."

"The master wishes to see you. He's waiting in the atrium."

She left the kitchen, but didn't rush to find Caros. After all, he had Adiona to amuse him. Bending to pick a sprig of jasmine along the path, she tucked the flower behind her right ear. She breathed in the sweetness, shamefully aware that one small bloom could not hide the odor of her unwashed clothes and person.

Once she entered the house, she straightened her shoulders and held her head high. As she made her way into the courtyard, she noticed the lack of Adiona's presence and breathed a sigh of thanks.

Caros met her beneath the columned porch. The sight of him stole her breath. He'd had his hair trimmed and was freshly shaven. The thick black waves of his hair curled around his ears and brushed his forehead. His white tunic looked new, as did his leather sandals. She'd never seen him more handsome. Had he gone to such trouble with his appearance to impress his beautiful guest?

He grasped her elbow in a light grip. "Where have you been? I sent a messenger for you almost half an hour ago."

"Half an hour?" She glanced at the sundial, then schooled her features in an innocent expression. "I'm surprised you noticed the time with such pleasant company to entertain you."

He looked startled. "You met Adiona?"

"I didn't meet her. I saw her when she arrived."

His lips spread in a slow smile. "She *is* pleasant, is she not? And beautiful enough to rival Venus, don't you agree?"

"She's remarkable," she answered, determined to sound congenial. Why, she couldn't pinpoint, but she waited for him to refute any serious involvement with the woman.

No denial came and she restrained herself from shaking one out of him. Jealousy buzzed in her head like an irritating fly beside her ear. She pasted on a smile to save her pride. "I hope the two of you are most happy together."

"Oh, we are," he assured her. "Adiona and I have known one another for years. Unlike you and me, she and I are of similar minds. Our relationship is everything I desire it to be."

She swallowed her heartache and reached up to tuck a stray wisp of hair behind her ear. The jasmine fell to the mosaic floor. Having forgotten she'd placed it there, she realized how pathetic she must seem compared to the luminous widow. With her hair unwashed and lusterless, the feed sack of a tunic she wore and dirt embedded under her fingernails, she was a broken stem next to an artfully arranged bouquet.

Caros bent to retrieve the sprig and handed it to her. "Is all well with you, Pelonia? You seem a bit disheartened."

Careful not to touch him, she took the flower. "If I seem down, it's because I'm confused."

"By what?"

"By you," she admitted. "If you belong to your widow friend, why did you attempt to woo *me?*"

He shrugged. "Why do you care? You're the one who claimed we're ill-suited. You should be delighted I've taken you at your word."

The flow of the fountain filled the silence. A reply froze in her throat. She searched his face, captivated by the deep blue of his eyes, the strength of his jaw, the fullness of his lips.

Her vision blurred with unshed tears. How much loss could she endure? First her father and household, now Caros when she was just beginning to understand how much she cared for him. It was cold comfort to realize she'd been right to withhold her heart since his had proven fickle.

She bowed her head. *Please, God, hold me together. Don't let him witness my despair.*

His warm fingers slid around the back of her neck. With a gentle tug, he pulled her toward him, but she refused to budge.

Voices carried from the direction of the guest rooms. Caros released her the moment Adiona entered the courtyard.

"There you are, my darling." The widow's bright smile curved her painted mouth. She linked arms with Caros and her amber gaze scanned Pelonia from head to foot. She frowned. "This isn't the one you suggested earlier, is it? She'll never do as a maid of mine. She looks like she hasn't bathed in a week. I might get fleas."

Pelonia's cheeks burned and with as much dignity as she could muster she walked away. Her vanity wounded, her feminine pride shattered, she clutched at the hollow ache in her chest.

"Where are you off to?" Caros called before she could escape indoors. "I didn't dismiss you."

Her steps slowed to a stop. Her mortification fresh in her mouth, she couldn't bring herself to turn around.

Caros watched her intently. Would she carry out a test of wills in front of his guest? He hoped not. It would be an affront he couldn't let pass. He counted to three, then commanded, "Come here, slave."

He saw her wince and regretted the order. He'd meant to make her jealous, not earn her hatred for all eternity.

She turned, her entire manner as stiff as an iron blade. Her dark eyes shimmered with anger…or was it injured pride?

"Yes, *Master?*" she said, her tone so cold, he suspected he'd catch a chill.

Easing from the widow's grasp, he moved halfway to Pelonia. This close he could see the emotion wasn't anger or injured pride in her troubled eyes. It was raw humiliation.

He released a sharp breath. What a fool he was. The one woman he wanted most in life and he was certain he'd just lost her.

Chapter Ten

P elonia struggled to hide her embarrassment behind a mask of indifference. Aware of the widow's scrutinizing gaze, she couldn't bear for the arrogant gorgon to see how deep her insult cut.

She crossed her arms over her chest, uncomfortable with Caros's probing stare. "If that will be all, *Master,* may I go? There's work to be done in the kitchen."

He raked his fingers through his hair and gave a terse nod of consent. "Go, then. I'll speak with you later."

Her back as straight as a pike, she fled indoors. Once out of Caros's sight she pressed against a wall for support, waiting for her trembling to ease. Her anger burned against Caros and his icy paramour. The woman in her wished for a way to teach the malicious beauty a lesson in humility.

Adiona's husky laughter rippled through the garden. "Amazing!" she exclaimed. "I do believe our undefeated champion has finally met his match."

"Adiona, don't—"

"And a slave girl no less. How delicious!"

Fascinated, Pelonia stilled though she knew she should walk away.

"Leave it." He sounded exasperated.

"No, you must tell me," the widow said with glee. "I'm intrigued beyond bearing. How did you, with women all over Rome vying for your favor, fall for such a scruffy little mouse?"

Pelonia bristled, her dislike of the widow and her mockery growing more intense with each passing moment. She held her breath waiting for Caros's response.

"I've never struck a woman before," he said darkly, "but you're tempting me."

The widow gasped. "There's no need to be cruel. I was jesting."

After a long, tense moment, his heavy footsteps sounded on the tile. "Forgive me," he said, his voice strained. "In my bad temper, I forgot your past misfortune. After all these years, you must know you're safe regardless of my threats."

Pelonia's brow furrowed. Had Adiona been abused once? Perhaps the widow's brusque exterior hid a core of inner pain? If so, she couldn't help but feel a twinge of pity for the woman.

"I *do* know," Adiona murmured, almost too softly to reach Pelonia's ears. "I'm sorry I teased you. Love is an affliction. I've seen the various ways the malady affects its victims and I know you're not the giddy sort."

He grunted. "Leave it, Adiona. I'm not in love with her. The girl's a slave. No more, no less."

A chill settled in Pelonia's bones. The widow spoke, but she didn't hear over the rush of recriminations swirling through her head. *What did you expect of him, you silly idiota? A declaration of undying devotion?*

She bowed her head, distraught to realize some sort of acknowledgment was exactly what she'd hoped for. *Brainless, stupid, foolish...*

Heavy with disappointment, she climbed the stairs to lick her wounds in the solitude of her chamber. With Caros otherwise engaged and dinner preparations reaching their zenith, she suspected no one would notice her absence.

An hour later, a small oil lamp illuminated Pelonia's room. The sun had said farewell and darkness enshrouded the city. She stood at the window. Every fiber of her being urged her to run, to escape the prison of her despair. Yet, she was trapped as much by the guards at every gate as her promise not to flee.

Her fingers gripped the sill until her nails made marks in the wood. She must have been deranged to make the bargain last night. Yes, she wanted to tell Caros about Jesus, but if she were honest with herself she had to admit her capitulation stemmed from other reasons as well. Had it been the tenderness she imagined in Caros's eyes or her own gullibility? Perhaps both had conspired to trick her into believing something more, something precious yet unexplored, existed between her and the *lanista*.

Not that it mattered what she thought. This afternoon he'd been clear in his denial of any affection for her.

The girl's a slave. No more, no less.

His words circled over and over in her mind, scalding her with each relentless pass.

The smell of roasted meats carried on the cool night air. She hadn't eaten since morning. Her stomach grumbled. The banquet would begin soon. She tensed, aware that if anyone noticed her absence it would be during the meal's first few courses. Once the guests were immersed in the party's merriment, no one would care if there were too few servants or not.

Lying down on her pallet, she tried to reach out for God's guidance, an inkling of peace. Instead, her mind tormented her with visions of Caros and his lady love. Jealousy hounded her. How had she come to care for him in such a short time? When had he wormed into her heart so completely?

Lord, how do I pluck him out?

She rolled to her side. The shadows on the walls flickered like evil specters laughing at her misery. She stood and began to pace.

Shuffling footsteps drew her attention. Someone knocked on the door. If she ignored them perhaps they'd leave her be? Another knock, this one more insistent.

"Open up!" a gruff voice demanded. "I have word from the master."

She glared at the portal and the harsh male concealed behind it. She might as well answer; there was no lock. She wrenched open the door…and stared in astonishment.

"The master sent this for you." The short, burly slave nodded to a wooden tub held by two other slaves behind him. Confused, she backed up and let them deposit the large, barrel-shaped container in the corner.

"They'll be back with water," the gruff slave informed as he tossed her a folded bundle of cloth. "You have instructions to ready yourself. The master's guests will be arriving within the hour. You're expected to help serve the meal."

Moments later, the slaves brought water, filled the tub and left. She closed the door and undid the bundle she held. Inside, she found a fresh tunic, a bottle of cleansing oils and two rough cloths to dry herself with. Delighted by the items, she placed the oils and cloths by the tub and draped the tunic over the room's lone chair.

With a sigh, she slipped into the steaming water. It was almost too hot after weeks of bathing in cold, but the glorious sensation of being immersed in sweet bliss relaxed her muscles and lifted her spirits.

Tipping her head back against the rim, she closed her eyes. Why had Caros sent her the gifts? Had Adiona's scorn shamed him enough to be generous? Or did he simply wish to avoid embarrassment in front of his guests? No doubt, his displeasure would soar if she entered his banquet as odorous as a "scruffy little mouse."

She refused to rile her temper with thoughts of the widow or her insults. Whatever Caros's reason for the bath and other gifts, she was grateful.

The water cooled. She reached for one of the cloths and spread it on the floor. Stepping out of the tub, she applied a thick layer of spice-scented oil over her skin and through her wet hair. At the bath complex, an attendant would use a strigil to scrape the dirt and moisture from her body, but in the absence of both helper and implement, she used one of the rough cloths to buff her skin until it shone with cleanliness.

By the time she heard Caros's first visitors arrive, she was rinsing her hair. Clean and refreshed, she wrapped the strands in one of the dry linens and, stalling for time, washed her other garments.

Faint chatter and the muted melody of a panpipe filtered through the open windows, signaling the start of the evening's entertainments.

She'd best hurry. Her hair finger-combed and braided, her teeth cleaned, she finished dressing, thankful for the new tunic and the softness brushing her body. She slipped on her sandals, tied the laces around her ankles, and headed for the first floor.

Caros noticed Pelonia the moment she walked into the dining room, a pitcher held in each hand. He willed her to glance his way, but she denied him even the slightest acknowledgment. The oil lamps provided a clear view as she made her way toward the low-lying couches surrounding the banquet table.

His longing for her so strong he could taste the bitter sweetness of it, he admired the sway of her hips and her supple, honey-toned skin. In different garments, no one would suspect her slave status. She possessed the bearing of a goddess and her natural beauty put every other woman in the room to shame.

The music shifted tempo. A kithara and lyre joined the panpipe. Had she enjoyed her bath? He wished he'd thought of her needs sooner, before Adiona's mockery had a chance to hurt her. Had his wits been quicker, he might have saved Pelonia a healthy dose of embarrassment.

His gaze followed her as she mingled with his guests. Filling empty glass goblets with fresh water or honeyed wine, she smiled often, speaking when spoken to. The easy laughter that followed her comments added to the party's jovial mood.

She conversed with Alexius, unaware of her effect on many of the males in attendance. Noticing how the eyes of the men lingered on his woman, Caros struggled to contain his temper. Perhaps he should have overcome his need to see her and left her upstairs away from lust-filled eyes.

Adiona moved beside him, her sweet perfume surrounding him like a thick cloud. She linked her arm with his. "It's going well, don't you agree? Marius Brocchus and his mistress are eating all the honeyed figs, but other than that everyone seems happy enough."

He looked down into his friend's kohl-rimmed eyes. "The evening's going as you planned. I'm glad we could help one another."

She rose on tiptoe and kissed his mouth. "You're the last man in the world worth a denarius. I would have sent Lucia to my country villa even if you hadn't agreed to this fete."

He groaned. "You might have told me sooner."

Squeezing his arm, she laughed. "You can admit you're enjoying yourself."

He located Pelonia near the banquet table. As long as she remained in the room he managed to be content. "You know I'm not one for parties."

"Indeed, I do. *Everyone* knows you've been a recluse this last year. I've defended you, but…"

Adiona chatted on. Caros listened with half an ear. He'd stopped his wild socializing when he realized how empty it left him. Without Pelonia's presence even this fine gathering would soon bore him.

He barely noticed when Adiona went to make conversation with Alexius. As the night progressed, he did his duty and spoke with a number of couples and a small group of senators debating the consequences of Emperor Domitian's new policies.

Throughout the night, his female admirers approached him, but with his attention focused on his slave, he dispatched the women with ease.

His brows pinched together. He'd lost sight of Pelonia again. It wasn't uncommon for drunken guests to claim a comely slave for a night's use and with many of his visitors swimming deeper in their cups, he worried for her safety.

A well-known soloist began a bawdy song. Cheers and applause filled the room. Revelers reclined on the couches, stuffing themselves with more of the delectable food.

Adiona came up beside him. She tugged on his arm. "Why are you frowning when Rome's most-sought-after entertainer is performing for your benefit?" She sighed. "Isn't he wonderful? He was so honored when I sent word you would be here tonight, he cancelled a previous engagement to sing elsewhere."

Another burst of laughter erupted in the far corner. Pelonia had been gone too long. He started to seek her out, but caught sight of her in the open doorway, on a return trip from the courtyard. His anxiety lessened. She must have gone to refill her pitchers or care for the guests sampling the cooler air outside. Either way it was time for her to leave.

"Excuse me," he said, withdrawing his arm from Adiona's grasp.

Pelonia froze when she saw him approach. He smiled and relieved her of the pitchers, handing them to another slave close by. Unmindful of the hush descending around him, he took hold of her hand. "Come with me, *mea carissima*. I believe we've both endured enough for one night."

Chapter Eleven

Uncomfortably aware of the sudden whispers and keen interest aimed in her direction, Pelonia followed Caros from the dining room and down the corridor.

"Did I displease you?" she asked. "Where are you taking me?"

"You please me," he said without slowing his pace. "I wish to walk with you."

"Won't your company be offended if you leave?"

"If they are, so be it. They're Adiona's guests, not mine."

Bemused, she continued beside him, relishing the heat of his large hand engulfing hers. After hours of torture watching him in the clutches of other women, she was both irked and elated he'd chosen to leave alone with her.

Outside, a few widely spaced torches illuminated the stone path. The party's music and merriment drifted from the house behind them, becoming fainter the farther they moved away.

The peach trees rustled in the cool breeze as she and Caros reached the training ground. One of the night guards opened the gate. With a curt nod to the Nubian, Caros led

Pelonia onto the sidelines. The gate clicked behind them as though enclosing them in a world of their own.

They crossed the sand to a bench at the edge of the moonlit field. "Sit here," Caros said. "You look like you need to rest. With all the mayhem tonight, this is the quietest place I could think to bring you."

Her bewilderment deepened. If he had no affection for her as he'd told the widow, why did he treat her with persistent kindness? Where had a man who trained gladiators learned consideration?

Exhausted from a day of labor and a night serving his guests, she eased onto the bench. He towered above her, making her nervous. She craned her neck to see his face in the shadows. "Won't you sit beside me?"

Their sides touched when he took the space to her right. The heat of his body warmed her bare arm and thigh through her tunic. He laced his fingers with hers. Startled by the frisson of sensation that ran up her arm, she stilled but didn't move away. Her fingers meshed with his and an unexpected, inexplicable sense of intimacy cocooned them.

"Did the evening go as you planned?" she asked, resisting the urge to rest her head against his shoulder.

"I didn't plan it. Adiona did. She believes a banquet here amongst my champions will make her the envy of the other city matrons."

Reminded of her rival, she released his hand, but he held firm. A vision of the widow kissing him not long ago reared its ugly head. A desire to send the woman on an extended stay in the wilds of Germania overwhelmed her. She looked toward the empty field and prayed Caros wouldn't see the jealousy she struggled to conceal. "Perhaps we should head indoors."

"Why? Are you cold?" He wrapped his arm around her shoulders and pulled her closer to his side.

Unused to being held by a man, she stiffened for an instant, then gave into temptation and leaned against him.

"Is that better?" His lips brushed her hair. She nodded against his chest. He pointed to a constellation in the northern sky. "Do you see those three faint stars and the brighter one slightly south of them?"

"Yes, I see them."

"Now, follow a straight line north from the single star to that bright one just...there. Do you see it?"

She nodded, loving that he shared her interest in the stars. "The picture is called Cygnus the Swan, is it not?"

"You study the patterns? But you're a woman."

"And being a woman I should have no interest in the heavens?"

His shoulder lifted in a slight shrug. "The women I know are interested in other things—clothes and jewels, and endless adulation."

"I like clothes and jewels. The adulation—" she wrinkled her nose "—I can do without."

She felt the heat of his gaze studying her profile. She pointed to another set of stars in an effort to distract his attention. "Do you know Draco the Dragon?"

He leaned closer and looked in the direction she pointed. "No. I've only learned The Swan, Orion and the Great Bear."

She gave him a sideways glance and grinned. "Then perhaps I can teach you a thing or two."

"By all means, proceed."

"All right. From those four stars, follow south along his tail." She moved her finger as if tracing a winding river. "It ends there between the Great Bear and its cub. Do you see?"

"I do. It's called the Dragon, you say?"

"*Draco* the Dragon. Don't forget," she teased with mock

seriousness. "If you do, he might slither from the sky and eat your tough hide."

His laughter rumbled low and deep. He tugged her back against him. "Am I to take it you wouldn't protect me?"

"It depends."

"On what?"

"On how poorly you'd treated me that day."

He chuckled. "As well as I treat you, you'd have to throw yourself in front of me and beg Draco's mercy."

"Ha! So you think."

"Did I not give you fresh tunics and divert my much needed slaves from the banquet's preparations to fill you a bath?"

"Yes, you did," she said, growing serious. "And I appreciate them both."

"You're welcome," he sounded pleased.

"Thank you for bringing me here. The stars are beautiful tonight."

"Not half as beautiful as you." The compliment heated her cheeks. He cleared his throat and changed the subject. "Most people study stars to worship them or predict their own future. I didn't know your sect—"

"We don't. Why worship created things when we worship the true Creator?"

"Then why your interest? I can see it's keen."

"Yes, it is. It stems from my father. He used to be a deeply superstitious man. He studied astrology and worshipped the stars, the full pantheon, anything to relieve his uncertainty of the future. A few years before my birth, he accepted Christ as his Lord. After that, Creation became a thing of beauty, a testament to God's loving power and he learned to fear no longer."

Her mind sifted through cherished memories and she smiled into the dark. "When I was a child, we used to walk through our fields late at night. Father pointed out the constellations and told me stories." She swallowed the lump forming in her throat. "He told me he loved me as far and wide as the heavens, but even that didn't compare with the depth of Christ's devotion."

"I know you must miss him."

The compassion in his voice brought the sting of tears to her eyes. "More than I can say."

"You always will, but after a time the pain will lessen."

"It doesn't feel like it." Grief weighed on her chest like a box of iron.

"I lost my entire family in the space of one morning. Believe me, I know of what I speak."

Stunned speechless, she searched his face, her eyes wide with shocked dismay. "Your entire family? What happened?"

The moonlight revealed his bleak expression, his haunted eyes. "My father served Galba when he was governor of Spain. When Nero discovered Galba planned rebellion against him, he ordered the governor's execution along with his followers and their families."

Reminders of Nero sent a shiver of disgust down her spine. Even now, seventeen years later, rumor held the insane emperor set the great fire that burned half of Rome. Later, he'd blamed and persecuted thousands of Christians to mask his own treachery.

"But the plot must have failed," she said. "Galba became emperor a few months after Nero's suicide."

"Yes, the plot failed." Caros glanced away. "Because my father defended Galba with his life. When the killers realized the governor escaped, they marched to my family's door and accused us all of being traitors. I fought them. I was fifteen at the time, a youth against four seasoned assassins. Of course, I didn't stand a chance. They raped my mother and two younger sisters, then crucified them in our atrium, while they forced me to watch."

"Women and children?" Tears coursed down her cheeks. "Dear God, how did you survive?"

A cynical laugh broke from his throat. "My fighting impressed them. They sought to make a few coin and sold me to the local gladiatorial school. They assumed I'd die my first time out. Most gladiators do."

Words failed her. She shifted on the bench and threw her arms around him. He hesitated, then almost crushed her in a tight embrace. "I'm so sorry," she cried against his shoulder. "I can't imagine how you must have suffered."

Caros squeezed his eyes shut and buried his face in her soft hair. Never before had he revealed his family's horrific story. The telling had left him weak and shaken to his core. Pelonia's love for her father and home reminded him of the one he'd treasured so well and lost. How could he stand by, witness her pain and not do what he could to ease her grief?

In sharing with her, wanting to help her, he hadn't guessed how much his own wounds would be soothed by her tears. She resented him as her master and distrusted him as a man, yet she wept for him as though her heart bore him the deepest affection.

After years of being surrounded by hate, injustice and violence, he marveled at the depth of her loving spirit. The sound of her tears pierced the inner armor he'd fashioned to protect himself. Some of the anger and despair he'd harbored so long seeped away.

Her sobs eased and quieted. She loosened her steely hold and sagged beside him. His arm curved around the back of her shoulders, he allowed his fingers to caress her upper arm. "Are you well?"

He felt her nod against his chest. She sniffed. "I'm sorry

for taking my bitterness out on you the last few days, but you seemed like such a stalwart target. Now, I'm ashamed of myself. As much as I've suffered, you've suffered three times worse in life."

"It's not a competition. Pain is pain. The next time you need solace from yours, come to me. I'm strong, I can bear it. It's true I failed in my past, but I'm no longer weak nor will I fail again."

Pelonia looked into his eyes and for the first time saw insecurity there. Did he think by sharing his history, by revealing he hadn't always been the unconquered champion he was now, he'd altered her opinion of him? Did he think she somehow found him lacking?

May it never be! She cupped his cheek and wished she could replace the lifetime of tenderness he'd lost. "You're the strongest man I've ever known. If I thought it before, after tonight I know it for certain."

"Pelonia, I—"

The gate creaked, forewarning someone's arrival. Aware there were too many rumors about her already, she removed herself from Caros's arms and slid to the far end of the bench.

One of the house slaves ran toward them. "Master, the widow Leonia requests your attention."

"Have the guests begun a riot?" Caros asked. "Is the *domus* in flames?"

Panting for breath, the slave shook his bald head, his face pinched with confusion. "No, my master, but she insists—"

"Then tell her she'll have to wait."

The slave didn't argue. He backed away, then ran for the house.

Pelonia stood, disturbed to realize she'd forgotten Adiona's presence not only in Caros's home, but in his life.

Remember he's not yours. "Was that wise? What if the widow ventures out here and finds us?"

"It wouldn't matter. She has no say over me."

She searched the shadowed angles of his face. He seemed sincere. "She acts as though she does."

He shrugged. "Adiona's concerned about the party, nothing more. I, on the other hand, am bored by the whole affair. I'd much rather spend my time out here with you."

A lion's roar echoed from the covered cages in the distance. Arms akimbo, she turned her back to gather her thoughts. Was she being duped? Had the story of his family been the truth? Or was Caros a man like her father often warned about? A charmer who would say whatever worked to bring a woman to heel? Hadn't Caros already promised to win the bargain between the two of them?

Trying to be fair and not suspicious, she recalled their conversation from earlier in the afternoon. He'd implied he and the widow were more than friends. Their kisses this evening confirmed it. At the banquet, he'd flirted with a gaggle of other beauties and she'd seen how he fanned the heat in their eyes with no effort at all.

She conceded he'd done nothing untoward. The women were responsible for their own actions. But was he a man who could never be satisfied with the attentions of only one female? The evidence wasn't strong enough to condemn him outright, but with her heart and virtue at stake, she had to be wise. "I'd like to retire now—alone."

The bench creaked behind her. His footsteps sifted through the sand until she felt his presence at her back. His hands eased around her shoulders as though he feared she might bolt. "I don't want you to go."

"Why, because you're bored with the festivities?"

"No, because I enjoy your company."

She closed her eyes, afraid she might weaken. God forgive her, she wanted to believe him.

"You're trembling."

"I'm cold."

He moved to wrap his arms around her, but she stepped beyond his grasp.

"What's happened here?" He eased her around to face him. "Why are you leery of me again?"

"I can't trust you."

All hint of softness left his face. "Is it because I'm a *lanista?* Just because I train gladiators, just because I fought as one doesn't mean…"

She waited, holding her breath for him to finish.

"Doesn't mean I have no heart."

Her lips quivered with unspoken words of comfort. She forced herself to stand her ground when she wanted to smother him with care. "I know you're not heartless. In truth, your kindness to me is more than I expected when I awoke to find I'd been enslaved."

"Then why do you run hot and cold? Do you think I'm so untried I can't see you have feelings for me? Why not yield and end this yearning between us?"

Fear shot through her. He spoke the truth. She was entirely too susceptible to his charm. Riddled with self-disgust, she despised her weakness. What was wrong with her that she could be tempted by a man whose question proved his sole motive was to conquer her will and seduce her?

How had she grown so weak, so needy to forget she was little more than a game to him? "I should have guessed what you were up to. It's little surprise you were undefeated in the ring. You don't give up."

He crossed his arms over his broad chest, stretching the fabric of his tunic. "Should I be ashamed of the fact? I assure you I'm not, but what does it have to do with the affection between us?"

Affection? Does he suspect I'm falling in love with him?

"How do you fare?" His expression shone with sudden concern. "Even in this dim light, I can see you've paled."

I don't love him, do I?

She pressed her hand to her queasy stomach, wishing she could deny the truth. She backed away. "I told you I need to retire. I'm too exhausted to match wits with you when I've worked all day with little to eat."

He followed after her. "Let me help you to your room."

"No, there's no need."

"I insist." He took hold of her arm and coddled her to the gate.

No longer able to bear his unsettling touch, she broke his hold and preceded him back to the house. Somewhere along the orchard's path, her queasiness turned to anger—anger with her own stupidity. They had a bargain. How had she allowed herself to love a man who viewed winning her affections as merely a challenge?

Back inside the domus, the party raged on. The music played louder, wilder. Drunken laughter rang through the house. Pelonia glanced over her shoulder at the same time Adiona latched on to Caros's arm. His intense gaze locked on Pelonia and the look in his eyes guaranteed he would seek her out later.

Chilled by the promised reckoning, she mounted the steps to the second floor. Gaius called her name, but she rushed up the stairs and pretended not to hear him. She'd played the part of a good slave for days, but now she'd had enough. *Let him come and fetch me if he must, but Lord, please prepare him for my ire if he does.*

She entered her room and slammed the door. The lamplight sputtered. The tub was gone. Her wet clothes had been removed as well, replaced by a stack of fresh garments on the chair.

Berating her traitorous heart, she unlaced her sandals and kicked them off. Out of all the men in the empire, Caros was the worst possible choice for her to love. At present, she was his slave and he was her master. When she escaped, and she had to, her family would never accept him or his violent past.

She stopped by the window, choking back her regret. Regardless of her growing affection, she promised to be more guarded, to use wisdom from here on out. No matter her feelings or those of her kin, an even greater wall stood between them. Caros disdained Christ. She had no future with a man who didn't share her faith.

A heavy hand knocked at the door.

"Who is it?"

"Gaius. The master sent me."

She opened the door, ready for battle. Her protests melted on her tongue when she saw the older man held a tray loaded with several dishes of fragrant food. Her stomach cramped with hunger. Why would Caros send his steward to fetch and carry like a common slave?

Gaius pressed past her and set the tray on the floor by her pallet. When he straightened, his dark eyes studied her from under bushy gray brows. "The master said you're to eat every morsel."

She glanced at the tray covered with plates of shredded meat, vegetables, fruits and bread. It was more than she'd eat in two days.

"Tomorrow is market day." He paused at the door. "The master wants you to go with him. He expects you to ready yourself by the seventh hour and meet him in the atrium."

"Why?"

"Who are you to ask why, girl? You will do as your master instructs."

She raised her chin. "And if I don't?"

"Then you're a fool and you deserve whatever you get."

Chapter Twelve

Caros rose early the next morning and dressed with care. The sun was out and the first nips of autumn blew in through the open window. Despite the abrupt ending of their talk the night before, he anticipated a fine day spent with Pelonia. He left to meet her, a smile curving his mouth.

He entered the courtyard and found Adiona perched on a bench instead. His good mood faltered, but he quickly subdued his disappointment and greeted his friend with a kiss on each cheek.

"You're awake early, Adiona. After last night's entertainments, I figured you'd be abed until well after midday."

"Shows how little you really know me, my darling. I'm never one to sleep late." She rose from the bench, her bracelets jangling, her vibrant yellow tunic flowing to her feet. She smiled. "You look delectable this morning. Are you on your way out?"

A quick glance around the atrium revealed no sign of Pelonia. "It's market day. I have supplies to purchase."

"You?" Her eyebrow lifted with amused disbelief. "In

case you're unaware, you have a capable steward. Why not send him instead?"

"Gaius is resting. You and your cohorts wore him out last night. He's not as young as he used to be and I don't want him to die on me."

"Of course not. Good slaves are hard to come by." She linked her arm with his and they began a slow turn around the covered porch. "Yesterday, while I waited for you to return from the baths, I noticed you have several new trainees. One in particular caught my interest. I wonder if you might sell him to me."

Caros eyed his friend with genuine surprise. He'd never known Adiona to notice any man except to slice him with the sharp edge of her tongue. "Which man?"

"One of your trainers called him Quintus Ambustus. He's a condemned man, one I'm sure you wouldn't miss if—"

"What price are you offering for him?"

Adiona shrugged a slim, silk-draped shoulder. "Whatever you wish, of course."

Caros clenched his jaw to keep it from falling open in amazement. Clearly Adiona was trying to hide a powerful interest in his slave. "Did the man insult you or commit some other crime against you? Is that why you wish to buy him, to see him punished?"

"No. What did I say to make you think so harshly of me? Am I really such a cruel woman?"

"To most men, yes," he replied bluntly. "I'm the only man in the city you're civil to."

Her lashes fluttered down, but not before he saw the flicker of shame in her eyes.

"Let's forget I asked about him, shall we?" Her bracelets jangled as she dismissed the subject with a wave of her be-jeweled hand. "It was silly of me. Slaves are as easy to come by as specks of dust and I already have a house full of them. The last thing I need is another mouth to feed…or back to whip as the case may be."

"I didn't mean to imply—"

"No, it's quite all right, Caros." All hints of vulnerability disappeared from her manner, but the bright smile she gave him didn't quite erase the chagrin from her eyes. "Let's discuss another matter, shall we? I know you'll find this a trivial one, but the banquet's success last night was even greater than I hoped for. Of course, I have you to thank. Your reputation is still unmatched in Rome. Most everyone came just to catch a glimpse of you."

"Relieving me of Lucia's presence is thanks enough."

"She's waiting outside in a cart as we speak. As I promised, she'll be sent to my country estate tomorrow. If you change your mind and want her returned—"

"I won't want her back. After what she did—"

"What she did was wrong, but understandable. Women can't help but love you."

If only that were true in Pelonia's case he'd be a contented man. As it was, his slave never failed to perplex him. Each time he thought she might waver in his direction, she slammed the door in his face.

"Even I love you, and as you pointed out I detest men."

"Not all of us are like your late husband." He kissed the back of her hand. "One of these days you'll find a good—"

"Don't say it!" She froze to the spot. "If one more *well-meaning* person tells me I'll wed again, I'll scream until the Forum crumbles."

He struggled to maintain a straight face. "Be warned, those who protest the loudest often fall hardest."

"Ha! I'll consider marriage as soon as you break your vow and return to the arena."

His humor evaporated. "I'll never be a slave again."

"Nor will I." She flipped her *palla* across her chest and over her left shoulder. "Slavery is all marriage offers a woman and there isn't a man alive worth sacrificing my freedom for."

Understanding her agitation stemmed from harsh experience and deeply imbedded fear, he plucked a rose from the bush climbing up the column beside them and presented it to her.

Her face softened with a smile that lit her dark eyes. "You're too kind. It's no wonder I can never stay angry with you."

"Be careful of the thorns."

"Don't worry." She lifted the red bloom to the tip of her nose. "I've been pricked so many times in my life, I'm immune to pain."

A movement at the edge of the porch's double doors drew his notice. Dressed in one of the new tunics he'd bought for her, Pelonia appeared at the bottom of the staircase just beyond the doorway. *Finally.*

Adiona followed the direction of his gaze. "Ah, the slave girl awaits."

He looked into his friend's knowing expression and narrowed his eyes in warning. "Remember what I said about being kind. If you insult her again our ties of friendship will be severed once and for all."

She raised her hands in surrender. "Who am I to find it strange the great Caros Viriathos is in love with a mouse."

"Don't make light of what you don't understand, Adiona."

"I understand all too well, my darling. Now go to the fortunate girl. I can see you're desperate to be near her."

He nodded and kissed the back of her hand in farewell. The widow murmured something, but with his interest fixed on Pelonia, he heard none of it.

Passing the porch's columns and potted palms, his quick

strides erased the tiled space between them. The closer he came to Pelonia the more distrust he saw in her eyes.

He crossed the threshold and stopped at the base of the steps. This early in the morning, a cooler temperature prevailed in the house. He rested his hand on the banister, his sandaled foot on the first step.

By the gods, she stole his breath. Her skin beckoned his touch. Her mouth was enough to drive him mad.

"Gaius said you ordered me to meet you here this morning."

He nodded. "You're going to the Forum with me."

"So he said."

Why was she acting indifferently when he could see the spark of interest she couldn't quite hide? "Are you ready to leave, then?"

She glanced at Adiona's departing back. "What of your guest?"

"She's leaving in moments. I've already said my goodbyes."

Pelonia's lips thinned, but she descended the last step. "You're the master. Lead and I will follow."

Her coolness rankled. "What ails you, Pelonia? Are you not well rested and properly fed? Is a day at the market with me less desirable than hours here scrubbing floors?"

"Nothing is less desirable than scrubbing floors…except perhaps, scrubbing the latrines."

Was she jesting or insulting him? "It's good to know how high I rank in your estimation."

"If someone's high regard is what you seek, perhaps you should spend more time with your lady love."

"My what?"

"Nothing. If you're ready, perhaps we should leave?"

He hid a smile, pleased by her jealousy. He took her by the elbow and led her outside where the morning's comfortable autumn temperature surrounded them. The street in front of his home was calm with only a few pedestrians and a passing horse cart. A stray dog sat on the corner scratching fleas.

"We're leaving later than I planned," he said.

"Perhaps you should go alone. I might slow you down."

And miss spending time with her? "No, it makes no difference."

He helped her into a waiting chariot and stepped up behind her.

"Your horses are exquisite," she said. "And this chariot has some of the finest wood carvings I've ever seen. The details of these tigers are superb."

Her compliment pleased him. "The craftsman was a friend from India."

"He's a true artist."

With a wave of his hand, he signaled the slave holding the bridles to move away from the pair of black Spanish stallions. Pelonia gripped the chariot's curved front panel before he flicked the reins. The horses whinnied and ambled down the drive, then entered the street at a steady clop.

As the chariot picked up speed along the stone pavers, the movement stirred a breeze that blew strands of her hair against his cheek. He savored the clean scent and its silken texture against his skin.

Unbidden, he wondered what it might be like to have Pelonia for his wife, to wake up with her soft and warm in his arms every morning.

"I've never ridden in a chariot before." She cast a glance over her shoulder, her dark eyes bright with excitement. "We always traveled by litter in town and by cart for longer journeys."

"Where are you from?"

"Iguvium." Her chest ached with a sharp, sudden pang of homesickness. She looked straight ahead. The dirty streets and multistoried living complexes on either side of the wide lane were a far cry from the rolling hills and sun-warmed villas of the Umbrian countryside she loved. "It's a small but beautiful place built up the side of a hill about six days north of here."

"I know of it. I fought there once."

"Did you? When?"

"About five years ago. I saw much of the amphitheatre, but little of the town."

He shifted his stance and his chest brushed against her shoulder blades. She gasped at the unexpected tremor that danced down her spine.

"Perhaps you'll visit there again someday and see its finer parts." Not wanting to encourage more peculiar feelings, she focused on the horses and the expert way Caros maneuvered the chariot through the thickening traffic of horse carts, wagons and other chariots.

"I remember the meadows were abundant with a wealth of red and yellow wildflowers," he said.

She nodded, once again surprised by the gentle spirit beneath his battle scars. For his sake, she wished she could turn back time and regain the years he'd lost to violence.

"You must have been there in summer," she said. "It's a beautiful time, but fall is my favorite. The harvest will arrive soon and everyone will be celebrating…"

"What's wrong?"

Her eyes burned with tears. "I no longer have a home there. My father is gone. All the loved ones of my household are dead. My uncle owns all that my father worked for. Our land, our villa…everything."

"The uncle who sold you?"

She nodded.

His lips brushed her temple. "Again, I'm sorry for your loss, Pelonia. The area seemed a peaceful place. The kind of town where a fortunate man settles to raise a family."

She cleared her throat and choked back her heartache. "Is it a town where *you* might want to raise a family?"

He slowed the horses to turn down an empty side street. "I never planned to marry. Some gladiators do, but I wanted no wife or children to leave behind unprotected if I died in the arena."

"Your sentiments are honorable, Caros. I believe my father would have acted the same in your circumstances." But what of Adiona? Her curiosity got the better of her. "What of these last three years? You've been a free man. Why haven't you wed?"

He shrugged. "Perhaps no one will have me."

"I can't believe—"

"I'm a *lanista* after all. Wasn't it you who reminded me my profession is the lowest of the low? Tell me, what decent woman ties herself to a barbarian?"

Her cheeks flamed. She knew she'd been wrong to judge him. She eyed him over her shoulder, eager for him to see her sincerity. "I misspoke and I'm sorry for my arrogance. The more I've come to know you, the more I think whoever you choose to wed will be a woman truly blessed."

Surprise flared in his deep blue eyes, but he said nothing. He flicked the reins, driving the horses into a faster pace while the road remained deserted. Wind whipped at the fringe of hair around her face and ruffled the edges of her tunic. Aware of his muscled arms around her, she allowed herself to brace against the solid column of his body to keep from falling backward.

His lips brushed her ear. "You're not frightened, are you?"

"I've never traveled this fast in my life," she admitted, a touch of anxiety heightening with the jolt of excitement she felt.

"There's no need to be afraid, this is hardly the races.

Perhaps we'll visit the Circus Maximus. With no obstacles to watch for, I could show you the true meaning of speed."

The cloud of sadness lifted from her slim shoulders, if only a mite. "Could we?"

"Perhaps another day." He indulged in the scent of her hair, glad to hear a spark of curiosity in her voice. "I know for a fact the races are on today and you wouldn't want to ride with a charioteer. They're nothing but insanity incarnate."

"As opposed to gladiators?"

He grinned. "We're not sane, either. We're killers, remember."

Her lips compressed into a prim line. "I thank you for the reminder."

He chuckled. "Here, take the reins. Perhaps I can teach *you* a thing or two."

Her hesitant smile told him she remembered saying the same words to him the previous night. She accepted the leather strips in a tight grip. "By all means, proceed."

The back of her head brushed the center of his chest. He drew her closer. His hands covered each of hers. "Hold the reins loosely. Let them ease through your fingers."

The chariot began to veer to the right.

"Caros!"

"Don't be afraid. Take control or your horses will feel your fear. To steer, pull back on the left or right rein like this."

He allowed her to drive unaided through the next few streets until they came to the city gate and the traffic began to back up.

"Thank you. I enjoyed that! For the first time in weeks I've felt free." She handed back the reins and gripped the chariot's front panel.

Her joy pleased him, but he didn't expect the twinge of guilt he experienced for holding her captive. He did have the power to set her free. He wanted her happy just as he was happy, yet to free her was to lose her—a prospect he refused to face.

It had been years since he felt alive—as if there were something valuable to wake up for each morning. He would have to try harder, look for other ways to please her until she no longer sought a life apart from him.

They neared the amphitheater. A gift from the Flavian emperors to the people of Rome, the massive arena had been dedicated the previous year with a hundred days of continuous spectacles. Standing four stories, the white travertine exterior gleamed in the morning sun. The day's first games were in full force. The mob's roar swept across the distance.

He felt Pelonia tense. "What's wrong?"

"We're not going there, are we?"

"Not yet. I have business with the editor this afternoon. I can't avoid it or I would. My business won't take long."

"The editor?"

"He arranges the games." He maneuvered past a cart that swerved to the road's edge, then guided the chariot in a westerly direction toward the Forum. The horde of wheels and horses' hooves clattered on the stone road, drowning out further conversation.

Caros reined the horses to a stop not far from the Via Sacra. People swarmed around the chariots and other forms of transport. "We'll leave the chariot here. I'll hire one of the boys over there to watch it while we're gone. The way isn't far."

He helped Pelonia to the ground. If not for her vow, the milling crowd would provide an ideal cover for escape. Coins exchanged hands. The chariot seen to, Caros led her along the Sacred Way, pointing out sites of interest. "There's the Palatine to our left. And up on the Capitoline there, the Temple of Jupiter."

With no interest in the pagan temple, Pelonia surveyed the Palatine. The hill was overgrown with elegant palaces of Rome's noblest families. Somewhere up there, her cousin Tiberia resided. An eager fascination gripped her. *Which home is it?*

The thought of her kin being so close overwhelmed her with happiness and…unexpected gloom. Her cousin was her dearest friend. Who better to share her feelings about Caros with than her closest confidant? Yet the moment she saw Tiberia again, she would be forced to cut her ties with the man who meant more to her with each passing day.

"Are you tired? Do you need to rest?" Caros' light touch on the small of her back made her realize she'd stopped walking.

"No, I'm fine." She picked up her pace, her turmoil increasing with every step. Their situation was intolerable. Each kindness he showed her made him dearer to her heart, but every day she remained a slave eroded her inner core of strength. How long would it take before she joined the other slaves with broken spirits and nonexistent wills?

"You're too quiet."

She looked into his blue eyes, her heart melting at the concern she saw there. Just a short time ago, she would never have guessed this rugged man capable of such gentleness. "I'm sorry. I have many things on my mind."

"Tell them to me. Perhaps I can help."

She shook her head. "No, I have to work them out for myself."

He wasn't pleased, but he didn't press her. They continued along the road without speaking. The din of the crowd surrounded them. Food stalls lined the street. The smell of spices, roasted nuts and exotic fruits tinged the air.

Caros cleared his throat. "Your unhappiness isn't related

to Adiona, is it? She has a wicked tongue. The way she mocked you in the garden yesterday was cruel. I told her so."

More concern for her feelings? "Thank you, but why did you bother? You know I plan to leave as soon as our agreement is finished. I don't want to cause trouble between you."

Anger flashed across his face. He led her to the side of the road, to a quieter spot between a large statue and a laurel tree. "You might as well abandon your thoughts of escape. You won't be leaving in two weeks' or two years' time. I can't let you go."

"Why? What is it about me that can't be replaced? Anyone can weed the garden. I'm almost useless in the kitchen and I refuse to warm your bed. If it's a matter of coin, my family will repay you. If you're in need of affection, why not seek it from…"

"From whom? My lady love?"

"Yes," she snapped, annoyed to have her own words thrown back at her.

"And who might that be? One of my admirers? One of my other female slaves? Why don't you enlighten me?"

"You know very well, it's Adiona."

"Come again? I couldn't hear you over all the racket in the street."

Her hands balled into fists at her sides. "*Adiona.* Considering what I saw this morning and what you told me yesterday—"

"This morning? What did you see?"

"You seemed most reluctant to let her leave."

His brow arched. "And yesterday? What did I say?"

"You said she's pleasant and lovely enough to rival Venus. That unlike the two of *us,* the two of you are of similar minds. That the relationship you share with the widow is everything you desire it to be."

That I'm a slave and nothing more.

His face inscrutable, he pressed closer. She stepped away until the tree trunk scratched her back. He gripped her upper arms and leaned over until they were eye to eye. "Finally a woman who listens. Why did you hear all the wrong things?"

"What do you mean?"

He sighed. "It's true I said those things and none were lies. I also said I think *you're* beautiful and told you of my family—something I've never told anyone else."

She glanced away. "I'm honored you confided in me. I realize you shared with me to help ease my grief. You're most kind for doing so."

"I'm not kind." He released her and raked his hand through his hair. "I told you because you're special to me."

"Special? Will you be more specific? I confess my thoughts are like jumbled string. I've wrapped myself in them until I fear I'll never break free."

"How shall I define it? I've already told you I want you."

"What does that mean? My father warned me of men who *want* every woman they see."

"*I* only want *you.*"

Her knees went weak. "Then what are your true feelings for the widow?"

"I care for her, but not in the way you think. She's been an excellent friend who's given me much. When I gained my freedom, she used her influence to help me establish the school. In return, I've been her friend and protector, nothing more."

"Then why did you lead me to believe otherwise?"

"We should proceed to the Forum." He turned to leave. "At this pace, the best wares will be gone and we'll endure second-rate meat for a week."

She grabbed hold of his tunic along with a few chest

hairs. He winced but froze to the spot. Her hand dropped away as though she'd touched fire. "Oh, no, we're not moving on until you tell me the truth. As it is, I feel you and your 'friend' have made me the back end of a joke."

"You're no joke to me." He groaned. "Adiona had nothing to do with it. I didn't speak to her about you except to tell her she'd been cruel. She suspects I care for you, but…" He combed his hand through his hair again. "In truth, you've found me out. I encouraged you to believe there was more between Adiona and me because I wanted to make you jealous."

Her mouth fell open. Caught between hot indignation and enormous relief, she realized he'd succeeded without a hitch. "How did you know I'd be jealous of her?"

"I didn't. She came when I summoned her to take Lucia. I had to think of something since you didn't want the wench whipped or sold."

"You amaze me," she said softly, her secret thoughts finding words before she realized she'd spoken them.

His expression warmed with pleasure. "The first time you spoke of Adiona to me, I knew you were jealous."

She felt her cheeks burn. "Only a little."

He chuckled. "I saw it in your eyes. You wanted me to deny all involvement with her. Your reaction gave me hope. After the speech you flayed me with the day before about how unsuited we are—"

"But we are," she interrupted. "Nothing's changed."

He waved away her protest. "Don't travel down that road again. Whether you acknowledge it or not, there's something unique between us."

She couldn't deny him, nor could she admit she agreed. No matter how much she was growing to love him, she still had to leave.

Chapter Thirteen

Pelonia followed Caros up the hill to the Forum. The pristine weather had lured a rambunctious crowd. Merchants hawked everything from food and plants to boat sails, while street musicians played tunes on various instruments, hoping to earn coins or gifts of food.

She'd never visited the world's capital and everywhere she looked Rome offered something new to delight the eye. The public buildings—temples, basilicas and various monuments outshone any she'd ever seen.

"What's that over there?" she asked, pointing through the milling throng to a unique circular building.

"The Temple of Vesta," Caros said, distracted by his attempts to lead her through the shifting sea of people.

"Where the Vestal virgins keep the flame of Rome alive?"

"The very same."

"You don't *really* believe Rome will fall if the flame burns out, do you?"

As he sneaked a glance at her, his lips curved in a mocking smile. "All good Romans believe it."

"But you're not a good Roman," she said as they walked

up the congested steps of one of the basilicas. "You haven't even adopted a Roman name."

"Out of respect for my father, I carry the name he gave me."

"You said your father served Galba, but did he resent the Romans conquering your homeland?"

"No, he was a citizen, just as I would have been had I not been forced into the gladiatorial trade. That didn't stop him from loving our Iberian heritage or wanting to pass on that heritage to me."

Caros tightened his grip on her hand when they entered the basilica by way of the main entrance. Rows of arched windows allowed light into the magnificent market. Two levels of shops lined both sides of the central pathway. The walls, floor and rows of support columns were all fashioned of polished white marble.

Lilting strains of a pan flute combined with hundreds of voices echoed through the cavernous space. The heavy flow of people jostled Pelonia, threatening to knock her over more than once. Caros steadied her each time and navigated the multitude with ease.

"What a marvelous place," she said in awe.

Caros grunted. "It's crowded."

"It's beautiful. All the craftsmanship is perfection."

"It stinks like a sty."

She laughed. "Who would have thought you'd have such a sensitive nose?"

"You enjoy teasing me, don't you, woman?"

"A slave must find enjoyment where she can."

He chuckled. "As must her master. Remember that the next time I try to kiss you."

The thought of him kissing her no longer unwelcome, she ducked her head to hide a shy smile of pleasure. Caros cleared the way for her as they entered the butcher shop. The smells of fresh meat surrounded her. Shouted orders and voices haggling prices competed with the bleat of lambs and a few mooing cows. Animal carcasses hung from hooks behind the long counter.

The shopkeeper looked up from a large pile of coins. His eyes bugged when he saw Caros. He swiped the coins into a drawer and hurried from behind the counter.

"You are the Bone Grinder, no?" the shopkeeper asked, his wrinkled face bright with excitement. "By the gods, it is an honor to have you in my shop."

The clamor faded into silence. Gaping mouths and curious eyes turned to stare.

Amazed by the people's reaction, Pelonia studied Caros. She'd never seen him beyond the walls of the school and it was an enlightening experience to find so many people revered him.

"The honor is mine," he said.

The shop owner's face took on a slight frown of concern. "I usually have dealings with your steward. Is Gaius well?"

"He's fine."

Pelonia allowed her attention to wander. Caros let go of her hand once the other customers returned to their business. While she waited for him to arrange deliveries to the school, she meandered around the shop, comparing the costs of various meats with the lower prices she would have paid at home.

Caros joined her near a table laden with buckets of brown eggs. He tucked a wisp of hair behind her ear, sending a shiver through her body when his calloused fingers brushed her cheek. "I was watching you," he said. "Not once did you try to run off."

"You're surprised? We have a bargain and I'm a woman of my word."

He opened the door and ushered her out into the press of

patrons. "We do have a bargain. Up to now, I wasn't fully confident you'd keep it if an opportunity arose for you to escape again."

"I assume I passed the test."

He nodded. "You're honest, I'll give you that."

Some time later, Caros finished his business with several other merchants. He led Pelonia into a different shop. Perfume sweetened the air. The skeins of white cotton hanging from the ceiling drew her attention, as did the vibrant bolts of silk lining the walls. Freewomen dressed in lavish tunics and *stolas* admired the feminine wares that covered the counters and shelves.

"I've brought you here because I realize you need certain items. If—"

"Caros!" One of the women, her hair covered in a fashionable blond wig, rushed toward them from a counter full of cosmetics. A delighted smile curved her painted lips and lit her kohl-rimmed eyes. "It's been months since I saw you last."

Pelonia bristled at the woman's too-familiar tone and the way she greeted Caros with a lingering kiss on each cheek.

"Cassia, what a pleasure to see you. I've been working," he said. "I have many new men to train and they've claimed my full attention."

"I missed you at my banquet last week." The blonde pouted as she gauged her effect on him from beneath lowered lashes. "I sent you a special invitation since my husband was out of town."

Pelonia's eyes rounded, then narrowed when Caros cast a guilty glance her way. Disgusted to find he would dally with another man's wife, she abandoned his side and sought out the counter farthest from him. Hating the ease with which Caros sent her emotions reeling, she forced herself to admire a set of ivory combs while the elegant shop mistress finished her business with another customer.

"I'll see you Sunday," the shop mistress said as she handed the other woman a folded bundle of yellow cloth.

"Sunday," the customer agreed. "At the seventh hour, down by the river."

A bell on the door rang as the customer left. The shop mistress turned her attention to Pelonia. Instead of ignoring her and treating her like a slave as the other merchants had done most of the morning, the older woman offered a pleasant, "May I help you find something?"

"Thank you, but I'm just looking. These combs are exquisite."

"And very expensive," the mistress said, though not unkindly. "I have others over here. They're carved of wood, and not as fine as the ivory, but some are quite nice."

Glancing to find Caros continued his conversation with the would-be adulteress, Pelonia followed the silver-haired shop mistress to the far end of the counter. The other woman pulled out a large wooden box filled with combs and began to pick out the best pieces.

Pelonia stopped her. "Please, don't waste your time on me. There are several customers here who need your help and I have no coin."

"I assumed you had no money." The shop mistress's expression softened with compassion. "I can see you're a slave of the *lanista* over there. You look so unhappy, I couldn't help but wonder if he's hateful to you."

"No, no, he's kind," she hurried to defend him, surprised the woman spared her a second thought. "But thank you for your concern when I'm no more than a stranger to you."

"It's important to be kind to strangers. Even the wicked are good to their friends."

Pelonia wondered if the other woman was a fellow believer. Jesus had taught a similar lesson and it was an uncommon one in a world where few people cared for anyone beyond themselves and their own families.

On impulse, she tapped the wooden counter, drawing the shopkeeper's attention to the spot. Pelonia traced the sign of the fish, a secret symbol Christians used to identify themselves.

The woman looked up, a huge grin parted her lips. She nodded and squeezed Pelonia's hand as though they were long-lost relatives. "What's your name, child?"

"Pelonia. And yours?"

"Annia."

Caros's footsteps warned of his arrival. The shopkeeper released Pelonia's hand and began to place the combs back in the box.

"Do you see anything you want?" he asked. "If so, let's buy it and be on our way. The editor is waiting for me at the amphitheater."

"There's nothing," Pelonia said, reluctant to accept gifts from him. She noted Annia's frown when Caros spoke of the arena. Like most Christians, the older lady would despise the games. Not for their barbaric cruelty alone, but because a multitude of their fellow believers had been tortured in them and slain for sport.

"Are you certain?" he asked. "I thought I saw you admiring those ivory combs. If you want them—"

She shook her head. "I have everything I need. Let's be on our way. I don't want you to be late on my account."

Pelonia shared a lingering glance with Annia. For the first time since her arrival in Rome, she didn't feel quite so alone. It was heartening to find another believer, to feel connected to the body of Christ again.

Outside the basilica, the sun shone brightly. The afternoon heat had erased the morning's fall breezes. Caros took her by the hand and led her quickly through the open market and back down the Via Sacra.

"You seem different since we left the Forum," he said. "Tell me, what did you and the shop mistress speak of?"

Pelonia hesitated. She wouldn't lie, but neither would she confess she'd found another Christian. She didn't think he would report Annia to the authorities. After all, he hadn't turned her in, but she couldn't take a chance with the woman's life either. "We spoke of many things I'm certain you'd find of no interest. And you? Did you and your *married* friend have much to discuss?"

"More jealousy. That pleases me," he said, laughing. "Cassia and I are no more than acquaintances. She's rich and bored. Like many women of her class, she thinks she'll find excitement in the bed of a gladiator. If nothing else, she'll have something to gossip about with her friends."

"And she wants you."

"I'm a champion of Rome. All the women want me."

Pelonia marveled at his conceit until she realized he was teasing her. With a gentle poke at his ribs, she laughed. "They must not know you very well."

"You wound me," he said in a lighthearted tone, but his intense blue eyes grew serious. "Perhaps I should have said, all the women want me, except the one I want most."

Unable to jest when words of tenderness rushed to her lips, she sought sanity in the distraction provided by the merchant wagons along the pebbled path.

As they neared the amphitheater, the crush of people thickened. The roar of the mob inside the gleaming torture palace grew louder, spreading through the air like constant thunder.

Pelonia's stomach rolled with dread. "Can I please wait

for you out here? You have my word I won't flee and I've proven I won't break our bargain."

His arm slipped around her shoulders and he pulled her tight against him. "No, it's too dangerous."

His refusal brooked no argument. He ushered her beneath one of the amphitheater's arched doorways, down a flight of concrete stairs and past the guards standing watch at the back entrance. From what she could tell as they walked down a long corridor, they were directly under the spectators.

"This way," he said when they came to a choice of direction. "Those steps lead to the arena."

No one offered Caros resistance when he bypassed the long line waiting outside the editor's office.

Caros pushed open the office door. The occupant barked, "By the gods! How dare...oh, it's you, Caros. Come in and take a seat."

A moment later, a wealthy man, by the looks of his fine white tunic, exited the office and took a place at the front of the line. That he seemed honored to give up his time with the editor spoke volumes of his respect for Caros.

Caros led her inside the dingy office. Large parchments advertising past competitions covered the walls. A barred window near the ceiling allowed noise from inside the amphitheater to filter into the dusty space. She sat on an up-ended crate in the corner, while Caros took the chair in front of the large wooden desk.

The editor, a rotund, pockmarked individual, lifted a glass and a ceramic jug. "Care for a drink, Bone Grinder?"

"I'll pass, Spurius. Knowing you, it's probably laced with hemlock."

Spurius chuckled. "I admit I'm not above tipping the scales in my favor, but you have no worries from me. As long as there's a chance I might lure you back to the ring, you're safe."

Pelonia tensed. She hadn't considered the possibility of Caros returning to the games. Fear for his safety rushed to the fore of her mind. Lacing her fingers together in a tight ball, she willed away the image of him hurt and bleeding.

"What's this about you contracting forty of my men for tomorrow, then amending it to twenty with less than three days notice?" Caros asked in a quick change of subject. "If you need no more than twenty fighters, so be it, but don't think you won't pay me for the original count."

The mob cheered. Feet pounded above them like thunder on the ceiling. Motes of dust danced in the stream of light allowed by the small barred window.

Spurius hefted his girth and reached to close one of the window's shutters in an effort to muffle the noise. "The executions have gone over long today."

Caros's hands fisted on the wooden desktop. "They usually finish long before now."

"Executions?" Pelonia sat forward on the bench.

Caros turned in his seat. "Thieves and murderers, nothing more."

"And a few deviants." Spurius frowned at Pelonia as though she were a dog who'd dared to interrupt. "They rounded up a group of Christians and the traitors have been pitted against a pack of wolves."

"That's enough," Caros warned the other man.

"The crowd has been wild today." Spurius continued with the undiluted glee of a man who found pleasure in butchery and torture. "The mob loves a good show and I make a fortune when the seats are full."

Pelonia shuddered at each horrible word. The room began to spin.

"What's wrong with her," Spurius griped. "She isn't one of them, is she?"

"No!" Caros snapped. "She has a tender heart. That's *all*."

"Then why is she here? A tender heart is the first thing to die in this place."

She launched to her feet and threw open the door before Caros had the chance to stop her. She pushed through the tangle of bodies blocking her path and ran down the hall.

"Pelonia, come back!"

Deaf to Caros's order, she took the steps he'd pointed out as a passage to the arena. On the first landing, she froze. A strangled cry broke from her lips as her gaze traveled the huge oval theater packed with an ocean of bloodthirsty spectators. The atmosphere writhed with terrible excitement and chants for human death poisoned the air. Never in her life had she seen such horror.

With the floor of the arena out of view, she pressed onward. A guard barred her path. "Woman, you're not permitted here. You'll have to find a place to stand with the other slaves in the top rows."

She ducked under his arm and raced to the rail, ignoring his command to halt.

In the center of the sand a pack of wolves circled a handful of men and one young woman. Terror lined the prisoners' faces, though their lips moved as if in prayer.

One of the beasts lunged at the woman. Raucous laughter swirled through the crowd.

"No!" Pelonia screamed just as a large gray wolf leaped at one of the men.

"You can do no good here," Caros said a short distance behind her.

She spun to face him and the guard standing a few paces behind his left shoulder. Tears coursed down her cheeks. "Please make it stop," she begged, knowing even *his* power didn't extend far enough to end the suffering below.

Caros's face creased with pity. He grabbed hold of her arms and drew her against him. "If I could end this for you I would, but those poor wretches are beyond human help."

The mob's frenzied cries erupted around them. Pelonia squeezed her eyes shut, horribly aware that each new cheer meant another slaughtered Christian.

Chapter Fourteen

Caros swept Pelonia off her feet, holding her tight while she wept against his chest. He'd witnessed numerous executions over the years. The scene below was no different except this time he observed the fray from above, instead of fighting in the thick of it.

The mob's wild chants swarmed like locusts as the last two men in the arena struggled to protect the woman—a woman who could easily be Pelonia if the Fates turned against her.

The thought soured his gut. He brushed a kiss across the top of her head. For the first time in years, fear coursed through his veins. Now that he'd found a woman to love, he refused to live without her. But what if someone uncovered Pelonia's secret and took the choice from his hands? What if someone threatened to throw *Pelonia* to the wolves for her Christian beliefs?

Bile rose in his throat. Anxious to leave, he sought out the exit. A storm of stomping feet pummeled the marble risers and a blast of wild shouting thundered around the arena.

With a last backward glance, he saw two of the wolves

begin to circle the woman. His feet froze. Time faltered and stood still. Riveted by the animals' cunning, Caros felt each of his muscles tighten with dread. He willed the Christian to deny her beliefs and save her life. A simple retraction of her faith would provide a way of escape.

Why didn't she grasp the opportunity and see herself freed?

The pack moved like a troop of gladiators, sizing up the weaknesses of their prey and how best to attack. It wouldn't be long before all of the Christians lay mangled in the sand.

A seasoned predator himself, Caros held his breath as the largest she wolf determined a precise moment to strike. The pack charged as one frenzied unit, downing the last three Christians in a single, simultaneous assault.

An unfamiliar ache took root in his chest. He closed his eyes and pushed the pain away as the mob's triumphant roar erupted around the arena, freeing him from his momentary trance.

Pelonia writhed in his arms and fought to look over his shoulder, but he tightened his grip, pinning her with his superior strength as he carried her toward the exit. "Don't look, *mea carissima*. It's a gruesome sight and we've both seen more than enough."

Neither of them spoke on the journey home. The senseless butchery in the ring disgusted Caros. He'd never enjoyed the public executions, but he'd grown calloused to them.

No longer.

His love for a Christian made all the difference, destroying his ability to look upon their deaths with the same resignation and complacence.

He stole a glance at Pelonia beside him in the chariot, her eyes red and swollen from tears. His breathing grew difficult. Long ago he'd become accustomed to all manner of physical pain, but her quiet sorrow filled him with helpless agony.

Tender feelings and emotions he'd buried years ago to

survive the bleakness of his existence rose up like a tide. Guilt for his part in past executions choked him. None of his usual excuses soothed his conscience. By the gods, how would she see him if she learned of his misdeeds? After witnessing her people die in the ring, she was certain to despise him. All hope of winning her affection would be forever lost.

He reined the chariot to a stop a few paces from his front door and waited for one of his slaves to lay hold of the bridle. He jumped from the chariot and offered to help Pelonia down. She alighted without touching him, as though she could see the stain of blood on his hands. Stung by her rejection, he closed his fingers and dropped his fist to his side.

He stepped toward her, but she retreated. Frustration gripped him. Was she in shock or had the few gains he'd made in earning her trust fallen by the wayside? "Come, Pelonia, let me help you. As long as there's breath in my body, I promise you won't be harmed. You must know by now you have nothing to fear from me."

Her glassy gaze rested on his face. "You think not, *lanista?* Why did you bother to stop me from seeing the truth? Do you think I don't realize all of you Romans are cut from the same bloodthirsty cloth?"

Caros held his tongue. Her bleak expression tore at his heart. If it eased her anguish to lash out at him, so be it. "I didn't want you to see your people killed. I suffered when I saw my loved ones butchered. The pain has stayed with me all my life. I hoped to spare you from a similar grief."

"If you wished to spare me grief, you should have thrown me into the ring with those beasts. But then again, you *are* one of the wolves. Why share me with your kin when you plan to win our bargain and have me all to yourself?"

Her bitterness gutted him. She saw him as an animal, a murderer…and she was right. He may not have been in the arena this afternoon, but he'd been a fixture in countless other fights. He cleared his throat. "You're upset and with good reason. Let's go inside before we say something we'll both regret."

Pelonia proceeded Caros through the front door. Gaius met them in the dim light of the entryway. "Master, you have a guest. She arrived a short time ago and asked if she could speak with you. She's waiting in the atrium."

"Who is she?"

"Her name is Annia. She claims to be a shopkeeper at the Forum."

Irritated by Annia's bad timing, Caros made his way to the courtyard. An older woman with gray at her temples sat in profile on the bench in front of the fountain. She stood and faced him the moment his sandals brushed the mosaic floor. He recognized her cheerful face from the shop where he'd spoken with Cassia.

"Good day to you, Madam." He gave a slight bow. "My steward says you wish to speak with me."

"My name is Annia." A smile crinkled the edges of her friendly brown eyes. "Thank you for seeing me unannounced."

He motioned for her to return to her seat on the marble bench and offered refreshment, which she declined.

"I know you're a busy man. I promise not to take much of your time. I met your slave, Pelonia, today in my shop." She adjusted the voluminous folds of her wine-colored *stola*. "She reminded me so much of my own daughter I've come to ask your permission for her to visit me. That is, if she agrees."

"Your daughter?"

"She passed on last year."

"You have my sympathy."

"Thank you." She lowered her gaze. "I know my request

is an odd one, but grant my appeal and you'll have my deepest thanks."

Caros spotted Pelonia half-hidden by the nearest column. Her troubled eyes pleaded with him to give his consent. After the events of the afternoon he wanted to please her. Yet he wasn't about to create a situation that might aid Pelonia with her plans of escape.

"No. The streets are too dangerous for a beautiful young woman to walk alone and the many claims on my time make it impossible for me to act as her bodyguard."

"I understand your wish to protect your property, but this is a gladiatorial school. Surely there's at least *one* other man capable of seeing to her safety."

No longer willing to debate the point, he offered Annia one of his most charming smiles. "Perhaps, perhaps not. Either way, Pelonia isn't free to leave these grounds without me."

"I see." Water splashed in the fountain while Annia fiddled with the folds of her *stola.* "Then may I visit her here on occasion?"

Caros considered the perceptive gleam in the shop-keeper's eyes. Normally, he'd dismiss an uninvited guest without explaining himself, but his mother had taught him to respect his elders and this woman's gentle smile reminded him of her. He tried a different tack. "I'll have to consider—"

"Please allow her to visit." Pelonia hurried from behind the pillar, making no pretense of her eavesdropping. Her cheeks held a renewed hint of color and her eyes begged for his consent. Further refusal withered on his tongue. How could he say no to such a beguiling plea?

He gave a slow nod. Her face softened with gratitude and the smile she gave Annia sent a jolt of relief through his veins.

He realized he'd feared she might never smile again.

Without another word, he turned on his heel and headed for the training field, in dire need of release from his tension.

Bemused by Caros's abrupt exit, Pelonia watched him disappear down the corridor that led to the rear of the house.

Anguish weighed heavy on her shoulders. She wished she could bite off her tongue. His shattered expression when she'd compared him to the wolves would torment her for the rest of her days. Her cruelty was inexcusable no matter how much the executions distressed her. Caros wasn't to blame for the evil she'd witnessed today. That he'd tried to protect her from seeing the worst of it proved once again what a man of compassion he was.

"Pelonia? Pelonia, child, are you all right?"

She blinked several times as if waking from a dream. "I'm better now that you're here," she said, striding forward. "Your presence is a lift to my spirit."

"I'm glad to hear it. At my shop today, I felt as if we'd known each other all our lives."

"I felt the same."

"I spoke no lie when I told your master you reminded me of my dear Phoebe."

Pelonia followed her friend to sit on the bench, careful not to crease the fine cloth of Annia's *stola*. She clasped the older woman's soft, warm fingers. "I'm sorry to hear you lost her last year."

Pain spread across Annia's gracefully aged features. "The authorities executed her, her husband and my grandson in the arena."

"How horrible! I saw the executions today. I—"

Further words failed her. A vision of the wolves made nausea roll in her belly. A jagged pain knotted in her throat. Annia put her arm around Pelonia and drew her close. "Don't fret, child. They're with the Lord, dancing at the feet of Jesus."

"As is my father," she whispered, resting her cheek against Annia's shoulder.

"What happened to him? Was he executed as well?"

A tear trickled across the bridge of her nose and onto Annia's *stola*. As quickly as she could, she told her friend of the marauders' attack, her uncle's treachery and her sale into slavery.

"My dear girl. How much you've suffered! No wonder the Lord sent me here to comfort you."

"You *are* a comfort. At times, it's been frightfully easy to think God has discarded me."

"Never." Annia patted her hand. "One of the most beautiful traits of our Lord is His ability to create joy from mourning. He always has a plan and it never fails to work for our good. Sometimes we may not like or understand His ways of achieving that good, but in those times our faith is refined and we grow stronger."

She sniffed and wiped her cheeks. "You speak the truth. My father used to say the same, but I confess I feel my faith is hanging by a thread. I've never been angrier with God or so overwhelmed by bitterness. Even when I repent or do my best to accept His will, I say or think things that make me cringe with remorse. Truly, a part of me wants to rail at Him and demand to know why He took everything of value from my life."

"We must remember our Father never takes what He doesn't return with interest when He owes us nothing at all."

"I know," she said in a small voice. "But how can He return my father or the loving home that no longer belongs to me? How can He return your daughter and your family?"

"I'll see my loved ones again when I join them in heaven, just as you will see your father. As for the rest, it's all part of the mystery that makes His ways a wonder to behold.

Wait upon the Lord and let Him renew your strength like an eagle's."

Wiping her tears away, Pelonia sat up and nodded. "I never used to cry. In Rome, it seems I cry every few hours."

"Tears cleanse the soul."

She sniffed and offered a weak smile. "Then mine must be spotless."

"And the *lanista?* What does he think of all this weeping?"

"Caros is ever kind."

"*Kind?* There's a word I didn't expect to hear when describing a man known for violence."

"He's gentle as well. And considerate."

Annia frowned. "Are you besotted?"

Sadness spread through Pelonia like a growing stain. She plucked a small frond from a potted palm beside the bench. "It matters not if I am. Caros and I have no future together."

"That's probably the wisest course of action, but why do you believe so?"

Pelonia wished wisdom could mend a broken heart. "He rejects our faith and I'll never let go of it. He's my master and I can't live as a slave forever. I *will* have to escape. When I do, he'll hate me for it."

"And what if God has planted you here for a specific purpose?"

"He has," she answered with assurance. "He's shown me I'm to be a light in this dark place. Why He chose me, I don't understand. My inner flame is flickering at best. I believe a worse failure would be difficult to find."

"Don't listen to the lies the Evil One would force on you." Annia stroked Pelonia's hair. "Who, in the midst of trouble, ever feels successful or doesn't question God's plan?"

"I suppose no one."

"The important thing to remember is that even when we are weak, our Lord is strong. Just because our prayers haven't come to fruition, doesn't mean the answers aren't already on the way."

Chapter Fifteen

Caros's third opponent of the afternoon landed on his back in a burst of sand. After years of conditioning himself to fight, he knew of no other way to relieve the tension that plagued him. His attempt to find release from the condemnation in Pelonia's eyes had proven futile. Like the tip of a red-hot poker, her accusations probed the raw sores of his diseased soul.

His lip curled at the unconscious gladiator on the ground. Supposedly a champion of more than a year, the Thracian had been a disappointment, and lasted no time at all. Where was Alexius when he required a challenge?

Fingers flexing around the hilt of a *gladius,* Caros searched the field for another man to bring down. His gaze landed on the trainee he'd purchased the same night as Pelonia. The Christian he was certain she'd find attractive if she learned of his presence here.

His eyes narrowed. Even Adiona, a woman known for her hatred of men, had found this particular trainee worthy of interest.

Unreasonable jealousy fueled his displeasure. He lifted

his weapon and pointed the bloodstained tip toward the slave. "You there. Quintus, is it not? Present yourself."

Quintus's intelligent eyes darkened with caution, but he made his way from the shadowed sidelines and into the late-afternoon sun.

Caros clapped his iron *gladius* against the slave's wooden sword. "You seem to be taking to a gladiator's life with ease. A few more weeks of training and you might survive a round in the arena."

The trainee kept up his guard. "Whatever God wills."

"God?" Caros swung the *gladius* with more force than necessary. "You think your God has a hand in the ring?"

Quintus blocked the blade with notable speed. "Nothing happens that my Lord doesn't allow."

A vision of the day's execution flashed in Caros's mind. "Then your God is a merciless tyrant."

"I've thought the same a few times myself."

"And yet you continue to serve Him? Would endure being made a slave and cast to the beasts rather than deny Him?"

The slave stayed alert, his sword at the ready. He nodded without hesitation. "I'm here in this pit for no other reason."

The conviction in the slave's green eyes leveled Caros. He stepped back and dropped his weapon to his side. The victims in the ring today had shared the same fervor or they'd have denied their beliefs and saved themselves. Like Pelonia, they believed in an elusive, compelling force Caros wished to comprehend, but couldn't quite grasp.

His thirst for battle drained away. He jabbed the *gladius* point first into the sand and strode toward the sidelines.

Silence fell across the yard. A quick glance over his shoulder revealed Quintus and the other trainees gawking in astonishment. No one was more amazed by his undisciplined behavior than Caros himself. He pulled a tunic over his head and pointed to the gate that led from the training ground. "Come with me, Quintus. I have a few questions for you."

As he walked to the egress, he ignored the quizzical looks of his assistants and motioned for them to resume training. Crisp orders followed by the clack of wooden swords sounded in his wake. A Nubian opened the gate. Quintus's quick steps trailed him through the arch and onto the stone path.

The gate clicked shut. The tranquility of the peach orchard did nothing to ease Caros's inner upheaval. He raked his fingers through his hair and spun on his heel, pinning Quintus with a terse glare. "I want you to tell me of your God."

Surprise notched Quintus's features.

"How does He command unwavering devotion among His followers?"

"Loyalty is the least we can give when compared to the gift of salvation Christ offers."

Caros scowled. "As far as I can see, the only gift you Christians receive is a shameful death in the arena."

Quintus stood taller. "There's no shame in dying for Christ."

"Have you been to an execution, slave? There's no glory in it, either."

"Compared to what?" Quintus asked, unable to conceal his contempt. "A gladiator who spills his lifeblood for mere sport and a drunken mob's amusement?"

"Gladiators don't die for entertainment." Caros knew he lied. "When one of our kind dies in the ring he does so to exalt the emperor and reaffirm the glory of Rome."

"Exalt the emperor? A flesh-and-blood man who will return to the dust at his appointed time? I'd rather praise an all-knowing, loving God. One who promises life eternal if I have the courage to live, and if need be, die for Him."

"If your God is as loving as you claim, why are there times when you think He's cruel?"

Quintus hesitated. The muscles along his jaw worked as he sought to control his inner strife. "The trials of my life of late have caused my faith to falter on occasion. But I'm confident the Lord's forgiven me for those weak moments."

"You speak of being brought here?"

"Yes, among other things."

"Yet, you believe your God is good?"

Quintus nodded. "Even when my plight makes me *feel* otherwise, I choose to walk by faith and believe all the trials I face are part of His greater plan for me."

The dinner bell rang in the distance. A gentle breeze blew through the orchard, rustling the branches and scattering the fallen leaves along the path. Caros's skin prickled despite the warmth of the early evening.

The Christians' sincerity impressed him, persuaded him their beliefs held merit. Both Quintus and Pelonia had suffered tremendous loss, yet they continued to believe their God cared for them in a personal way, that He hadn't abandoned them no matter how dark their circumstances.

He longed to experience that kind of peace, but the jeering faces of those he'd slain stomped through his mind like a barbarian horde. An endless parade of regrets condemned him to a life of turmoil. How he wished life had allowed him to chart a different course than one of constant slaughter. Perhaps then he could cast off his guilt and accept that forgiveness existed.

Convinced he was irredeemable, he tried to brush aside his torment. Pride kept him from asking more questions. It was easier to pretend he didn't care about his place in eternity than reveal his deepest fears. "If I believe in your God, I might find myself tossed in with the wolves. Who needs the aggravation?"

A resigned smile touched the trainee's lips. "If *you* ended up in the arena, I'd pity the wolves."

Caros forced a laugh, but his guilt weighed heavier than a slab of marble. The reminder of his experience in the ring returned him to the core of his dilemma. Not only did his past actions stand like a yawning chasm between him and the Christians' intriguing God, but Pelonia would despise him even more if she learned of all the believers he'd killed.

He would just have to keep the specifics of his past a secret from her.

Sitting heavily on the nearby bench, he braced his elbows on his spread knees. He may not be able to accept Pelonia's God, but he would do his best to earn her affection. A difference in religion shouldn't stand between them. She was his match. His heart's desire. At the moment, he represented everything she despised, but there had to be a way to change her mind and win her love. He didn't know how to stand aside and let her go without a fight.

He eyed Quintus through the twilight. The trainee shared Pelonia's beliefs, had read the Christian texts. Perhaps he understood something she didn't that would allow her to share her life with a nonbeliever.

He stood and paced several steps before wheeling around to find Quintus beside one of the lantern posts. "I have a slave—a woman I purchased the same night I bought you. She's also a follower of your Jesus. She was with me today and witnessed the executions. Indeed, she blamed me for them."

The trainee shook his head, his expression a combination of anger and anguish. "Did my brothers and sisters endure much pain?"

"No," he lied. "They went quickly."

"God be praised." Quintus rubbed a weary hand across his eyes. "Is this woman the same girl whose uncle sold her?"

Caros nodded. "What do you know of her?"

"Very little. I heard a man haggle a price for her. A thousand denarii if I remember correctly."

The slaver had made a tidy profit off him with Pelonia, but Caros felt he'd gotten the better part of the bargain.

"Why did she blame you for the executions?" Quintus asked. "Did you arrange the killing or provide the wolves?"

"No…. Not today."

The hoot of an owl filled the silence as Quintus absorbed the full implication of the statement. The slave's mouth twisted with unconcealed repugnance. "I see."

"Do you?"

"I believe so."

"Then explain it to me."

"It's simple enough," Quintus said. "You're in love with a Christian, but you've killed her kind. Now you're laboring with the question of how to win her affection without having to admit your guilt or share her faith."

Caros flushed at the accuracy of the slave's assessment. Was the trainee some sort of sage? His insight bordered on clairvoyance. "What makes you think I have any affection for Pelonia?"

"I can read the symptoms. A calloused man like you wouldn't be burdened by a woman's bad opinion unless he cared for her."

Caros flinched, stung by the unpalatable truth. Unable to bear the scrutiny in the other man's gaze, he looked toward the remnant red and gold streaks that stretched across the deep purple sky. In no time at all, total darkness would descend, blanketing the city as completely as the regrets consuming his blackened soul.

Footsteps from the direction of the main house pulled him from of his thoughts. A slave ran to him, gasping for breath. "Master, please come quickly! Gaius collapsed. With Lucia gone there's no one left in the household who knows how to help him."

Caros cursed as he ran for the house. What else could go wrong?

While other slaves swept the floor and tidied the kitchen, Pelonia finished stacking the last dishes from the evening meal. Her hands scalded from the water she'd used to wash the trainees' mountain of platters and bowls, she toweled perspiration from the back of her neck and tossed the damp cloth into a laundry basket beside the back door.

Her conscience pricked her. Since Annia's departure an hour before dinner, she'd thought of little except how unfairly she'd accused Caros. The Lord had brought her here to share His light, not add to Caros's guilt or burden him with condemnation. She ached for the brothers and sisters she'd lost to the wolves today, but it did no good to blame Caros for the violence, nor did it aid God's purpose to wound him with her spiked tongue.

Leaving the kitchen, she relished the brisk night air against her heated skin. She arched her back, stretching the muscles made stiff from an eternity bent over a steaming bucket of water and admired the clear sky and bright stars overhead.

Where had everyone gone? The sound of insects hummed through the night, but no human voices. Lanterns glowed in the windows of the house. Torches burned along the path that led to the training field, but the whole place seemed eerily deserted, which was nonsense given the number of trainers, gladiators and slaves living within the compound's walls.

Vowing to apologize to Caros the next time she saw him, she wandered through the orchard, careful to stay in the shadows lest anyone see her. There were enough rumors milling about her already.

A gust of air extinguished two of the torches along the walkway. Tree limbs swayed above her like long arms beckoning her deeper into the night.

She made her way to the marble bench she'd shared with Caros the previous day. Her hand lingered on the spot where his had rested. A bittersweet sensation settled over her. She wished she could revisit their time together on the training field and revel in the unique closeness she'd shared with him as they gazed at the stars. Those few hours alone in his company had been some of the sweetest of her life. If she believed in the Roman gods or were prone to superstition, she might think he'd whispered incantations to steal her will.

Sensing she wasn't alone, she left her seat and squinted into the darkness. A mysterious figure approached from the direction of the gate that separated the orchard from the training area. "Caros?"

"No." A tall stranger stepped from the shifting shadows, his sculpted features strong and handsome in the torchlight. "Don't be frightened. My name is Quintus Ambustus. The *lanista*'s no longer here."

Recognizing a trainee by the cut and coarseness of his belted tunic, she backed away. "Why are you out here by yourself?"

He motioned toward the field behind him. "The gate is locked and the guards have gone to keep watch at the barracks."

She half turned toward the main house, aware it was a mistake to remain in the man's presence unattended. Not only was the situation dangerous, but her instincts warned of Caros's wrath if he found the two of them alone together. "Do you know where your master is?"

His deep-set eyes narrowed with rejection. "I call no man master, but as for the *lanista,* one of the other slaves called him to the house."

With a murmur of thanks, she started back the way she came.

"Wait." He stayed her with a light grasp on the shoulder. "Are you Pelonia?"

She shrugged off his touch. "How do you know my name?"

"The *lanista* said you attended the executions with him today."

A sharp pain cleaved her chest. "Yes," she managed in a choked whisper. "I'll never forget the terrible sight or the sound of thousands demanding murder."

"I'm sorry." His bright green eyes brimmed with empathy. "I understand you're a Christian."

Her eyes snapped back to his face.

"Don't be alarmed. I am also."

His unflinching gaze convinced her of his sincerity. Gratitude flowed through her from the unexpected gift. "Praise be to God. You're the second believer He's placed in my life today."

The strain eased from his tall frame. "The Lord is good indeed. When the *lanista* mentioned you earlier, I prayed for a way to meet you, and here you've appeared. It seems an age since I spoke with another of our faith."

"Caros told you of my beliefs?"

"Yes, but you needn't worry. Your secret will stay with me."

"I wasn't worried. Caros must be aware you're a fellow believer. He's far from careless."

He nodded. "I've seen little of him in the few weeks I've been here, but I've gleaned the same impression."

"How did you come to be here in the gladiatorial school?" she asked, her curiosity piqued.

"You and I arrived the same night, though I had no idea if you'd been kept here or taken to serve elsewhere."

"The worst day of my life," she said sourly.

"I've enjoyed better myself." His dry tone made her laugh. "In all seriousness, I'm sorry to remind you of harsh memories, but believe me, I understand the trials you've faced. I've endured similar circumstances myself in recent months."

Her brows pinched. "How do you know anything about me? Surely Caros didn't discuss—"

"No, he said very little about you. I was chained in one of the wagons close enough to hear your uncle offer you to the slave trader."

She frowned, still unable to comprehend Marcus's hatred.

"He told the slaver what happened to your camp. The fresh graves spoke for themselves."

"I see." Her throat was tight and scratchy. She didn't want to hear more. She continued to struggle with her loss on a daily basis. Her uncle's betrayal only added to the cauldron of grief and rage that kept her at odds with the life of faith she desired to lead.

"What of you?" She swallowed down her hurt and anger. "How did you come to be here?"

"I was condemned to die because of my faith, but the jailer sold me to the slave caravan."

"I'm sorry." Empathy ran through her. "But as you still live, God must have a plan for you yet."

He glanced over his shoulder toward the training field. "At times the Lord's ways are difficult to understand and accept."

She recognized the pain and thread of ire in his voice. Her fingers tightened around his with sisterly compassion. It was her turn to offer encouragement and comfort, she realized, just as Annia had done for her earlier in the day. How like the Lord to bring each of them a friend to bolster their faith in times of trouble.

"Quintus, believe me, I don't always understand the Lord's ways or means of bringing about His plans, but I do know He's trustworthy. Our circumstances may make us *feel* alone, but I believe He'll never forsake those who love Him."

"I know you're right." He smiled and stood taller. "I said the same to the *lanista* and I believe it in my heart."

"You spoke with Caros about living by faith?"

He nodded. "He asked me to tell him about God. I have a strong suspicion his interest stems from your example and a desire to understand you. We all have a purpose and I think yours at the moment is to win your gladiator."

"Yes," she agreed with growing confidence. "I believe I am, too. I pray for him daily and do my best to share the Good News. I realize some may think I'm an odd choice, but—"

"No, you seem the best choice to me." He squeezed her hand, offering reassurance and friendship. "Anyone with eyes can see you've made a good impression on the man. He cares for you. It wouldn't surprise me if you're the only person in the world capable of piercing the armor around his heart."

Hope warmed her like the sun after a frigid rain. "If what you say is true, then it's worth the loss of my freedom. I'll consider myself blessed that the Lord has chosen to use me."

With his elderly steward resting in comfort, Caros went in search of Pelonia. She wasn't in her room, or the slave quarters, the atrium, kitchen or herb garden.

A nagging fear drove him toward the orchard, the last place he could think to look before he called the guards and began a search within the school and beyond the compound's walls.

If he'd trusted her only to learn she'd duped him long enough to escape, he'd…

His feet ground to a halt. His heart slammed against his breastbone. The sight of Pelonia holding hands with the one man he didn't want her to meet caused his stomach to heave with a violent need to retch. As he stalked forward, his eyes narrowing on Quintus, he regretted leaving Cat in his cage. It had been a long time since his tiger had had a human to toy with.

"Slave," he snarled at Quintus. "Step away from her unless you wish to find yourself entertaining the lions at first light."

Pelonia whirled to face him, a look of astonishment, or was it guilt, stamped across her expressive features. A sheen of red clouded Caros's vision when the defiant trainee took his time to back away and put a suitable distance between the two of them.

Jealousy shredding his reason, Caros locked fingers around Pelonia's delicate wrist and pulled her against his side. His hostile gaze flicked back to Quintus. "Leave us, worm. If I see you near her again, I'll slay you where you stand."

"Caros, please, let me explain!" She thrust herself in front of him, her small hand splayed against his chest. "You're behaving like a lunatic. I won't allow you to harm him."

Allow? Icy rage slithered through him. "You aren't strong enough to stop me."

"I know, but—"

"Why do you care? Is this slave more than a stranger to you? Have you somehow discovered he's your perfect man in so little time?"

Bewilderment scored her features. She eyed him as though he'd gone mad. "No. I'd try to stop you because tomorrow you'd regret your idiocy and the death of an innocent man. You're burdened by enough guilt as it is. I'd want to save you from piling more on yourself."

Feeling like a cobra in the hands of an expert charmer, he dragged his gaze back to Quintus. "Take this path back to the *domus.* Report to the guard on duty by the back door and have him take you the long way around to the bunkhouse."

Quintus offered no acknowledgment of the order other than to tip his head in a respectful nod to Pelonia. "Good night, sweet lady. I hope the Lord answers your prayers with all possible haste."

Seething at the man's audacity, Caros waited until the trainee was out of earshot. "What prayers, Pelonia? Already my slave knows more of your secrets than I do. Share them with me."

She stroked his chest as if to soothe him. "I can't until you're ready to hear them."

The heat of her palm reached through the thin fabric of his tunic. He lifted her other hand to his chest and held both tight against him, his heart pounding from the powerful effect of her touch.

His anger began to fade though his jealousy continued to roar like a bonfire. He refused to share her or give her up. Every part of his being longed to draw her against him, to kiss her until she agreed to be his woman for the rest of her life. Their bargain could burn Hades' fires for all he cared.

"I'm ready now, Pelonia. I want no barriers of *any* kind between us."

She winced at his tight grip on her wrist. "Let go," she said, softly. "You're holding me too tight."

He relaxed his fingers without breaking the contact. "Why do you think the idea of you choosing Quintus drives me insane?"

"Quintus? I just met him."

"He's better suited for you than I am," he said gruffly. "He shares your faith. His true occupation is one of a learned and respected man, not death. No scars mar his face or form. He's—"

"Not you," she replied with simple honesty.

His mouth snapped shut. A mix of expressions crossed

his chiseled features—astonishment, uncertainty, and finally…hope.

His vulnerability shattered her remaining defenses. His height and nearness surrounded her. The spicy scent of his skin and the night's peach-infused air robbed her of protest as he gathered her against him.

"There's no man I prefer over you."

She felt the last traces of hostility drain out of him. His lips brushed the top of her head. Gooseflesh prickled her skin. She snuggled closer, resting her cheek against the center of his chest. Lulled by the solid thud of his heart beneath her ear, she chose not to examine the oddity of finding so much peace in the arms of such a violent man.

"Must I beg or is your silence how you intend to punish me?" he asked against her hair.

"Punish you?"

He leaned back and waited for her to look at him. "Yes. For being a 'bloodthirsty' Roman."

She flushed with guilt. "I don't blame you for the executions. I regretted what I said to you even before you left me alone with Annia. Now, once again I find I'm in the wrong and needing to apologize for the meanness of my tongue."

"No." His fingers cupped her cheek, then slipped into her hair at the nape. "You did nothing."

"I said horrible things. I wish it weren't the case but I only seem to lose control of my temper when I'm with you."

"You were in shock and I'm not the easiest of men."

"Please don't make excuses for me." The kinder he became, the worse she felt.

He opened his mouth to argue, but seemed to think better of what he planned to say. "You're right. I shouldn't make excuses for you. Your insults ripped through my heart like flaming arrows, causing more pain than I've ever endured.

Then, when I could bear your scorn no longer, I searched for you to discuss the matter only to find you sharing secrets in the arms of another man."

Remorse rolled over her in waves. Not for her innocent behavior with Quintus, but for the hurt she'd caused Caros with her angry accusations. Never in her life had she wounded anyone as much as she had him—the one soul she wanted most to see healed.

"Caros, I…" Her voice rasped over the lump in her throat. She lifted her gaze, ready to apologize, to plead for forgiveness and offer a fresh start between them, but amusement gleamed in his eyes. "I…why are you laughing?"

Chapter Sixteen

Caros endeavored to keep a straight face. "I'm not laughing."

"You lie." She swatted his chest and tried to break free of his hold. "Tell me why you're laughing at me or I'll have to twist your arm and make you."

"Vicious woman." He closed his eyes. At the moment she almost escaped, he tightened his arms, not ready to relinquish the exquisite torture of holding her so close. "All right, I admit it. You have a face as easy to read as an open scroll and it makes me happy to see how concerned you are for me."

"Happy?"

"You say the word as though you've never heard it before."

"I've heard it." She burrowed back against him, her arms wrapped around his waist, her cheek pressed against his heart as though she meant to stay with him forever. "You just surprised me, but then you always do."

He stroked her hair, loving the silken tresses that made him grateful he had hands to touch her. "I wouldn't want to bore you."

She grinned up at him, her doe eyes sparkling like the

stars above them. "You make me feel many things, *lanista,* but boredom has never been one of them."

He squeezed her until she squealed and merry giggles filled the cool, autumn evening. "If I confessed to the feelings you stir in me, you'd run for the hills in maidenly fright."

Relaxing back against him, she sighed from what he hoped was contentment. "Then confess nothing, for I'm pleased where I am and too tired to run anywhere."

"The woman is finally satisfied." A chuckle rumbled in his chest. "If exhaustion is the ingredient needed to make you stay with me, I'll have to devote more time to thinking up chores for you."

She yawned. "You best hurry, then. Our bargain ends in twelve days' time."

The reminder spiked him in the heart. Despite the tenderness between them, she clung to her plan to escape at the first opportunity. The knowledge hurt more than he cared to admit. "Why do you remain so adamant to leave? Have I not treated you well and shown you as much respect as any man can show a woman?"

She stilled like the night surrounding them. "Let me go."

Cursing the end of what had become an enjoyable evening, he released her. Her shoulders thrust back, she aimed for the bench several paces away. Already his arms missed holding her.

Never one to admit defeat, he decided to double his efforts to convince her of her place by his side.

"My wish to leave isn't swayed one way or the other by how well or ill you treat me," she said, her tone as stiff as her small body. "As I've told you before, I want my freedom because to live as a slave is abhorrent to me. This degraded state is not who I am. Would you be willing to change places with me? To take on a mantle of slavery once more?"

"I swore the day I won my freedom, I'd never lose it again."

"Then how can you expect me to abide the loss of *my* freedom just because you will it to be so?" She kicked a fallen piece of fruit with the toe of her sandal. "It also troubles me greatly to know my cousin must be worried sick…or worse, mourning me if she believes I'm dead. If you felt a tithe of my pain when I think of Tiberia suffering, you'd let me go this instant."

"And what of *my* pain?" he asked quietly. "What am I to do once you leave here? I'm not naive enough to believe you'd return to me if I released you."

Distant voices carried through the crisp night from the direction of the house.

"You're wrong," she said. "I'd come back to you. I want you to know the Lord."

"Of course." He threw up his hands in exasperation. "Why didn't I guess? If not for your absurd need to see me believe in your God, you'd be seeking escape at every possible turn."

"Most likely," she agreed. "But then, without my hope for your soul, there'd be no bargain between us in the first place."

"Without your silly beliefs, you'd already be in my bed and there'd be no *need* for this cursed bargain between us."

"No. My father taught me to be a woman of honor. Christian or not, I wouldn't share your bed without first being your wife."

A bitter laugh erupted from his throat. "Wife, slave, what's the difference? Either way I own you."

Pelonia paled until her luminous skin shone as white as a pearl in the moonlight. "There's a difference, Caros. If you don't realize that simple truth, then regardless of whether or not you believe in my God, there's no hope at all for us."

* * *

A rooster crowed, waking Pelonia from a dreamless sleep. Her lashes fluttered open. It was the first day of the week. Three days had passed since the executions, three nights since she and Caros had quarreled in the orchard.

Disheartened by the situation between them, she rose from her pallet, noting the rising sun. The chill in the air reminded her of Caros's attitude toward her. He hadn't spoken to her since they'd argued, but every once in a while she would catch him studying her with a fierce gleam in his eye that turned to ice the moment he realized she'd seen him. She'd offended him greatly and though she was sorry she'd hurt him, she took solace in the fact she'd told him the truth.

Washed and dressed, she made her way to the herb garden. She'd developed a routine over the last few days and found she enjoyed caring for the plants as much or more here than she did at home. Along with pruning the existing plants, she'd marked out a vegetable garden on three sides of the fountain and planted seeds from a variety of root vegetables to see how they'd take in the rich, black soil.

Cat met her inside the gate. No longer afraid of the tiger since the day he almost shoved her into the fountain, she scratched his head and rubbed his ears, laughing when he closed his eyes in contentment and nuzzled her chest with a gratified grunt.

Hearing footsteps, she looked up to find Caros's steward picking his way toward her.

"How is your health, Gaius?" she asked once he stopped a few arm lengths away from her. "The color's returned to your face but should you be up and back to your duties so soon after your collapse?"

The old man offered a grim smile that pleated the wrinkles of his thin face. "I'm well enough thanks to your garlic concoction. I believe the culprit for making me ill was a poorly prepared joint of mutton. It smelled less than fresh when I ate it. I should have known better."

"I suspected as much. Who hasn't suffered the consequences of eating bad food from time to time? I believe the mixture I shared is fairly well-known. I was surprised no one here knew how to fix it for you."

"This is a gladiatorial school. Lucia excelled at gentle remedies, but our physicians are better at binding wounds than mixing potions."

"I'm sorry the healer is gone because of me."

"She was wrong to behave as she did," he said without mercy. "I've found the master to be a wise man who handles situations in the best possible manner. Don't concern yourself any longer. Lucia was sent away because she deserves to be, but she'll be fine."

Pelonia nodded. "I hope you're right."

"I am, but I didn't come to fetch you to make small talk about Lucia. You have a guest."

"Who is it?" she asked, no longer surprised by Gaius's brusque manner.

"Annia, the shop mistress from the Forum." His mouth turned down in clear disapproval. "The master informed me she might visit, but he said nothing of her bringing a mob along with her."

She patted Cat on the head in a quick farewell. "Where did you tell them to wait?"

"In the chamber just off the front entrance," he called as she hurried toward the house.

She found Annia and her companions waiting patiently on the plush couches in the sitting room.

Annia hopped to her feet the moment Pelonia rushed across the threshold. "I trust you don't mind my bringing friends."

"Of course not," she assured her. Annia's soft perfume surrounded Pelonia as she gathered the elegant older woman in a hug.

"Then let me introduce you."

Gaius's "mob" turned out to be two couples—one, a fresh-faced pair of newlyweds dressed in matching shades of yellow, the other a plump middle-aged husband and wife, both with graying hair and dark eyes.

Annia took the older woman by the hand. "You may remember Marcia here from my shop the other day."

"Yes. I believe you mentioned meeting by the river this morning."

Annia nodded, her good mood infectious. "The five of us meet to worship God and discuss the texts this time each week. After I told them of your dreadful plight and that you weren't able to join us in our usual spot, I suggested we visit with you here instead."

"How wonderful." Pelonia beamed with happiness. "You're all an answer to prayer. It's been over a month since I've gathered with anyone to praise the Lord. I couldn't be more pleased you're here."

"What of the *lanista?*" Marcia's husband, Festus, asked with marked concern. "Forgive me, but it seems strange to worship in the home of a man known to kill Christians. Is he here? Are we safe?"

Pelonia's smile faded. Her first instinct to defend Caros, she tamped down a forceful reply and kept her voice as mild as possible. "What do you mean *known* to kill Christians? It's true the *lanista* trains gladiators, that he fought and killed for several years but he's been retired from the games for a long time now. He's never even fought in Flavian's amphitheater…"

An uncomfortable silence fell over the group. The visitors

exchanged uneasy glances. Festus cleared his throat. "Forgive me, dear sister, I spoke out of turn."

"No, I'm certain you didn't. Please don't treat me like an outsider. What has Caros done?"

Festus shifted nervously from one foot to the other. "You're newly arrived to the capital. There's little chance you know of your master's history before the mob demanded his freedom. He was the best gladiator this city's ever seen. Before I chose to follow the Way, I used to enjoy the games. Back before the Flavians built the arena, the editors set up fights in squares, back alleyways, even the middle of the Forum on feast days. The Bone Grinder, as the *lanista* was called then, never failed to rouse the crowds who gathered just to see him kill."

"He was known for his speed and tenacity," Geminius, the other male guest added. "The spectators loved him because no one stood a chance against him, and he rarely showed mercy. He played the crowd and made them dream of being him. Unfortunately the victims included many of our sect who were charged with treason and brought in for execution."

Trembling, Pelonia sank into the seat behind her. Perhaps she'd been naive, but she hadn't allowed herself to consider just how many Christian lives Caros had ended.

Annia coughed and left the comfort of her pillowed chair. "That's enough, men. Can't you see what you're doing to the poor girl? We didn't come here to add to her distress."

"No, we didn't," said Geminius.

"Shall I get you a cup of water, Pelonia?" his young wife, Vergilia, asked.

"No, I'm fine," she insisted, her head throbbing with tension. Her concern for Caros blotted out all rational thought. A distant part of her admitted she was horrified by the

number of deaths at Caros's hand, but armed with the knowledge of his past, how could she condemn him? He'd once
told her he'd learned to survive under the threat of kill or be
killed. Loving him as she did, she was only too thankful he'd
been strong enough to live.

"Whatever Caros did, it's in the past." Pelonia met each
of the other's uncertain gazes with a direct look of her own.
"As far as I'm concerned the past is where it will remain."

"I agree," Marcia said. "No one is blameless. The Lord
says to forgive. Like Pelonia, I intend to follow His instructions. Now, perhaps we should pray. We've started off badly.
Let's begin afresh."

The others murmured in agreement. Pelonia joined them
in prayer even more firmly convinced Caros needed the
peace of Christ in his life if he ever hoped to overcome the
horrors he'd known.

Dripping with sweat from his morning sword practice,
Caros toweled his face and bare chest before slipping his
favorite old tunic over his head. As he made his way down
the hall toward the atrium, he stopped midstride, caught off
guard by the chorus coming from somewhere in the house.

It couldn't be Alexius singing. He heard more than one
voice. Besides, his friend sounded like a mule with a cold
when he sang. Was it the other slaves? He doubted it. As far
as he knew they'd never before felt the need to burst into song.

In the sun-drenched courtyard, the voices grew louder,
competing with the splash of the fountain. Discernible words
caressed his ears and drew him across the covered porch
toward the front of the house.

The Lord is my Shepherd; I shall not want.

Locating the source of the soothing hymn, he crossed his
arms over his chest and leaned against the doorframe, won-

dering if a mirage had sprung up in his sitting room or if a group of Christians really had been audacious enough to gather under his roof.

He makes me to lie down in green pastures.

He leads me beside the still waters.

He restores my soul.

The last words caught him by surprise. He listened more intently, his interest keen to learn who might restore his soul.

He leads me in the paths of righteousness for His name's sake.

Yea, though I walk through the valley of death, I will fear no evil: for You are with me…

His eyes sought out Pelonia where she stood worshipping her God, an expression of intense love and peace making her even more lovely than usual.

As the group continued to sing, Pelonia's eyes fluttered open. Once again she caught him staring at her. This time he didn't feel angry for being found out or trapped and ashamed by his inability to keep his eyes off her. This time, he felt…welcomed.

She smiled at him, a glorious display that lit up her face and allowed him a deeper glimpse of her beautiful spirit. The hope of reconciliation shone from her eyes.

Stretching out her hand, she beckoned him to join her in front of the shuttered windows. He took a step forward, surprised by his eagerness to share in the atmosphere of peace their worship created.

The song ended. He peeled his gaze from Pelonia to find the other believers gaping at him. He saw in their faces, they knew who he was. Worse, what he'd done to their kind. To their credit they tried to hide their distrust, but the trepidation etched in their expressions severed the tenuous thread reeling him over to Pelonia's side.

The temptation to join them evaporated. What madness to think he could leave his old life behind when everyone except Pelonia knew the full extent of his brutal past.

With a terse shake of his head in answer to Pelonia's invitation, he turned on his heel and left the house.

Pelonia flinched as the heavy stone door closed with an angry thump. Owl-eyed, her companions stared at her in speechless alarm.

"He isn't going for the authorities, is he?" Festus yelped, his voice reed-thin with fear.

"Don't be too anxious," Geminius warned. "If he wanted us dead, he wouldn't bother to contact the authorities. He'd have killed us himself."

Annia and the others launched into an agitated debate about their safety, but Pelonia didn't weigh in. Every nerve in her body demanded she go after Caros. She rushed for the door, nearly tripping on her tunic's hem in her haste to catch up with him. The guard moved to bar her way, but her new friends closed ranks around her, sweeping her past the guard and out onto the front steps. Blinking the sun's glare from her eyes, she spotted Caros just before he disappeared into the thick flow of pedestrians on the street.

Frantic to be heard over the clack of horse hooves and wagon wheels, she called Caros's name as she sprinted down the steps before the guard had a chance to follow her.

Caros whipped around. His eyes flared, then narrowed. Walking back to her, his steely disapproval gripped her by the throat. "How did you get out here?"

"My friends—"

"You mean those fools abandoning you?"

Pelonia craned her neck to see behind her. Wringing her hands, Annia waited by the school's tall, iron gate, but the other two couples fled in the opposite direction.

"Your surliness frightened them."

"Cowards," he sneered, grasping her hand and dragging her back toward the house. "At least your friend Annia seems to possess a bit of courage."

"So do the others." Offended on her friends' behalf, she did her best to pull free. She didn't appreciate his snide attitude or his overreaction. After all, she hadn't been trying to escape. She'd followed him because she'd been worried about his feelings. "It took great courage for them to worship in the home of a *lanista*."

"Great courage or tremendous stupidity?"

Pelonia bit back a tart reply. Marching up the steps, he berated the guard for his carelessness and hauled Pelonia through the front door. Annia close on their heels, Caros blocked the door with his arm. "You've 'visited' long enough today, mistress."

With a decisive thud, he closed the door in the older woman's indignant face.

Chapter Seventeen

Annia descended the school's front steps, her maternal instincts running rampant. Until now, she'd believed Pelonia's assurance she was well treated, that she felt the Lord had placed her in the gladiator's home for a purpose. She didn't want to question Pelonia's calling, but she feared the *lanista*'s anger might lead to violence.

Her mind already forming a plan to help Pelonia, she realized she may not have known the young woman long, but she'd come to think of her as a daughter. Perturbed for provoking Caros's temper, she wished she'd used better judgment and come alone this morning. With the damage done, she had to do something to correct her lack of foresight.

Calling for the litter she'd arrived on, she gave her servants swift orders to be taken to the Palatine hill. Pelonia had mentioned her cousin's marriage as her family's reason for venturing to Rome in the first place. Perhaps her cousin's important husband wielded enough influence to see Pelonia freed from the *lanista*'s hold.

Annia hopped from her litter the moment it arrived in front of Senator Tacitus's palace on the Palatine. The huge marble columns and grand portico reminded her of a religious temple. Taking a deep breath, she lifted the hem of her tunic and *stola* enough to keep from stumbling on any of the myriad steps leading to the front door.

At the top of the stairs, she noted the wool marking the doorposts, an indication of the bride and groom's recent marriage. She knocked and breathed a sigh of relief when the palace caretaker allowed her entrance.

Inside the cavernous entryway, she waited, the smoky-sweet scent of incense drifting from the family's shrine in the atrium behind the long blue curtain to her right. She caught her breath at the vibrant frescoes decorating the walls and the numerous busts of the senator's illustrious family lining the brightly hued edges of the mosaic floor.

The curtain parted and a slender young girl stepped from the shadows of the atrium.

Annia surged forward. "Forgive my intrusion this morning, but I must know, are you Tiberia, wife of Senator Antonius Tacitus?"

Her manner severe, the girl nodded. "I'm Tiberia. My caretaker says you have news of my cousin."

Confused by the cold, almost hostile tone, Annia began to question the wisdom in coming here. Perhaps Pelonia bore her cousin more affection than Tiberia returned? Fearing she'd made yet another error this morning, she eased back toward the exit.

"Where are you going?" Tiberia waved her hand and two slaves moved to block Annia's escape. "Do you or do you not have news of my cousin?"

"I believe I may have made a mistake."

"Why? Did you think to come here, demand a reward for your information and leave without any of us being wise to your deceit?"

"Reward? You misunderstand. I want nothing from you. I wish only to tell you of your cousin Pelonia's whereabouts. I fear for her safety and pray you and your family will be gracious enough to rescue her."

The girl hesitated, her small, slightly uptilted eyes narrowing with indecision. The curtain rustled again. A feminine voice called from behind it, "That's enough, Asa, I'll see to our guest myself."

Annia watched the girl bow toward the curtain and scurry off down a side hallway. The curtain parted again. This time an aristocratic woman stepped into the entry. Appearing slightly younger than Pelonia by perhaps a year or two, the newcomer's red *stola* and white undertunic gave her a dramatic air that went well with her above average height and patrician features.

"I am Tiberia, the person you seek. I trust you'll forgive my small deception and understand the need for it. When Pelonia disappeared, my husband offered a reward for news of her whereabouts. We've been swarmed by charlatans bearing lies simply to gain a few coins ever since. Now, please," she said urgently, "tell me of my cousin. My husband commissioned the best scouts to find her. They brought news she was dead."

"The scouts were mistaken," Annia assured her, relieved to find she'd made the right decision to come after all. "Her family's camp was attacked by thieves and everyone killed except Pelonia and her uncle. That same day, her uncle sold her to a slave caravan."

"No! I can't believe you," Tiberia said, the color draining from her face.

"It's true, my lady. She was sold to the *lanista,* Caros Viriathos. She's being held in his compound even as we speak."

"I've been such a fool," Tiberia whispered, staring at the floor. "I believed him."

"Who did you believe, my lady?"

Her full mouth pinched into a thin line, Tiberia shook her head, unable or unwilling to share more. She clasped Annia's hands, her unsteady fingers clutching tightly. "I've been so distraught. I blamed myself for Pelonia's death. Please, you must take me to her this instant. I *must* see her for myself."

"That may not be easy, my lady. I believe you will need your husband to attend with you. The *lanista* is a difficult man from what I can tell. I'm certain he won't let you see her without being forced."

"Nonsense." Tiberia snapped her fingers and called for a litter. "My husband is a senator of Rome. No one refuses me entrance. Least of all a filthy gladiator trainer who dares to think he can keep me from my cherished kin."

Unsure of his status as far as Pelonia was concerned, Caros found her under a lemon tree in the herb garden a short time after the noonday meal. Cat lay stretched out on the ground beside her, basking in the cool autumn afternoon. Deep in thought, her chin resting on her raised knee, she idly stroked the tiger's ear.

Pleased by the peaceful sight of his woman and pet together, he admired Pelonia's courage. In small ways and large, she proved her immeasurable worth. Few people viewed his tiger as anything more than a vicious beast, but she possessed a talent for seeing deeper into a person—or tiger, as the case may be. In less than a week, she'd overcome her initial fear and accepted the animal, treating Cat with as much affection as if he were her own. He lived in hope of the day she would accept him with as much ease and openness. Though why she would ever find him worthy of her was a mystery after the way he'd treated her and her friends earlier in the morning.

Dry leaves crunched beneath his sandals, drawing Pelonia's attention. Her expression unreadable, he continued toward her. The idea of entering a ring full of lions held more appeal than facing her and admitting his guilt.

Unpracticed in offering apologies, he'd spent the last hour devising the best strategy to win her forgiveness for his heavy-handed behavior. Why had he become so unreasonable over a few judgmental glances? Most of society condemned him as next to nothing because of his profession. Why, all of a sudden, did the opinion of a few weak-livered Christians cause him the slightest concern?

Because Pelonia will side with them.

He crouched beside her in the shade, his fingers folding into the short coarse mane around Cat's neck. The quiet disappointment in her regard made him regret his earlier actions even more than he already did.

He rubbed his chin, waiting for her to berate him. When she said nothing, he assumed her silence was meant as some form of feminine punishment. Usually blessed with the ability to ignore a woman's sulks, he found the idea of Pelonia thinking badly of him an herb too bitter to swallow.

"How long do you plan to be angry with me?" he asked, his attention focused on his dozing pet.

"Have you done something to make me angry with you?"

"Don't play games, Pelonia."

"I'm not." She shifted to her knees, then rose to her feet, brushing the flecks of dirt and leaves from her tunic. "Nor am I angry with you. I thought *you* were furious with me."

"No, not in the least," he said, standing.

"I find that difficult to believe. Your fierce looks of the past three days have said otherwise. And this morning—"

"I behaved like a mad dog."

"No, you were hurt and I'm truly sorry for it. Believe me, I'm upset with my new acquaintances enough for both of us."

"You'd side with *me* against your fellow believers?"

"I'd side with you against anyone except God."

Astonishment rattled him to his core. The bright color blooming up her slender throat told him she'd spoken secret thoughts with an unguarded tongue. She never ceased to surprise him. Grateful to find so unique and generous a woman, he thanked her God for bringing her into his life.

"Why do you think I followed you this morning, Caros? To cause another argument between us? No," she answered for him. "I chased after you because I saw your expression when the others judged you. They didn't give you a chance. They should have known better. If they claim to be followers of Christ, they ought to show His love to all of those in need of it."

Astounded by her attitude after the way they'd parted three nights ago and then his harshness this morning, he couldn't believe his good fortune. Even more convinced she was the finest person he'd ever known, he brushed his thumb over her smooth, rosy cheek, loving her more with each passing moment. "I need no one's love but yours."

A startled gasp broke from her lips. More heat stained her cheeks until they glowed bright red. "You're wrong. We *all* need Christ's love and forgiveness. At this moment, you most of all. I believe you're suffering from a strong case of conviction."

He raked his fingers through his hair. "Conviction, eh? Conviction of what?"

"Jesus taught—listen to me, don't shut me out," she said when he rolled his eyes and opened his mouth to interrupt her. She waited until she held his full attention before she continued. "Jesus taught that no person comes to the Father unless the Holy Spirit draws him. The Spirit is drawing *you,* whether you accept it or not. The road to believing in Christ as Savior and living by faith can be a rocky one if a person refuses to follow the truth he knows in his heart."

"Is that why I berated your friends and slammed the door in Annia's face?"

She reached for a lemon leaf and split it into strips. "I think you overreacted out of fear."

"I fear nothing." *Except losing you.*

"That's not true." She stepped closer. "You wanted to join us this morning. Don't deny it. I saw it on your eyes. It wasn't until you noticed the others' reactions that you changed and became defensive. Are you concerned if you turn to Christ the other believers won't accept you?"

Being Romans, her friends knew truths about his past that she didn't. "Their opinion matters to me as much as the dirt beneath my feet."

"If you say so."

"The only opinion I care about is yours."

She pinned him with a knowing look that made him feel she possessed the talent to read his thoughts and divine the secrets of his soul. "Is that why you haven't told me of the Christians you've killed?"

She might as well have kicked him in the stomach. "Who told you?"

"It's not important. Why didn't *you?*"

"Why would I? Especially after your reaction to the executions."

Her soft hand reached up to caress his cheek. "Only now do I comprehend how much my words must have hurt you. I'm sorry."

"Then you don't hate me for what I did to your kind?"

"No! When I heard what happened, I remembered what

you said about learning to kill or be killed. I'm just grateful you survived all those years."

He nuzzled her palm, overwhelmed by her sweet spirit.

"I'm ashamed of how I dragged you down the street like a common slave this morning."

Clearly he'd caught her off guard. "Why? Don't you think of me as a common slave?"

"There's nothing common about you." He kissed her fingers. "In truth, I believe I haven't thought of you as a true slave since…the first time I found you in this garden."

Astonished, she didn't know whether to laugh with glee or to screech at him. Her fingers tingling from the brush of his lips, she stepped away. "Then why threaten to bend me to your will and force me to accept my bondage? Why do we have a bargain at all? Why not release me to find my cousin?"

"Because I want you here with me, within arm's reach. I want you here where I know I can see you every day, every *hour* if I choose."

She turned her back on him, but not before he saw her tormented expression. "What of *my* wants, Caros?"

"I'll give you anything except your freedom."

"Every other gift pales in comparison."

He inhaled sharply, desperate enough to offer all that he had left of himself. He grasped her shoulders and eased her back around to face him. "What if I give you my heart?"

Her lips began to tremble. The muscles of her face twitched as she worked to maintain her composure. Her huge dark eyes watered with unshed tears. "Please don't, Caros. As much as I want to, you know I can't accept any part of you as long as we have no future together."

Chapter Eighteen

Tiberia waited impatiently in the covered litter while one of her slaves announced her arrival and obtained entrance into the gladiatorial school. Surrounded by thick, gray stone walls and a massive iron gate, the school reminded her of a military fortress—perfect for training men to kill or die in honor of the emperor.

Without a hint of softness to be seen from the front street, the formidable compound sent a quiver of unease through her already agitated nerves. Perhaps Annia had been correct when she'd recommended bringing Antonius along with them. A part of her wished she'd listened to the older woman she'd sent home earlier, instead of simply sending word to the senator by way of a messenger.

Her fingers tapped a rapid tattoo on the fat silk pillow she reclined against. Through the thin lavender veil shrouding her litter, she watched the throng of pedestrians scurrying to and fro. If her slave didn't return soon, she feared she might burst from all the restless energy frothing inside her. She couldn't wait to see Pelonia again.

Spying her slave the moment he stepped outside the gate,

she held her breath in eager anticipation as the tall Lycian sprinted toward her. It didn't bode well that sweat beaded his upper lip despite the afternoon's mild weather.

She snapped her fingers. Her bodyguard pulled the curtain back and helped her alight. "Well?" she demanded of the slave. "What news do you have for me?"

"The steward, Gaius, welcomes you, but he warns the *lanista's* mood is far from pleasant. He recommends you return another day."

Her lips thinned into an agitated line. "He does, does he? What day does he suggest?"

A trickle of sweat seeped down the slave's temple. "The ides of December, my lady."

"The ides of *December?* That's six weeks away!" Infuriated by the obvious rebuff, she drew her shawl tighter around her stiff shoulders and marched toward the massive front gate, her slave hard-pressed to keep pace with her.

"Open up!" she commanded the guard at the gatehouse. "I am Tiberia, wife of Senator Antonius Tacitus. I'm here to speak with your master."

After much debate, the guards opened the gate, its hinges creaking from the weight of the massive iron piece. The Lycian ran ahead to announce her presence, gaining admittance into the *domus* just as she arrived on the doorstep.

"It's an honor to welcome you, my lady." The elderly steward bowed low as she crossed into the entryway.

"Where is your master? He has much to answer for," she said, biting her tongue to keep from calling the old man a liar. *The ides of December indeed!*

"In the herb garden, my lady." He led her to a sitting room off the atrium. "Please, make yourself comfortable. I'll inform him you're here."

Refusing to be put off any longer, she pursued him at a

short distance, careful not to draw his attention to her presence behind him. Leaving the cool interior of the *domus,* they followed a path past the kitchen, through a gate and into a connecting garden rife with lemon trees and an abundant variety of herbs.

The delicate scents of rosemary and mint mingled with the sound of voices emanating from a spot around the kitchen wall beyond her view.

"Pelonia, wait!" A deep male voice sliced through the warm afternoon.

Tiberia ran toward the voice, concern for her cousin pressing her onward.

The sight that greeted her could have been plucked from a tragedy. The *lanista's* hands clutched Pelonia's shoulders like the talons of a great winged beast. An expression of such forlorn agony creased Pelonia's visage, Tiberia felt her own throat close over and her heart pinch from the pain of it.

"What are you doing to her?" Tiberia demanded, racing to her cousin's rescue. "Get your vile hands off her this instant!"

The *lanista* stilled, but didn't release his prey as commanded. Pelonia's gaze darted toward her, her eyes wide with shock. As recognition dawned, her countenance brightened by degrees with elated disbelief. With little effort, she shrugged off her captor's hold. "Tiberia? Is it really you?"

The steward began an immediate round of apologies to his master for not having known she'd followed him.

"Fetch Cat before he frightens our guest," said the gladiator. "He's in the corner beyond the fountain."

Unconcerned about a cat, she held out her arms to Pelonia in welcome. "Yes, dear cousin, I'm here for you. I came the moment I learned of your whereabouts."

Pelonia launched herself into Tiberia's embrace with a jubilant shriek. "The Lord be praised for bringing you here!

You can't imagine how happy I am to see you. Marriage must agree with you. You're even lovelier than the last portrait you sent me."

Unwilling to let go, Tiberia held on tighter, tears of thankfulness burning the back of her eyes. "I believed you were dead. I can't thank the gods enough you're alive."

"How did you find me?"

"I…" Momentarily struck speechless, she watched in amazement as the steward led a tiger from behind the fountain and up the stone path. "By the gods, what is that beast doing in the garden?"

"The tiger is Caros's pet. He's fairly harmless."

"Fairly?"

"He *is* a tiger." Pelonia laughed. "You should have seen the look on your face just now."

"And how did you react the first time you saw him?"

"I confess, much the same way. The tiger sneaked up behind me and breathed down my neck. It was a curious sensation to say the least."

Regaining her wits, Tiberia giggled. "I can imagine."

Pelonia linked arms with her, apparently unconcerned by the *lanista*'s black expression. "Now, tell me, how did you find me?"

"Your friend Annia visited me this morning. I didn't know whether or not to believe her at first, but any positive word of you was most welcome. Marcus, that weasel, led us to believe you were kidnapped. I lost countless nights' sleep, I was so worried about you. The scouts we sent to search for you reported you were dead. I've been racked with grief for weeks, blaming myself for—"

"No, no, you mustn't blame yourself. You aren't responsible for anything that's happened," Pelonia assured her. "I'm sorry I didn't send word of my good health. You were never far from my thoughts, but circumstances prevented me from contacting you."

Understanding perfectly, Tiberia narrowed her gaze on the *lanista*. She'd heard stories about Caros Viriathos. Her husband enjoyed the games and was an avid admirer of the great champions. This close to the infamous former gladiator, she could guess why he'd never been beaten. He was a colossus—battle-hardened, massive and formidable. A long scar ran down his cheek and his tunic did little to hide the marks of battle on his arms and legs. She imagined the hostile gleam in his eyes alone had sent many confident challengers into early graves.

Silently reminding herself of her position, that the man wouldn't dare harm a senator's wife, she began to lead Pelonia from the garden.

"Wait," Pelonia said, not so easily led. "I want you to meet Caros."

With no desire to greet the man who'd enslaved her favorite relative, Tiberia wrinkled her nose with distaste, but submitted to propriety for Pelonia's sake.

"Caros," Pelonia beckoned with an outstretched hand. "Come and meet my cousin, Tiberia, my dearest friend in the world."

Struck by the informality between them, Tiberia marveled at the way the *lanista*'s severity softened each time he glanced at her cousin. Was it possible Annia had been mistaken in thinking he'd kept Pelonia as a slave?

"It's an honor to meet you," he said.

Sensing his insincerity, she inclined her head, but didn't return the sentiment.

Pelonia attempted to fill the awkward silence. "Tiberia is a recent bride."

"Yes, Pelonia was to be one of my special guests." She

didn't bother to dull the edge of accusation in her tone. "Apparently she was otherwise detained. How long have you had her enslaved?"

"Almost three weeks," Caros replied. "She was unconscious when the slave trader brought her here. I had no way of learning who she was or who awaited her."

"And, of course, you searched for us the moment you learned her true identity?"

He shrugged. "No."

"You honestly planned to keep her as a slave?"

"My plans are none of your concern."

Incensed by his audacity, she glanced at Pelonia, who watched from beneath one of the lemon trees, arms akimbo, her eyes fixed on the *lanista,* her expression unreadable.

"Whatever your plans, you must realize they've been altered," Tiberia said, at the end of her patience. "No relative of mine will be chattel in your possession."

"How do you intend to take her from me?"

"Through the front door, of course."

As though he enjoyed baiting her, he smirked with infuriating calm. "I'll warn you now that's a risky scheme. *If* you make it past me, there are armed guards at every exit who've been threatened with severe punishment if she escapes."

"Don't toy with me, *lanista.*" She stamped her foot in vexation. "What kind of fiend are you? You can't honestly hope to imprison her here now that you know who she is and the importance of her family. My husband, the senator, will never tolerate it."

"Obviously, you place more value in your connections than I do. I broke no laws when I bought her—"

"If it's a matter of coin—"

"It isn't."

"I'll gladly repay you with interest."

"I've no need of your money."

"You're just being stubborn!"

Pelonia joined the fray. "That's enough, both of you."

Caros reached for Pelonia and led her to a spot by the fountain, too far away for Tiberia to overhear their conversation. Confused by the gentleness in the brute's manner toward her cousin, she acknowledged there was a stronger tie between the two of them than she'd originally been prepared to admit.

Her lip curled in disgust at the idea of *her* relative being entangled with anyone of the gladiatorial trade. Her friends and neighbors, even her husband, might be consumed with the games and its champions, but only from a spectator's distance. The gladiators were revered for their skills and entertainment value, but they were still lowly slaves and their *lanistas* did little more than pander flesh.

A jewel like Pelonia deserved a man similar to her own dear Antonius, a man of prominence and wisdom who knew how to appreciate a woman of Pelonia's rare qualities and strength of character.

At the first possible opportunity, she'd see that Antonius arranged a proper marriage for Pelonia. Her gentle cousin deserved nothing less than the best.

Certainly *not* an animal like Caros Viriathos.

Still overwhelmed and giddy with happiness from Tiberia's unexpected appearance, Pelonia sat beside her cousin on the long cushioned couch in the house's main sitting room. Warm sunlight filtered in through the open shutters, bathing the frescoed walls and potted plants with a golden hue.

"What did he say to you just now?" Tiberia asked, feigning an interest in the folds of her *stola*.

"Nothing dire, I assure you." In truth, Caros had reminded her of their bargain, that she'd promised not to leave.

"Are you certain?"

"Of course, I…ah, here's Gaius with some refreshments for you."

Gaius placed a glass goblet of spiced wine and a charger filled with oatcakes, honeyed dates and fresh grapes on a low table within Tiberia's reach.

"What's the meaning of this?" her cousin demanded. "Did you intend to insult *me,* or Pelonia when you thoughtlessly brought a single glass?"

"Tiberia," Pelonia groaned. "Don't—"

"I meant no insult, my lady. I'll fetch another."

"See that you do, and be quick about it."

Once the steward left, Pelonia shook her head at the younger girl. "I appreciate you taking my part, but I wish you hadn't berated him. His manner is a bit distant, I admit, but Gaius carries out his tasks with great care. He thinks of me as a slave. Naturally he didn't bring me any refreshment."

"That, my dear, is the crux of the problem." Tiberia reached for one of the smaller oatcakes and placed a fig on top. "You're not a slave. You're the victim of an outrageous misunderstanding. If that twice-cursed gladiator weren't such a stubborn brute, you would have been returned to the protective bosom of your family weeks ago."

Or found myself in a brothel. Pelonia flicked an imaginary piece of lint from her tunic, while Tiberia enjoyed her treat. "Don't speak ill of Caros. You don't know him. He's an honorable man."

"Yes, honorable enough to enslave you and *honorable* enough to refuse your freedom." Tiberia snorted. "I don't understand how you can defend him. Has he threatened you? Or worse, has he beguiled you?"

"Neither," she denied a little too vehemently. "But I've

come to know him over the past fortnight and I…I think I understand him."

"Not a difficult task, I'm sure." Tiberia brushed the crumbs from her fingers. "A mindless barbarian can't be too difficult to read."

"Tiberia, stop."

Her cousin shrugged, unbothered by the warning. "What's this about a fortnight? Is the dolt unable to count as well? He claimed you've been here almost three weeks, not two."

Pelonia prayed for patience and tamped down her aggravation. She was finally in the company of Tiberia again. The last thing she wanted was to cause an argument, though she'd forgotten how opinionated her cousin could be. "Caros is a successful man of business. His sums are fine. I don't recall much of my initial time here. Uncle Marcus beat me senseless. I was unconscious the first several days. After I awoke, it took another week to get me on my feet and recovered enough to be useful."

Tiberia's face puckered with remorse. Her fingers clenched the ample folds of her scarlet *stola*. All traces of flippancy disappeared. "Tell me of Marcus's treachery. Annia shared what she knew with me before I sent her home and came here."

Pelonia told her the full extent of Marcus's duplicity.

"I was a fool." Anger radiated off the younger woman. "I believed him when he claimed you'd been kidnapped and welcomed him into my family as a true relative. Knowing he betrayed you into slavery is heinous enough. Realizing he did so within hours of your dear father's murder has me tempted to hire an assassin. I'm certain the world would be a far better place without an insect of his ilk."

Despite the painful reminder of her father's death, Pelonia bit her lip to suppress a chuckle. "I admit the thought of revenge holds a great deal of appeal, especially if Marcus's punishment is slow and painful, but let's leave the matter in God's hands, shall we? I don't want you guilty of murder on my account."

Tiberia sighed and a slight smile played about her lips. "I know you don't mean it. If a fly were dying you'd look to make it more comfortable in its last moments. But it does my heart good to see you've retained some of the playfulness I love most about you."

Not wanting to spoil the reunion with more woeful talk, she squeezed Tiberia's hand. "I'm truly glad to see you, cousin. I don't think I'll ever be able to express how much."

"Of course you are. Even if you didn't love me so well, weeks enslaved in a gladiator *ludus* must have set your teeth on edge. I imagine you'd be pleased to see any unscarred and smiling face."

"You're probably right." A sidelong glance at her cousin's indignant expression made her laugh. "In truth, I've had little exposure to the school. I've helped in the kitchen, but my chores have been contained to the garden for the most part. Caros says it's too dangerous for me to be around the men."

"*Please* don't say any more. I can't abide the thought of you toiling like…like a common *slave!* By the gods, I think I'm going to be sick to my stomach."

More of Pelonia's laughter filled the sitting room. She made a show of examining her cousin's soft, unblemished hands. "Nary a mark in sight. You are a senator's wife for certain."

"I'm glad you're amused, but seeing you in this shapeless rag of a garment is a travesty. The moment we leave this place I'm taking you to the Forum. We're going to replenish your wardrobe with the finest silks available. You always had superior taste. I want your opinion on a new set of *stolas* for me as well. In fact, shopping will be the extent of your labor for at least a month."

"It sounds grand," she said, realizing she lied. Certain she'd be bored senseless without Caros to spar with, she did her best to deny the twinge of panic she felt at the thought of not seeing him every day. She forced a bright smile. "Tell me of your new life. Is marriage as blissful a state as you wished for?"

"It's even better." With a wistful sigh, Tiberia fell against the back of the padded couch. "Antonius is all I've ever dreamed of in a husband. He treats me with honor and more kindness in a day than Father ever gave me or Tibi in a decade."

"How is your sweet sister?" she asked, delighted by her cousin's blessed state. "Tibi must be, what, thirteen or fourteen by now?"

"Fifteen last June." Tiberia scowled. "Honestly, I don't know what Mother and Father are going to do with the brat. When she doesn't have her nose in a scroll, she's spouting philosophy and forever arguing with their houseguests—and mine. She refuses to marry and her reputation has preceded her until no suitable man will risk taking her on. Lately, she's threatening to wear a man's short tunic and cut her gorgeous flaxen hair. I told her, no matter what she does to fashion herself as a son, Father will pay her no more mind than he ever has. Thank the gods, Antonius is a wise and patient man or he'd forbid her presence to darken our door."

"I'll pray for her," she said, concerned for her younger cousin. Having been blessed with the best of fathers, she despised the thought of Tibi suffering from a lack of paternal affection.

"Yes, do. Perhaps your God will succeed with her where mine have failed."

"I'm praying for you, too, you know."

"You needn't bother. I'm pleased with Juno's blessings on my house thus far."

Pelonia nodded, mindful of her cousin's resistance to Christ. Tiberia would come to Christ when she was ready. If she'd learned one thing from her father and Uncle Marcus's relationship it was that a heart commitment to the Lord couldn't be forced.

"Enough about me, Pelonia. I want to hear about you. What is the cause for this queer sensation I get when I watch you and the *lanista* together? He doesn't behave toward you like I'd expect him to treat a slave, yet he claims he owns you and refuses to release you to my care. For your part, you defend him as though he's your lover."

Flushing with embarrassment, she prayed Tiberia remained ignorant of just how much she did love her supposed master. At a loss of how to explain her unusual relationship with Caros, she left the couch and feigned interest in a figurine of a centaur atop the side table. "As I said before, he's a good man. He's treated me well."

"Are you saying he hasn't seduced you?"

She shook her head. Eyeing one of the large ostrich fans in the corner, she wished for one small enough to cool her hot face. "No, he hasn't."

"Nor raped you?" Tiberia asked delicately.

"No! I told you he's an *honorable* man."

"The gods be praised again." Tiberia rose from the couch, her *stola*'s heavy folds of red silk falling to her feet. "Mother told me it was much easier to find a virgin a suitable husband and I believe she's right. With your beauty and the dowry I'm certain Antonius will bestow on you, I've no doubt we'd find a decent man regardless, but I want you to have a husband of the highest caliber."

Pelonia ran her finger down the smooth figurine's cool

marble spine. She wanted Caros or no one. "I don't believe I'll ever marry."

"Of course you will. Don't you want children? What of having your own home and social position? You wrote once not long ago telling me how you wished with all your heart to find a loving mate. What's happened to change your mind?"

I've given my heart to a man I can't have.

Gaius passed the sitting room's door. Intrigued by the steward's curiously quick pace, Pelonia stepped out into the atrium. Moments later a deep male voice rumbled across the entryway.

"Antonius!" Tiberia exclaimed, rushing into the atrium. "He must have received my message. I've every confidence he'll see the entire matter between you and the *lanista* resolved in no time at all."

Following her cousin into the entryway, she spied Tiberia's new husband, his white, purple-edged toga proclaiming his senatorial status. A hair's breadth shorter than her cousin, Antonius possessed a lean, muscular frame, a prominent blade of a nose and intense dark eyes. His regal posture and the haughty jut of his chin proclaimed his innate confidence.

Here's a man who can force Caros to free me.

The happiness brought by Tiberia's reemergence in her life began to dwindle. Why, after weeks of praying for a reunion with her family, did she suddenly wish they'd never found her?

"Come, Pelonia. Meet my magnificent husband."

Her legs heavy with guilt from her disloyal thoughts, she did her best to ward off the cloud of dejection descending upon her. As was custom, she inclined her head. "It is an honor to meet you, Senator."

"No, the honor is mine, my lady," he said without a hint of falseness. "My fair wife has been overwrought in her concern for you. To claim Tiberia's high regard is no easy task and I dare say she favors no one higher than you."

"Thank you, Senator, but I must respectfully disagree." She grinned at her cousin who stood with her arm entwined with her husband's. "You are the person she values most in the world. She's sung your praises since last spring in her letters to me and even more so since her arrival here this morning."

The newlyweds exchanged an intimate glance of mutual admiration. Antonius looked back to Pelonia. "From my wife's message earlier, I understand the *lanista* is under a false assumption about you. I've met Viriathos on more than one occasion. I don't think there's cause for alarm. He's a clearheaded and reasonable man. Don't fret any longer. I'll have you freed within the hour."

Chapter Nineteen

Caros prowled the confines of his study, cursing the Fates for delivering Tiberia to his door. Outside, the air grew ripe with the promise of an early fall storm, but the most powerful squall was no match for the tempest of fury and fear swirling inside him.

Like a chain squeezing him ever tighter, the possibility of losing Pelonia threatened to choke the heart from his chest. If the senator's wife had her way, all the vows he'd made to keep Pelonia within his reach would be shattered.

"Ahem."

His steward stood framed in the doorway. The old man's uncharacteristic nervousness knotted the cord of muscle across Caros's shoulders and up his neck. His teeth on edge, not that it took much to irritate him since the invasion of Pelonia's pugnacious cousin an hour ago, he prepared to hear the worst.

"Don't dither like an old woman, Gaius. What have you to say? Has Hades arrived yet?"

His eyes downcast, Gaius nodded. "The senator is waiting in the courtyard, Master. Shall I show him in?"

Caros uttered another fervent oath. A frequent guest of Adiona's lavish parties, the senator and Caros had met on previous occasions. The head of his powerful family since his father's death the previous year, Antonius Tacitus was one of the few men in Rome with enough influence to see Pelonia released whether Caros forbade it or not.

His mouth pressed in a firm line, he threw himself into the chair behind his desk. Once he'd recognized Tiberia in the garden, he'd expected the tall beauty's husband to make an appearance sooner or later.

By the gods! *Why* did Pelonia's cousin and the senator's new wife have to be one and same?

Gaius fidgeted with the rope belt around his waist. "He told Pelonia he'll have her freed within the hour."

Caros's brow arched at the man's gall. "How arrogant of him. And how like a politician to make a promise he can't keep."

"Are you certain he speaks false, Master?"

He wasn't certain at all. He surged back to his feet, his temper as black as the approaching storm clouds. Like all good politicians, the senator could be a crafty swine when it suited him, but in most cases he used his talents for the good of all Romans. His genuine concern for the masses had won him great popularity. He was respected as much by the common plebs as his own patrician class. His marriage less than a month ago had been a grand occasion with much of Rome's aristocracy in attendance.

Caros stopped by his desk and picked up a stylus, rolling the slender writing implement between his palms. The fact that Pelonia was a member of the senator's family and, by rights, under the powerful man's protection, shot a dart of cold panic through his veins.

God, please don't let me lose her.

The stylus snapped between his fingers just as a harsh blast of thunder shook the walls. Wind whipped at the curtains, yet Gaius continued fluffing the blue pillows on the couch as if spring had come to call.

"I trust you don't plan to scrub the floors before you fetch the guest?"

"No, Master." The steward lit a bowl of incense on the mantel.

The sweet aroma invaded Caros's nostrils and made his head ache. "Enough fussing," he snapped. "Fetch Antonius and take that noxious incense with you."

Moments later, Gaius returned with the senator. Caros wondered if the other man had worn his ceremonial toga as a silent means of intimidation. He forced a smile. "Senator, it's been overlong since I saw you last. Allow me to congratulate you on your recent marriage and welcome you to my home."

His eyes shining with excitement, the senator gave a vigorous nod of his head, seemingly oblivious to Caros's less-than-eager manner. "As always, it's an honor to meet with you, *lanista*. You know I've been an admirer of your accomplishments for years."

Caros murmured his thanks.

"Much to the chagrin of my new wife, your champions continue to draw me to the arena much too often. In fact, I ventured to the Colosseum just a few days ago because I thought your men were scheduled to fight. I was disappointed when I found I'd gone the wrong day. To add salt to the wound, the executions lasted longer than usual. I had other unavoidable business to attend to and in the end, missed the afternoon's entertainment altogether."

"I recall the day you speak of." Caros indicated a chair in front of his desk for Antonius to sit down. "I was there for the end of the executions. The mob seemed pleased enough by the wolves and their prey."

"True, but the punishment of a few deviants doesn't excite me. I prefer the combat of trained men. Otherwise, all one has is carnage and what pleasure can be found in common gore?"

"None, I suppose." Noting Antonius considered Christians deviants, Caros waited for the senator to make himself comfortable before claiming his own place behind the desk. "As a *lanista*, I'm gratified to know there are still a few spectators interested in more than raw butchery and blood."

"Of course. A true connoisseur understands a gladiator's greatness is in his technique and stamina. Since you are their teacher, it's little wonder your men are so magnificent to watch." The senator arranged his toga to flaunt its wide purple edge to best advantage. "However, you must know I'm here to discuss an even more important, though less enjoyable, subject than the games."

The rain came down in earnest. He nodded. "I assumed as much."

"My wife says she's spoken to you about her cousin."

His fingers dug into the arms of his chair. "Yes, she's quite adamant I free Pelonia and negate my claim on her."

"It seems only right. You must admit there's been an error concerning her presence here. I assured her you're a reasonable man—"

"You were mistaken…at least where that particular slave is concerned."

"I see." Antonius pursed his lips. "Surely you understand my wife and her cousin are closer than sisters. You must realize Pelonia can't stay here any longer."

"Pelonia is well cared for. There's no reason for her to leave."

"You jest," the senator scoffed in disbelief. "In the absence of her uncle, the girl is under my care, my protection. No member of *my* family will ever serve as a slave."

"The three thousand denarii I paid for her says otherwise. And as I reminded your wife, I broke no laws when I purchased Pelonia. What grounds, other than your pride, do you have for attempting to wrest her from me?"

The senator gawked at him with bug-eyed dismay. "Why so much? Are you mad?"

Caros shrugged. "Perhaps. People have said as much on more than one occasion."

"I believe it." The senator considered the information while he strummed his fingers on the desktop. His previous amicability was replaced with a flintlike gleam in his eyes. With a wave of his hand, he seemed to dismiss Caros's claims. "It matters not. This is a question of family honor and my wife's happiness. I'll pay whatever your price up to double your original cost, plus fifty denarii to reimburse what you've paid for the girl's food and upkeep."

"As much as it pains me to disappoint you or your lovely wife, there's no price worth the loss of Pelonia. She's mine. I intend to keep her."

"She's not a bone for us to fight over like a pack of hyenas," Antonius derided.

"No, she's the fairest prize imaginable."

Dawning flared in the senator's gaze. "You're in love with her, *lanista*."

He didn't deny it.

"You can't marry her," Antonius said, his tone matter-of-fact. "And it's impossible for her to continue on here as if she's a mistress. Her father was a citizen. A woman of Pelonia's stature must wed a worthy and like individual. That is, unless you've prostituted her or passed her among your men."

"What I've done with my slave is none of your concern."

Adopting a haughty air, the senator sat back and glowered. "What have you done to her?"

"I've treated her with respect."

Antonius looked doubtful. "Have you used her for your own pleasure?"

"What do you think?" Caros began to see a way out of the mire. Given time, Antonius was shrewd enough to deduce a girl with a questionable reputation was certain to become a family embarrassment. Pelonia was no matron to be excused of having other lovers. Any man Antonius deemed worthy enough to join his family's ranks would want an untouched bride—or at least one not sullied by a lowly gladiator.

"I suppose it was too much to hope you'd kept from spoiling her. Pelonia is beautiful. What man wouldn't try her if given half a chance?"

Caros gripped the cool wooden back of his chair. He glared in warning. "I assume a happily married one."

"Of course. That goes without saying."

"Of course," he said flatly. "I'll consider this discussion closed. Pelonia is mine and it's easier for all concerned if she stays here with me."

"I wish it were that simple." Antonius shook his head. "I'm afraid I can't abandon her here. Given you're not married, I doubt you'll understand, but I've no wish to fall into my wife's bad graces over an issue as trivial as this."

"It's not trivial to me."

"I'm sorry, but my own comfort comes first." The politician in Antonius rose to the fore. "The simple fact is this. Either you release Pelonia into my care or I'll take you to court. I have many friends there and many favors to call in if necessary. Who do you think will win the case?"

A nerve began to tick in Caros's jaw. The injustice of

the threat galled him. He clinched his fists, calculating the ease and swiftness of snapping the senator's neck. "What of Pelonia? A trial will turn into a spectacle. You seem overly concerned by appearances. Have you no care for her reputation?"

"That's rich coming from you." Antonius's snide laugh raised the hackles on the back of Caros's neck. "You have the power to save her name or ruin it, *lanista.* Thus far, no one important knows she's been a slave in a gladiatorial school. If the gods are kind, we might be able to salvage her yet. Force me to take you to court, and..." Antonius shrugged eloquently, then stood to leave. "It's up to you how we proceed from here. Either have Pelonia delivered to my home by tomorrow morning or meet me in court at the ninth hour midweek. If you care for her, as I believe you do, release her into the arms of her family. Allow her to recover from the tragic circumstances responsible for bringing her here and wed the kind of respectable man she deserves."

Antonius swept from the room, leaving Caros to contemplate the pounding rain and his less-than-acceptable options.

"You can't be serious!" Tiberia wailed in distraught exclamation. "Pelonia *must* leave with us tonight, husband. Who knows what that miserable cur will do to her if she's forced to stay another night in his clutches?"

"I'll be fine," Pelonia said, exchanging an uncomfortable glance with the all-too-perceptive senator. "Caros won't harm me."

"You don't know what he'll do for certain." Tiberia began to pace, her hands gesticulating to stress her point. "He's a seasoned competitor and a violent man. He hasn't faced the threat of losing you before. Up to this point he may have been long-suffering where you're concerned, but who's to say his patience won't snap? We really must see you safe before another tragedy befalls you."

"I think it's best if I leave in the morning," Pelonia insisted, determined to speak with Caros and promise to return to visit him. "The men have come to an agreement. Do you want your husband to break his word?"

"Oh, Antonius," Tiberia said, her face pinched and mournful. A man's word was his bond. "Why didn't you bargain for her release today instead of tomorrow?"

"I thought it best." The senator's voice conveyed his absolute certainty. "If I believed for one moment your cousin faced potential harm, she'd be leaving with us now."

"I don't like it." Tiberia pouted. "How can anyone expect me to leave her here when I've just found her again."

Antonius clasped her upper arms in a soothing manner. "The simple fact remains the *lanista* owns your cousin. You must brace yourself for the worst. If he chooses to meet me in court, Pelonia may not come home for several days."

"He's not that stupid, surely?" Tiberia asked Pelonia.

"He's not stupid at all." She tried not to let Tiberia's constant stream of snide remarks about Caros bother her. Tiberia's vehemence stemmed from loyalty. Her cousin was acting out of love in wanting to see her swift release. The younger girl had no way of knowing her main concern at the moment was not for herself but for Caros and how shaken he must feel.

Guilt snapped at Pelonia for the endless anxiety she'd caused her cousin. By rights, loyalty belonged to her family, not the master who intended to keep her enslaved. She should be as eager to go with them as they were to take her home. Yet, the silken bonds of love kept her more firmly tied to Caros than the strongest iron shackle. Yes, she craved freedom, but the cost of leaving Caros suddenly seemed a precipitous price to pay.

"I think it's time we left," Antonius announced.

"We can't. The rain has yet to die down," Tiberia said grumpily.

"A little rain won't harm us." His firm tone brooked no disagreement. "Tell Pelonia goodbye, my dear. You'll see her tomorrow one way or the other."

With a quick bow to Pelonia, he started for the door, leaving his wife to give her a hasty embrace and follow in his wake.

Once they left the house, Pelonia sank into the chair behind her and dropped her face in her hands. *Dear Heavenly Father, thank You for bringing my family to me, but what am I to do about Caros?*

Lost in his thoughts, Caros leaned against the study's doorway, facing the inner courtyard. The pouring rain had mellowed to mist and drizzle. Light from the lanterns in the interior rooms glimmered on the wet pavers. The twilight air was cool and refreshed, but Pelonia's imminent departure meant darkness was descending on him in more ways than one.

Across the courtyard, he saw Pelonia's tiny form exit the sitting room, her light colored tunic glowing like a beacon in the day's ebbing light. With her head bowed, she didn't see him, giving him a chance to observe her unhindered. The air of melancholy she wore disturbed him, churning up regrets he didn't want to address.

She leaned against one of the pillars and stretched out her hand to catch the rain dripping from the roof tiles. Her beauty held him in thrall. The shine of her hair, her creamy skin, made him long to touch her, even as the loneliness surrounding her lanced him with guilt.

Tiberia's appearance must have caused her to miss her family, freedom and the life of privilege she'd known with greater fervency than usual. What madness had possessed him to believe he'd ever be enough to replace what she'd lost?

He left the doorway, the back of his hand brushing the cool raindrops off a potted palm as he cut his way through the courtyard. Her family's invasion today had shaken him out of his selfish dream world. The money he'd paid for Pelonia gave him the legal right to keep her and he'd convinced himself she would be better off with him because he loved her. But after today's revelations he understood that if she chose him, he had nothing to offer but a demotion in social status and her family's endless disappointment.

He'd made the right decision in the hours since Antonius left. It hadn't been easy to come to terms with losing her, but in the end he wanted Pelonia's happiness above his own.

He heard her call his name. A smile played about her lips. "Caros, there you are. I'd like to speak with you."

"I want to talk with you as well. It's your last night here, after all."

If he hadn't been watching her so intently, he would have missed the way her bottom lip quivered before she steadied it between her teeth, or how she dropped her gaze to hide all traces of her true feelings. Either reaction may have been caused by happiness or sorrow; he couldn't divine which. He had more reason to believe she was elated to leave, but the hope that she possessed even a shred of lasting emotion for him, and wanted to stay, was hard to kill.

The mystery of how best to proceed knotted his tense muscles to the breaking point. He strangled the impulse to shake her until she admitted her thoughts on the matter and probed for answers using a different tack. "I imagine your joy is boundless at regaining your freedom. I made a mistake not to insist Antonius take you away tonight and save us both the hassle of packing you off in the morning."

"Yes, why didn't you? Tiberia was most upset to leave me here." Her eyes sparkled with a glassy sheen in the lantern's light. "I suppose you didn't think of it because it's not *your* back that endures a hard pallet every night."

"I offered to share my comfortable bed, but you declined."

"And rightly so given this sudden wish of yours to be rid of me."

The last thing he wanted was to be free of her. From the moment he'd seen her in the slaver's wagon, she owned him. For the first time since his family's murder, he'd dared to love another. Had he been wiser, he would have dismissed the ardent feelings she stoked in him. Relinquishing her hurt the same as severing his sword arm.

"I took the hint this afternoon when I offered my heart and you denied me," he said, willing his pain not to betray him. "You'll be better off with your family."

She glanced away, but didn't try to convince him otherwise. "Strange how my refusal didn't matter to you until the senator called me kin."

Suspicion rang in her voice. He raked his fingers through his hair. "I admit I chose to ignore the claims you made about your father and the ties you held to an important family because it suited me. I'd have been obliged to return you to your cousin and, at the time, I didn't want to let you go."

Rain dripped on the mosaic tiles as Pelonia considered him. "Because, *at the time,* you were determined to prove your mastery over me."

"You misunderstood—"

"No, I think I understand perfectly. Victory is what you care for most in the world. Admit it, you didn't want to give me up because you were determined to win the pact between us. Even the offer of your heart today was just a ploy to overcome the last dregs of my resistance."

The coldness in her tone was so unlike her, he flinched.

"But you want to lose the senator's goodwill or a court case even less than the game between us," she said bitterly.

He fought the instinct to pull her against him and show her how much he wanted her above all else. "If you believe so…"

Her eyes brimmed with misery and doubt. "I don't know what to believe, Caros. Either you lied to me when you said you cared for me or you're deceiving me now. I came out here with promises of my own…if you cared for me half as much I care for you—"

She gasped as his strong arms banded about her, dragging her against the marble column of his body. His lips silenced her with a kiss that plucked every thought of resistance from her mind. Her eyes drifted closed as his clean, spicy scent filled her senses. Her knees grew weak. Dizzy and shaking from emotion, she locked her arms around his waist to keep from falling.

A tremor ran through the corded muscles of his back. Through the thin linen of his tunic she felt the bumps and indentations of the scars from countless whippings. Her heart bled for the pain he'd endured. She held him tighter, the need to spend the rest of her life showering him with love and tenderness expanding inside her until the ache in her chest robbed her of breath.

The feeling was so intense, so poignant a sob built in her throat and a tear slid down her cheek.

How can I live without him?

He softened the kiss, drawing her even closer. "Look at me," he rasped, his warm breath caressing her ear. "Look me in the eye."

Her lashes fluttered open. His blue gaze burned with a light that singed her to the marrow, branding her his forever whether he chose her or not.

"Don't ever think I don't care for you." He cupped her face in his large palms and brushed her tears away with the pad of his thumb. "You're *all* I care about. I'd forgotten how to love… No, I'd forgotten love existed until I saw you lying there in the slaver's wagon. I wanted to keep you even if it meant forcing you to accept me because life without you was dark and empty. Believe me, I've thanked your God more than once for bringing you here, though now the time has come to let you go."

"You *do* believe in Him."

He shook his head. "It's too late for me, but it's not too late for you to enjoy the kind of life you were born to with the kind of man you deserve."

"*You're* the kind of man I deserve!" Her voice cracked. "If you'd stop being stubborn—"

"No. Today I accepted you have to go. I've nothing to offer you except your family's eternal disappointment and a foreigner's name. If you stayed with me you'd lose your rightful place among the exalted families you'll mingle freely with when you return to your cousin."

"I don't care."

"You will. If not today, then when our children are born and must bear the stigma of having a father who was once a slave. What will you tell them when they ask why people look down on them?"

"The same thing I'll tell them when they ask why we don't visit the pagan temples or participate in the pagan feast days or accept the emperor as a god. I'll teach them we're a people set apart by our Heavenly Father who don't need society's mark of approval."

He caressed a strand of her hair between his fingers. His eyes were soft and tender. "I've said it before and I'll say it again. You are truly a unique woman, Pelonia. I've never met your like. When you leave here tonight and return to your cousin, remember you always have a friend in me. If you or your loved ones need a sword to fight for you, I'm here."

"Tonight?" The cold evening air seeped into her bones. He spoke with finality, as though he hadn't heard her...or refused to.

He nodded and called for a litter. "This is goodbye, *mea carissima*. There's no reason to wait until morning."

Chapter Twenty

"Don't look," Tiberia said in a hissed whisper. "Adiona Leonia is standing over there by the statue of Mercury."

Pelonia froze in a moment of instant dread, her gaze darting around the Forum's chaotic central market in search of Caros's obnoxious friend.

Her sudden tension palpable, Tiberia latched on to Pelonia's arm. "She's that beautiful creature in the golden tunic. She's rich beyond imagination. My husband jokes that even the gods owe her coin." Her smooth forehead pleated with frustration. "I've given it my all to glean an invitation to one of her parties. So far she's rebuffed and ignored me, but I'm determined not to give up."

"Why is an invitation from her so important?" she asked, her eyes settling on the elegant Adiona and the bright purple *palla* draped around her slender shoulders.

"She's one of the city's leading matrons. Antonius assures me I'll know I've been accepted into the highest social circles once I've been received by her."

"I don't know why you bother. You're lovely in your own right. You have a wonderful husband and home—"

"You don't understand," Tiberia said, clearly distressed. "My husband is a powerful and important man. It's my duty to add whatever honor I can to his house. If I don't, Antonius might think he's made the wrong choice of bride."

"Never." She squeezed Tiberia's hand. "Antonius loves you. As far as the widow Leonia is concerned, *you're* a senator's wife. It seems she'd be the one to vie for your attention."

"Senators are voted in and out of their position, but Adiona—"

"Lingers like an unshakeable cough?"

Tiberia's lips twitched with laughter. "You're too kind. Adiona's more like a plague. Unfortunately, if I don't earn her approval I'll be a social pariah." She lost a shade of color. "*Please* tell me she's not coming this way. I'm not prepared to meet with her."

Pelonia angled in front of her cousin to give the girl time to collect her wits. Her massive bodyguard trailing close behind, Adiona sailed through the crowd seemingly unaware of all the slacked-jawed males and disapproving women she left in her wake. Her kohl-rimmed eyes took on a perceptive gleam of recognition the closer she came.

"What a surprise, Publia, is it not?" The widow's bejeweled bracelets jingled as she came to a standstill.

She felt Tiberia stiffen behind her. "My name is Pelonia."

"Oh, yes, forgive me, will you? I'm rather shocked. It's not every day one returns from a sojourn in the country to find a peacock has taken the place of a mouse."

Refusing to give the widow the satisfaction of seeing her upset, she soothed her palms down the pale blue silk of her own tunic, deriving a measure of comfort from the fact she no longer wore slave's garb. With her hair fashionably arranged and pinned with sapphires, and her skin back to its usual health from a month of daily treatments at the baths, she reminded herself she was no longer the trampled weed she'd been the last time she'd suffered Adiona's presence.

"How is Caros?" the widow asked. "I went by to see him when I returned to Rome yesterday. Gaius told me he ventured to Neapolis a week ago and has yet to return."

"I don't know. I haven't seen him in a month," she admitted once she absorbed the shaft of pain the sound of his name caused her. "I hope and pray he's well."

Adiona's eyes flared with surprise. "You haven't seen him? Judging by your transformation, I assumed he'd made you his mistress."

Pelonia's cheeks burned. Tiberia shrieked at the insinuation, drawing attention to her presence as she stepped to the fore. "My lady, you may not remember me. My name is Tiberia—"

"Yes, I know who you are." Adiona settled a tolerant smile on the younger girl. "We met shortly before your wedding to Senator Tacitus, correct?"

"Yes, my lady. It's an honor to meet you again." She slanted a terse glance rife with questions at Pelonia before returning her smile to the widow. "I really must assure you my cousin was *never* that man's mistress."

"Your cousin?" Her exotic eyes danced with mischief. "How intriguing. My steward mentioned you'd had a relative return from the dead."

"Yes, we're grateful the gods brought her back to us."

"The gods?" Adiona's husky laughter mingled with the din of the milling crowd. "When exactly did Caros achieve divine status?"

"The *lanista* is hardly divine, my lady, but after the way he treated Pelonia, the gods below may want to enlist his help in learning a trick or two."

"Really?" Adiona's manner cooled. "I've never known Caros to mistreat a woman."

"He treated me well," Pelonia said, eager to nip any gossip before it bloomed.

Adiona shifted her gaze to Pelonia as though she'd forgotten her presence altogether. "Marvelous, I'm glad to learn you won't spread lies about him."

"Never, I—"

"We missed you at our wedding." Tiberia quickly changed the subject, drawing the widow's attention back to her.

"I sent my regrets when family matters kept me from attending," Adiona said. "I was loath to miss such a special occasion."

"Thank you." Tiberia managed to look serene. "I did receive your kind regards. Both my husband and I were saddened you couldn't join us."

"I hope you'll let me make it up to you. I'd love to give a celebration in your honor next Tuesday night if you and the good senator are free."

Tiberia beamed, her discomfort obviously forgotten in the face of being handed her dearest wish. "I'll have to speak with my husband, but I'm fairly certain we have no previous engagements."

"Excellent." The widow nodded to both of them as she took her leave. "I'll look forward to seeing all of you then."

"No. Try this," Caros instructed Quintus. "Lunge forward with your right foot. Use the force of your weight to bring the *gladius* through in an even arc, slicing your opponent's face or middle. If you have two opponents and one is behind you, follow through with the swing, careful to keep control of your sword arm. Otherwise get out of the way as though your life depends upon it. Stand around twiddling your thumbs and you'll end up with a blade in your throat."

"Perish the thought!" a female voice burst from the sidelines.

Caros glared at Adiona. "When did you arrive?" As stunning as always, his friend couldn't seem to take her eyes off Quintus. Quintus, on the other hand, didn't look pleased to be standing there in nothing more than his sweaty tunic.

Intrigued by Adiona's continued interest in his slave, he realized the increase in Quintus's breathing wasn't entirely due to the morning's exercise.

Caros shook his head. The trainee was well on his way to becoming another of Adiona's love-besotted fools. "What are you doing out here tempting my men, woman? Do you mean to cause a riot?"

Her husky laughter reached across the golden sand. She cocked her head at a flippant angle; the bejeweled hoops adorning her ears glinted in the sun. Her eyes slid back to Quintus and captured the Christian's gaze. "There's only one man I'd like to tempt into anything."

Quintus turned his back on her, the veins in his sword arm popping from his tense grasp on the *gladius*. A crimson tide of embarrassment rose up Adiona's cheeks. Seeing the hurt in her eyes, Caros groaned under his breath. Her seductive behavior made it easy to forget she wasn't nearly as jaded or wanton as she pretended. A victim of Cupid's arrow himself, he pitied her.

Leaving Quintus with instructions to continue the morning's practice, he dried himself off with a nearby towel and made his way to Adiona. "Let's go indoors. I'll have refreshments prepared for you."

"There's no need," she said as they walked through the gate and into the shade of the peach orchard. "Gaius brought my favorite cinnamon buns and sweet wine before I ventured to the field to watch you."

"Ah, now I understand the intoxication in your eyes when you gazed at Quintus."

Scarlet crept up her neck. "I don't know what you're talking about."

"No? I half feared you were going to pounce on him."

"Nonsense. If I happened to pay attention to him overlong it's because the man's ineptness with a sword is mesmerizing."

"He's much improved."

"Possibly, but I worry he's going to impale himself."

He laughed for the first time since Pelonia's departure. "I see. So it was your *concern* that made you proposition him?"

He held the door for her as they entered the domus. "You're hateful," she said, slapping him on the arm. "I did no such thing. To think I came here as soon I heard you'd returned from Neapolis because I feared you were in the doldrums. Obviously your mouse was right to leave you."

His humor fled. "You know nothing of it."

"Oh, but I do. I saw her in the market three days ago. She looked splendid. I doubt she misses you at all. Truth to tell, I hardly recognized her."

Envy snaked through him. He'd tried, by the gods, he'd tried to cast her from his mind, but Pelonia was embedded in his heart like a thorn he couldn't pluck free. He'd left Rome hoping a change of scenery would help distract him from constant thoughts of her. It did no good. Each night he dreamed of her only to wake restless, unfilled…his heart broken by the weight of his loneliness. "She's a diamond. Exquisite and rare."

"How sweet, a poet gladiator. It's unfortunate you let such a prize slip through your fingers."

His lip curled at her sarcasm. "It wasn't by choice, you hag."

Her laughter grated on his nerves as she preceded him into the inner courtyard. Seating herself on the marble bench beside the largest fountain, she fluffed the generous folds of her vibrant blue *stola.* "The senator must have arranged her departure then. No one else but the emperor has enough sway to force your hand. With Domitian new to power he has more important things to attend to, I'm sure."

She surveyed him from beneath her lashes. "I understand there's a plot to wed her off to Minucius Brutus. Such a pity, considering your high regard for the girl. Minucius is upstanding enough, but as dull witted as the Brutus name implies."

Jealousy chilled his blood. "Where did you hear this?"

"My steward. I quizzed him about the situation after I saw your little mouse at the Forum. You know how he keeps me informed of the city's most interesting tidbits. It seems someone began a rumor that Pelonia was a prostitute in a gladiator *ludus.*"

He slammed his fist into his opposite palm. "Who started the lie?"

"I know not. Even if I did I doubt I'd tell you. From the flare of rage in your eyes, I'd be signing a death warrant. I can do without the blood on my hands. It's such a chore to wash off."

"Does Antonius know the deceiver?"

"I don't believe so." She brushed a wisp of dark hair behind her ear. "I suppose anyone who attended the party we hosted might be the culprit. At any rate, it seems there are too few agreeable men willing to wed your slave because of the report. From what I understand the senator had to double the massive dowry he'd originally settled on her before even Minucius expressed an interest yesterday. He's in desperate straits, you know. If you recall, the Brutus family suffered a major financial loss two years ago when their holdings in Pompeii were buried in the ashes."

He felt like Vesuvius on the brink of eruption. The irony of the situation hit him hard. He hadn't returned Pelonia to her family to see her married off to some weakling who wanted her solely for coin. Where was the justice when he'd gladly give half his fortune to see her once more, and the other half just to hear her sweet voice again?

"I'm going after her."

Adiona looked doubtful. "What good could you possibly do? You'll never make it past the senator's front door. You must accept you've lost her."

He sat heavily on the bench beside her, too tormented to care if she saw him in such a low state. "I released Pelonia to Antonius because he promised to find her a husband worthy of her."

"Why didn't you wed her yourself?"

"Don't vex me any more than I am, Adiona. Why do you think I didn't marry her when she's what I want most in the world?"

"I honestly don't know."

Her genuine bewilderment made him angrier. "I'm not good enough for her. Don't you see? I spent most of my life a slave, good for nothing but killing and violence. I have riches, yes, and invitations to the grandest homes in the empire, but only because I'm a novelty, an oddity for my hosts to show off before their friends like some two-headed bull."

She entwined her arm with his and placed her head on his shoulder in sympathy. The water splashed in the fountain beside them as they sat together for long moments without saying a word.

Somewhere in the house a door closed and the smoky aroma of the cook fires drifted in the air. Adiona sighed. "I don't believe in love, but *if* I did and a man loved me as you love Pelonia, I'd give up all that I have and consider myself blessed by the gods to have found him."

A bitter laugh burned in his throat. *Her God is the other reason she won't have me.* "I thought you hate men."

"Oh, I do. In my opinion, you're the last good one and clearly your heart is taken."

"Quintus is a good man, too."

"He might as well be a eunuch for all the notice he gives me."

"I think he notices you too well."

"You do?" She sat back, her expression guarded. "Why do you think so?"

"Because he's a healthy man and you are a fantastically beautiful woman."

Her nose crinkled in disagreement. "You saw him turn away from me."

He debated whether or not to tell the true reason for Quintus's rejection. Deeming her trustworthy, he shook off her hold and stood. "I imagine he turned from you because he's a follower of Jesus the Nazarene. To Quintus, I imagine, you're temptation in flesh."

"A *Christian?*" She began to laugh uncontrollably. "Leave it to me to fantasize about a deviant!"

He frowned. "From what he's told me, there's nothing strange or perverse in their beliefs."

"They eat human flesh and blood! If that's not unnatural, what is?"

"I asked Quintus why." He leaned against a pillar and crossed his arms over his chest. "He explained they aren't cannibals like so many believe. They have a custom where they take bread and wine as a remembrance of their God's death for them."

"*You've* been asking him about his beliefs?"

He nodded.

"Why? You know their sect is illegal." Understanding

dawned in her large amber eyes. "It's Pelonia. She's one of them."

"Yes," he admitted slowly. "It's the main reason she won't have me."

"Stupid woman. She cast aside the man who loves her and for what? Minucius? I assure you he has no Christian bent." She went to Caros and embraced him. "You know I love you as my dearest friend?"

He hugged her back. "Of course. And I care for you as a friend."

"Then I must beg a favor."

He released her and stepped away. "Why is it I've faced hordes of gladiators determined to kill me with less trepidation than I feel when you turn all winsome and womanly?"

"Will you favor me or not?"

"When have I ever refused to help you?"

"Good." She smirked. "I'm having a fete Tuesday night and I'm in need of a two-headed bull to display."

Chapter Twenty-One

The soft notes of a panpipe drifted in from the courtyard as Pelonia reclined on one of the low couches surrounding a table laden with the evening meal. Tiberia sat back on her own couch to Pelonia's left, the senator across from them. A variety of boiled vegetables, roasted lamb and salted fish made up the bulk of the dishes.

Tiberia selected a piece of spiced lamb. "Antonius, my love, don't forget we're to be celebrated by Adiona Leonia tomorrow evening. I'm wearing a blue tunic and silver *palla,* so I've had matching garb prepared for you."

"Whatever you wish, my dear, as long as the garment's not fashioned of wool. This heat is enough to blind me." Antonius snapped his fingers and motioned for slaves to wave huge plumed fans to cool the lantern-lit room.

"The warmth reminds me of late summer," Pelonia remarked, disliking the use of slaves, but unable to complain when she was little more than a guest in the palace.

"Indeed, but October was comfortable enough. Perhaps it will cool back down and become more seasonable in a few days' time." He raised his glass chalice and drank a long draught of sweet wine. Not for the first time that evening, his pensive gaze settled on Pelonia. She picked at a morsel of lemon-seasoned fish, leery of his hesitant manner. Did he have some misfortune to share?

He heaved a heavy sigh. "I've pondered how best to tell you I have news concerning your uncle."

She dropped the spoon she held. Fear winded her as she recalled the last time she'd seen her uncle and his hatred toward her.

"Marcus returned to Rome earlier today and sought me out this afternoon at the Forum."

Pelonia's heart kicked back to life with a jolt.

Tiberia sat up, her knees hitting the table in her haste. "I hope you carted him off to the amphitheater! I'm certain there's a least one hungry lion willing to tolerate rancid meat."

"What did he want?" Pelonia reached for her water and tried to drown the acid rising in her throat.

"The cur was in a fine mood, actually. He has no idea you've returned to us."

"What are you going to do with him?" Tiberia asked. "His villainy can't go unpunished after the harm he caused our family."

"Don't worry, he'll regret his treachery." A sly smile curved the senator's lips and for the first time he appeared to Pelonia as a true politician. "Before he left Rome several weeks ago, he and I struck a bargain," Antonius said. "He borrowed five thousand denarii from me and offered the property in Iguvium as collateral."

"You mean my father's property?" Pelonia asked in disbelief. At the senator's nod, a wave of anger doused her fear with fury. She pushed the dinner plate away as she swung her legs over the edge of the couch and surged to her feet.

"How dare he! My father toiled his entire life to make a home for us. And Marcus thinks to squander it? For what purpose?"

"He plans to open a wine shop and make himself a notable man of Rome." Antonius laughed. "It's ludicrous. Can you imagine? As if there aren't enough wine merchants in this city already."

Pelonia sensed she was missing an important detail, but her indignation blinded her. "Many times Father tried to give my uncle business responsibilities, but Marcus proved to be unsuccessful every time."

Tiberia sent her husband a queer look. "If the venture was bound to fail, why did you lend him the money?"

Antonius motioned for his wife to sit back down. "Don't fret, my love. You can trust that all is well. Marcus expected me to introduce him to key buyers and help insinuate him into our social circle. The *idiota* thought to use my reputation and my coin to set him up in grand style, yet he didn't think to offer me a partnership or a share of the profits. He must have taken me for a fool, but he'll soon learn who the imprudent one among us is. Even without the harm he caused Pelonia, I'd planned to teach him a lesson he won't soon forget."

Pelonia sank back onto the low couch. "What do you intend to do? I admit I'm having difficulty not hating him for what he did to me, but you aren't going to have him maimed or…or worse, are you?"

"He deserves worse," Tiberia said with an indelicate snort.

"No." Pelonia weighed her reaction with care, mindful of how she thought the Lord expected her to behave.

"What do you mean, cousin?" Antonius took another drink of wine. "I'd think you'd want Marcus dead after he sold you into slavery."

"I don't want him dead."

"You intrigue me, truly you do. Every other person I know would be demanding Marcus's head on a stake. But not you. Why? What makes you different?"

"I'm not so different. If I were to live by my impulses and feelings alone I'd wish for his death—no, I think I'd help you plan it. But I seek to walk a different path, one not always easy to follow."

"The way of your Christian God?" he asked.

"Yes. I want to serve Him and cultivate forgiveness in my heart."

"Have you forgiven Marcus, then?" Skepticism darkened his hawklike eyes.

"I'm trying." With her temper still blazing, she understood his doubt. "I've asked the Lord to help me, but I've yet to fully succeed."

The music shifted to a softer tempo, carrying on the warm breeze that fluttered the wispy drapes flanking the open doorway to the courtyard.

"Forgiveness is a nice sentiment," Antonius said. "But have a care who you admit your religion to. Being Tiberia's kin and mine by marriage you're safe here, but if you were anyone else I'd be forced to report you to the authorities."

The warning duly noted, she lowered her gaze and nodded.

"The truth is, whether you excuse Marcus or not is of little consequence to me," Antonius mused aloud. "The man is headed down a painful and well-earned road." He chose a round of flat bread from a stack within his reach and tore it in two. "I'm certain you and my dear wife will both enjoy the outcome once my plans have come to fruition."

With the help of a slave, Pelonia alighted from the litter once Tiberia and the senator stood on solid ground. As her gaze wandered up…and up…and up the wide stretch of steps leading to the palace of Adiona Leonia, she was convinced the edifice was the most lavish structure she'd ever seen other than a few of Rome's grandest public buildings.

Lit by a succession of tall bowl lanterns blazing with fire on every third step, Adiona's Palatine home boasted three stories graced with marble Corinthian columns and artfully arranged statuary. Bougainvillea, deep orange in color from the fire's glow, spilled from the series of arches along the second floor.

In the lush front garden interspersed with statues of Roman deities, jugglers entertained some of the early arrivals, while wandering musicians filled the night with festive songs.

"Isn't this wonderful?" Tiberia exclaimed with pleasure as she tugged on her husband's arm. "Can you believe all of these preparations are for us?"

"I'd expect nothing less from widow Leonia. There's no better hostess in all of Rome." A swirl of laughter, music and merriment surrounded them. "I'm proud of you, my dear. Not everyone is capable of earning the widow's favor, but this grand showing means she must have been impressed by you."

Pelonia drew her sheer white *palla* closer around her shoulders. Numerous well-wishers arrayed in colorful fabrics and sparkling jewels stopped to give their regards to Antonius and Tiberia. Pelonia followed the evening's honored couple, careful not to draw attention to herself. It had been months since she'd attended any kind of social function as a guest. Before she'd come to Rome, she'd always loved a merry occasion, but here she felt strangely out of her depth.

Perhaps she shouldn't have come. Though she tried to accept God's will and learn the lessons she thought He wanted to teach her, the tragedies of recent months had stolen her usual good cheer. She was lonely without her father to talk to and the constant, intolerable agony of missing Caros seemed to increase by the hour.

"Why are you frowning?" Tiberia asked. "This is the grandest of occasions. Please smile, if only for me."

Tiberia was right. The evening was meant to be a triumph for the newlyweds and Pelonia refused to dampen the festivities with any more of her dreary spirits. Determined to be an asset to her cousins, she plastered on a pleasant expression, nodded politely when necessary and made appropriate comments when Tiberia or Antonius introduced her to various acquaintances on their slow progress up the steps.

By the time they reached the final landing, Pelonia was a touch more confident she could put the *lanista* out of her mind for once and maintain her cordial façade—at least until she saw the large fountain twinkling with hundreds of tiny floating oil lamps. Without warning, the arrangement reminded her of the stars she'd gazed at with Caros during the party Adiona hosted at his home. The thought, so unexpected and fierce, overwhelmed her with memories of his arms wrapped around her and the intensity of his kiss.

"How beautiful!" Tiberia exclaimed beside her. "Have you ever seen such a glorious sight?"

Pelonia's answer lodged in her throat. She was floundering in a deep well of pain that threatened to drown her. A hollow ache was expanding inside her until it threatened to swallow her whole. With the exception of her father, she'd never missed anyone as much as she missed Caros. But where her faith promised she'd see her father again one day in heaven, the loss of Caros burned like true death, stealing away all the joy she'd ever know and stretching her life out before her like a lonely, colorless road.

"You're thinking about *him,* aren't you?" Tiberia asked. "You must put troubling thoughts behind you, dearest.

You won't have to face him again. The widow Leonia may be friends with that horrid *lanista,* but she knew you were attending with us tonight. I'm certain she didn't invite him."

"Caros Viriathos has been absent from this sort of gathering for more than a year," Antonius added, craning his neck as though looking for someone.

"Except for the party Adiona hosted at his home not too long ago," Tiberia said. They crossed the threshold of the palace. "I confess, at the time, I was jealous. Everyone heard of the fete and I can't think of anyone who wasn't overcome with envy if they weren't invited... By the gods, isn't this stunning?"

Pelonia gulped. The grandeur on display was indeed magnificent. From the flower petals strewn across the mosaic-tiled floor to the sweet scent of incense, consideration had been paid to every detail. But it wasn't the beauty of the large circular entryway with its rare yellow marble or the valuable bronze statues that drew her attention. It was Caros standing in profile just beyond the arched doorway leading to the palace's inner chambers.

She began to tremble. To her starved gaze, he was even more handsome than she recalled. The tallest man in the room, his black, wavy hair curled around his ears and nape. His lean jaw clean-shaven, the embroidered tunic he wore and the gold bands circling his wrists highlighted the deep bronze of his skin. Captured by the undeniable pull of his appeal, she took a step forward.

"Don't go." Tiberia latched on to her arm to stay her. "I'm surprised Adiona invited him tonight. Truly, I believed she'd exhibit better taste. Still, you must stay here. You'll look like a prideless *idiota* if you run to him when he's speaking with that gorgeous dancer over there."

He was talking to someone? Through the shifting bodies of the milling crowd, she strained to see the "gorgeous dancer."

"I've tried to shield you from the ugliness," her cousin continued in an embarrassed whisper, "but the gossip has been rife about you since someone let it be known he enslaved you for weeks at the school. Fortunately, Antonius has found a fine man who's willing to overlook your…past."

Registering the dancer's elaborate wig, heavy cosmetics and transparent costume, Pelonia paid no attention to Tiberia. The sensual delights the beauty's gaze offered Caros knotted her stomach with jealousy. That he seemed captivated by the woman and didn't rebuff the obvious invitation shattered Pelonia and broke her heart.

"Perfect. Our honored guests have arrived." Adiona Leonia approached, her breezy manner one of an accomplished hostess. The smile she wore seemed genuine. She welcomed the three of them with a kiss on each cheek, then clapped her hands to draw the attention of her other guests.

The music and conversation died down. Pelonia forced herself to look interested in her hostess's introductions, though her entire being danced with the awareness of Caros such a short distance away.

When she was finally able to glance at him again, he acknowledged her presence with a slight nod before he turned away. His lack of regard stung the same as a slap in the face.

Pierced through the heart, she lifted her chin in a valiant effort to maintain her dignity. The urge to flee into the night was strong. Inside, she felt herself crumbling. Tears scratched the back of her eyes and her chest locked up, making it difficult to breathe.

Thankfully, the introductions were over and her cousins' attention had been claimed elsewhere. They were too caught up in chatting with other guests to notice her plight. Mur-

muring her excuses, she sought out a quiet corner of the huge palace to calm her nerves in private.

Blinded by the need for a hasty retreat, she ran into a solid male chest. "Excuse me, I—"

"What are *you* doing here?"

Speechless, Pelonia stared into the livid face of her uncle.

"Marcus," Adiona exclaimed, covering the few paces it took to join them. "So good of you to come when you've only returned to Rome yesterday. The senator will be delighted you're here. He feared you might not make it. I see you've already found your niece."

Chapter Twenty-Two

The sight of Pelonia jolted Caros with a mix of pleasure and pain so intense it almost felled him. After five weeks and two days of missing her, he had to turn away or fall at her feet.

The sound of blood rushing in his ears drowned out the music and flirtatious banter of the dancer who'd approached him. Heart slamming against his ribs, every instinct urged him to toss Pelonia over his shoulder and carry her back to his home where he could keep her all to himself. Half mad with longing, he'd been in torment living without her.

His willpower at an end, the craving to see her forced him to seek her out. In an instant, he located her in the center of the entryway. Dressed in slave's garb, he'd found her beautiful, but cloaked in silks and finery she was a feast for the eyes, an unspoiled oasis to a man dying of thirst.

A pained frown marred her brow. She spoke to her cousin, then pivoted toward the exit. He followed her, his feet carrying him across the tiled floor as though they possessed a will of their own.

He was too far away to stop Pelonia from colliding into the burly newcomer a few steps ahead of her. The man's expression brimmed with recognition. His eyes flared with instant hate, his mouth twisted in a snarl.

Caros abandoned any pretense at politeness and began to shove his way through the thick crowd. From the corner of his eye, he saw Adiona abandon the clutch of guests she was speaking to and rush to Pelonia's side.

"I see you've found your niece," Adiona said at the same time Caros joined them.

Niece? "Marcus?" Caros's right hand balled into a fist.

"Yes, I'm Marcus Valerius. Who wishes to know?"

"If you're the man who abused Pelonia and sold her into slavery—" Caros swept Pelonia behind him and looked down on her worm of an uncle "—then I do."

Marcus's bravado began to fade until he noticed the circle of inquisitive onlookers forming around them. He puffed out his chest, determined, it seemed, to scrape together a show of strength, no matter how meager. "And…and who might you be?"

The music died on a discordant note and the din of conversation faded to shocked whispers. Adiona entered the fray. "You'll have to forgive Marcus, my friend, he's new to Rome." To Marcus, she said, "Let me introduce you to Caros Viriathos, undefeated champion of Rome, *lanista* of the Ludus Maximus—"

"And the man who's going to make you suffer ten times for every hurt you caused my lady."

The bystanders gasped in unison. Adiona snickered. Antonius stepped forward to wrangle Marcus from danger, but it was a halfhearted effort at best. Caros felt Pelonia's cool hand on his upper arm, heard her say his name, but he ignored everything except the maggot in front of him.

With malicious pleasure he watched her uncle squirm, aware that all of Rome's finest citizens would think Marcus a coward if he bolted. Judging by the nervous twitch in his left eye, Marcus knew it, too.

The tension mounted until a shout went up from the crowd, "I'll wager a thousand denarii the old buzzard ends up dead."

Laughter and more wagers broke the brittle atmosphere. "Thank the gods someone has a sense of humor," Adiona muttered. Distracting her guests by calling for more music and refreshments, she exclaimed, "I'll make that three thousand if anyone's game."

Pelonia tugged on the back of Caros's tunic. She was having a difficult time focusing on the seriousness of the situation when all of her senses were dizzy with the delight of being so close to the man she loved. That her uncle was keeping them from a pleasant reunion added to her dislike of him.

"Caros, my darling," Adiona said blithely. "If you must shed blood have a care for my floor and take the violence outside, will you?"

"With pleasure." He caught Marcus by the scruff of the neck and ushered him down a side hall.

"Caros, don't hurt him." Pelonia chased after the two men, vaguely aware of the group of revelers following on her heels.

The corridor led outside to a small garden. A few torches provided enough light for safety's sake, but the simple arrangement of benches and flower beds surrounding a whimsical fountain spoke of a private sanctuary vastly different from the public areas of the palace.

Wasting no time, Caros let his fist fly. Her uncle squealed in pain. Cupping his face as blood gushed from his nose, Marcus fell backward into the fountain, splashing water over the garden's pavers. The scent of blood encouraged the spectators. Excitement whipped through the air. More wagers were shouted.

The Romans' love of violence sickened Pelonia. Caros's bloodlust frightened her. No matter what she tried, he ignored her pleas for reason. Fearing he would murder Marcus and end up in prison or worse, she threw herself in between the two men to beg for mercy just as Caros threw another punch.

His fist clipped her forehead. Pain shot through her skull. She staggered back.

"Pelonia!" he shouted.

At the same time, the crowd heaved a collective groan.

The ground shifted. She felt as though she were spinning. She stumbled and started to fall.

Caros caught her before she hit the pavers. He lifted her, cradling her against his chest. Ashen with regret, his face blurred before her eyes. "I'm sorry, *mea carissima,* I'm sorry."

She rested her head on his shoulder. A feeling of safety, absent since she left him, enveloped her. "I…I'll be all right."

As he carried her through the stunned onlookers, he murmured, "I pulled back the moment I saw you, but you were too close."

"I know. It's not your fault."

"We're going inside. I'll have you more comfortable in moments." He groaned under his breath. "Your cousins are here."

"What have you done to her?" Tiberia screeched.

"Not now, girl."

"She's *my* cousin." Tiberia trailed them down the hall. "You *will* tell me what happened."

Caros walked on without comment, but Pelonia heard Adiona relay a quick report of events.

"By the gods!" Tiberia railed. "You were warned to keep your hands off her, *lanista!* Now look what you've done. I should have known you'd resort to brute force—one of your sort always does. Do you think her betrothed is going to stand still for this?"

Betrothed?

Pelonia felt Caros go rigid. Her cousin must be mistaken. She mused her hearing must have been affected by the blow or else her brain had been loosed from its moorings because she'd made no agreement to wed anyone.

Caros was the only man she'd accept.

"Is it true?" he asked for her ears alone.

She shook her head, sending another blast of pain through her skull.

He relaxed and brushed a kiss across the throbbing spot on her brow. "That's good. You're mine. You won't marry anyone if you don't wed me."

His high-handedness should have irked her, but she snuggled closer. Why be upset when he was simply confirming what she wanted and already decided for herself. If only he would come to believe in Christ…

"If you weren't such a barbarian, this would never have happened," Tiberia rattled on behind them.

"Cease your prattle, girl. You're paining my head," Adiona snapped impatiently. "If anyone is to blame for tonight's fiasco, it's your husband."

"What do you mean?" the younger woman demanded. "I didn't see Antonius assaulting your guests."

"No, but he came to me yesterday and requested I invite Marcus tonight."

A door opened. "Take her in here, Caros. There's a bed she can have for the night," Adiona said.

Pelonia lifted her head long enough to peer over Caros's shoulder and watch as everyone followed them into the room.

"Caros told me of the uncle who'd sold Pelonia, but I didn't realize it was Marcus." Adiona continued with Tiberia's set-down. "Of course, your husband did. I suspect he *knew* something like this would happen, didn't you, Senator?"

"Is it *true,* Antonius?"

She heard the distress in her cousin's voice and hated having a part in the cause of it.

"Yes," he admitted.

Caros tightened his arms around her.

"But why? You *knew* how important this evening was to me. You must have guessed Marcus's presence would ruin it."

"It depends on your definition of ruin, my dear. *You* see bloodshed and a wrinkle in the festivities. *I* see that Marcus has been humiliated beyond repair. All of Rome will shun him for the rest of his days without my having to say a word."

"But how did you know—?"

"I took a chance our hostess would invite Caros and another chance his feelings for Pelonia would demand he act in her defense."

"You're as crafty as Marcus," Adiona condemned.

"Hardly," Antonius said. "However, I am an opportunist. One doesn't become a successful politician without learning how to manipulate circumstances to one's benefit. But unlike Marcus, I'd never sell my own kin into slavery nor lie to them for financial gain."

Adiona snorted. "Perhaps not, but it's clear you'll manipulate and lie to those who *aren't* your kin. What did you plan to do if your gamble failed?"

"I'd have confronted Marcus. This lofty assembly is the ideal place to ruin a reputation. Thankfully the *lanista*'s temper is predictable enough I didn't have to do the unpleasant business myself."

Pelonia stopped listening to the others quarrel as Caros placed her gently on the bed. She opened her eyes, grateful for the dim light. He crouched beside her and brushed her hair back from her cheeks. She smiled, loving the gentleness in his eyes.

"I regret all of this," he said. "I'll never forgive myself for striking you. Tell me, why did you throw yourself in front of Marcus?"

"There's nothing to forgive. It was an accident, one I caused. I trust you'd never hurt me, but I thought you were going to *kill* him."

He kissed the back of her hand. "That's what he deserves after he sold you, but I only intended a good thrashing."

She cupped his cheek and allowed her thumb to caress his warm lips. "I admit I don't like how he cast me out, but I'll be forever thankful the Lord brought me to you."

Caros swallowed the lump in his throat. Tenderness washed through him. "I'm grateful He did, too."

"Caros, are you listening to this tripe?" Adiona's inflection strongly suggested he say something. "Antonius has arranged for Pelonia to wed Minucius Brutus. Do you have an opinion you'd like to share on the matter?"

"His opinion doesn't matter in the least," the senator injected. "He has no claim or rights to her."

Clamping his anger, Caros gave Pelonia's hand a reassuring squeeze before he stood to face the other man. "I may have no right to her, but I *have* claimed her. I trusted you to find her a suitable husband. Minucius Brutus is not acceptable. Given your failure to meet the terms of our agreement, I'm taking her back into my care. If she'll have me, I'll wed her. If she won't, then I'll wait until she does. She's mine and no one else will lay a hand on her."

"I won't give my permission for her to wed a *gladiator*."

"Then I won't seek it."

The senator grew red in the face. "How dare you?"

Caros had had enough. He launched forward, grasping

Antonius and Tiberia each by the arm. Before they realized his intent, he pushed them through the door and shut the portal behind them. His hand on the latch, he turned to his friend. "Adiona, leave us for a few moments."

"Need I remind you this is *my* house?" she sputtered.

Fists pounded on the other side of the door.

"Need I remind you I can pick you up and deposit you in the hall like I did the others?"

Adiona began to argue for principle's sake, or so Caros suspected, then thought better of it and sauntered toward him. She reached up and patted his cheek. "May Fortuna be with you, my darling, I do believe you're going to need her."

Once they were alone, Caros returned to Pelonia. With great care he removed her sandals and covered her with a blanket before kissing her gently on the cheek. "Go to sleep, *mea carissima*. Tomorrow is a new day and we have much to discuss."

Chapter Twenty-Three

Abandoned by the guests who'd witnessed his disgrace, Marcus berated the Fates. A few jeers wafted back to him, branding him with shame. Soaking wet, he levered himself out of the fountain. The agony emanating from his nose and up through his eye sockets was enough to blind him. Humiliated in front of the very citizens he'd planned to impress, he swore to wreak vengeance on all those who'd ruined him.

Staggering back up the path, he gingerly cupped his swelling face in an effort to stem the slow, yet steady, stream of blood. He'd spent the last five weeks establishing his business. With the money he borrowed from Antonius he'd rented an expensive location in the Forum to set up shop.

It was a natural assumption to think the senator had arranged his invitation to Adiona's tonight to fulfill his promise and introduce him to the influential contacts he needed to lure a wealthy patronage.

Perhaps if he'd stayed in Rome he might have been better prepared to meet Pelonia. As it was, he'd been slow to recognize the trap closing around him.

And it was a trap—a neatly set one. Though Marcus had

yet to figure out the connection between his niece and the *lanista,* he harbored nary a doubt that Antonius had engineered the night's events in an effort to avenge Pelonia. Once again the twice-cursed wench and her blasphemous beliefs were the catalyst for all his troubles. He'd thought he'd taken care to remove her from his path, but the gods must be testing him—and his patience—to see if he were truly worthy of their blessings.

Shivering, he gritted his teeth, then winced at the burst of pain behind his battered nose. He'd lost everything. He needed no oracle to see Antonius intended to demand his investment back. With the money spent, his savings gone and no way to make a quick return now that he was a pariah, the property in Iguvium was forfeit.

Soaked to the skin, he ordered a slave to fetch him a fresh tunic and a cloth to dry himself.

The longer he waited outside like a beggar, the more his fury grew. Shamed by how easily his enemies surprised him tonight, he likened Antonius and the *lanista* to a beast he must slay if he ever hoped to regain his pride. Pelonia was its heart. Cut her out and the beast would topple.

Fortunately for him, his niece was an easy target. Rome was an unhealthy place for a Christian.

"Pelonia, wake up!" Tiberia said. "We must get you out of here. Soldiers are at the front door demanding your arrest."

Her cousin's urgency acted the same as a cup of cold water splashed in her face, waking Pelonia from a sound sleep. A dull ache throbbed behind her forehead, but she thrust back the luxurious bedcovers and jumped up instantly, her feet hitting the floor before she even had her bearings. She shook her head to clear the grogginess. "What? Why?"

Tiberia passed her a servant's tunic. "Hurry, change into

this. Perhaps you won't be as noticeable. Antonius and the *lanista* are buying you time, but we don't have long before the soldiers surround the palace."

"We stayed at Adiona's," she said aloud, glancing about the room Caros had put her to bed in the previous night.

Now fully awake, the gravity of what was happening filled her with fear. "Why am I being arrested?"

"Can't you guess?"

"Marcus told the authorities I'm a Christian."

Tiberia nodded. "I left to warn you before I heard the full story, but it seems he reported you for sedition."

Exchanging the silks she'd worn the previous night for the tunic, Pelonia hurried to tie her sandals. The charge against her made the threat more real. Because followers of Christ refused to accept the emperor as a god, Christians were executed for being traitors of the Empire.

"One of Adiona's trusted slaves is waiting in the corridor to lead you through a secret passage to the street. He'll accompany you to the gladiatorial school. Antonius and I aren't pleased with the situation but we agree the *lanista* can protect you better in his own domain."

"What about Caros? I can't endanger him. If the authorities find he's hidden me, he'll be imprisoned."

"He's willing to take the risk."

"I'm not," she said stubbornly. "He's sworn never to be enslaved again. If he's imprisoned his old master will buy him and send him back to the arena for certain."

"If you don't leave he's bound to kill someone defending you and end up with the same fate." Tiberia pushed her toward the door. "Don't be an *idiota*. I want you safe. *Caros* wants you safe. Escape to the school and give us a chance to work out a plan to protect you."

Pelonia felt like a coward, but she couldn't find a hole in

Tiberia's reason. At the door, she stopped just long enough to hug her cousin. "I love you, dearest. I want your every happiness. Tell Caros I love him, too. In case the worst happens—"

"Say no more." Tiberia's throat worked to swallow back tears. "I refuse to listen. All will be well. Just go before they find you!"

A tall, dark-skinned slave by the name of Aram led Pelonia through the dimly lit bowels of the palace. "Look there," he said in his thick Syrian accent, once they emerged outside.

She glanced over her shoulder to find the sun-washed steps leading to Adiona's palace a short distance away. A handful of soldiers, their red capes flapping in the breeze, waited on the top landing, near the front door. Others were already fanning out to surround the property just as Tiberia predicted.

"Come," the slave said, "we must walk. A cart or litter may draw added attention and we want to remain in the shadows."

After what felt like hours at a punishing pace along Rome's littered streets, Pelonia and Aram came to the school's massive front gates. The place seemed quieter than usual, but she'd been away for almost six weeks. Perhaps the throbbing pain in her head made her remember things differently than they actually were.

A guard opened the iron gate, his face solemn. The yard was a mess, not the neat, efficient space she recalled. Crates and barrels were stacked at odd angles. Shards of broken ceramic were strewn across the gravel.

An air of foreboding seized her. "I think we should leave, Aram. This doesn't feel safe."

It was too late. Soldiers converged from behind the stacked crates and surrounded the two of them. Fear exploded within her. One of the uniformed men knocked Aram to the dirt. Propping his sandaled foot on the back of the Syrian's neck, he pinned him to the ground.

Encircled by soldiers, she had nowhere to run.

A sinewy arm clamped around her waist from behind. "You're a slippery little thing, aren't you?" His harsh laughter rang in her ear.

"How did you find me?"

"We were warned you'd be at one of three places. The widow's palace, the senator's home or—"

"Here," she finished for him. Panic rising ever higher, she worked to remain above the abyss of terror that promised to drag her deeper into its depths.

As the soldiers bound her wrists behind her, she gave herself over to prayer. *Dear Heavenly Father, if it's Your will I die for Your name's sake, please let me do so with honor.*

Her ankles shackled with a short chain, one of the men lifted her off her feet and tossed her face-first into a wagon. Her head, already sore from the previous night, bounced against the rough wooden floorboards. Lewd comments and rough caresses on her bare calves prickled her skin with revulsion.

"Enough of that, men," said a voice of authority. "She was supposed to be delivered by the noon hour. Unless you want to face his ire yourself, we'd best take her to the magistrate as ordered."

The wagon rolled to a halt. Orders were barked and two of Pelonia's captors were assigned to guard her. Calloused hands hefted her from the wagon and stood her on the ground. Hot, queasy and faint from the long, bumpy ride in the sun, she trembled uncontrollably. She'd had too long to think about the horrors of her possible fate. Like the wolves snapping at the Christians in the amphitheatre, images of torture and untold agony plagued her.

The taller of her guards bounded up the steps leading to

a public building in front of her. A chiseled stone sign above the entrance read, Magistrate.

Perspiration broke out on her brow.

"Get moving." The second guard shoved her and she proceeded him at a hobbled pace up the steps. The taller man returned from indoors, his red cape flowing out behind him. "Hurry it up, woman," he bellowed from the landing. "The magistrate's in a foul mood. He's been waiting all afternoon to hear your case."

Why? Why was the magistrate waiting for her? What was so unique about her situation?

The rope chafing her wrists, she entered the office. Her shackle rattled against the concrete floor and echoed off the barren gray walls.

Where is everyone?

Except for a few dour-faced clerks behind tables to her left, there were few witnesses. She'd never been to a magistrate's building and had no firsthand knowledge of how legal proceedings were carried out. Perhaps all suspected criminals were tried in relative private? No. Something was wrong.

A clerk stood and read her name and supposed crimes from a small scroll. A guard pushed her forward. The shackle caused her to stumble. With her hands cinched behind her back, she almost fell. Biting her lip, she prayed for courage and crossed the austere room to stand before the magistrate.

A rotund man with deep lines in his forehead, he smacked his lips and scrutinized her from behind laced, sausagelike fingers. Nerves stretched to the breaking point, Pelonia began to fidget under the weight of his glare.

"I think I've been lied to," he finally said with disgust. "I was told you were dangerous, a deviant intent on influencing a senator to commit treason against the emperor."

The seriousness of the charges made her tremble. No

wonder she'd received a rapid trial. It was bad enough to be tried as a Christian, but inciting others to rebel meant instant death.

Suddenly the lack of observers gained new meaning. She suspected the office had been cleared to protect Antonius's honor, not her privacy. With so few witnesses, there was less chance of gossip to sully the powerful senator's name.

"You look more like a harmless butterfly to me." The judge licked his thick lips and allowed his eyes to roam up and down her person.

Repulsed, she lifted her chin and met his gaze with a cold stare. His suggestive smile faded. His expression hardened. He picked up a stylus and scribbled notes on a piece of parchment. The chair he sat on creaked as he leaned back to sneer at her. "So tell me, is your accuser a suitor who wants revenge because you've shunned him? Or are you truly a follower of that crucified agitator, Jesus of Nazareth?"

The temptation to lie called to her. Her own sense of self-preservation betrayed her. The fear of torture and death played havoc with her reason. An insidious voice whispered inside her head, *Won't God forgive you if you deny Him just this once?*

The magistrate's brow pleated with impatience. "Come on, tell the truth, girl. You've nothing to fear if you're a faithful subject of the emperor."

She tugged at the ropes binding her wrist. "I…"

"On the other hand, if you're a follower of Jesus, you'll follow Him straight to the arena."

Her head began to throb. Judging from his blunt tone, she didn't doubt he'd sent many Christians to their deaths. She struggled not to show her terror. A simple denial and her life would be hers again. As would the chance to be with the man she loved. Every facet of her being demanded she set aside her faith and follow her heart.

"Well, spit it out. I have other cases to try today."

Her resolve hardened to flint, she released a pent up breath. "I...I'm a loyal subject of the emperor."

"Silly wench. Why didn't you just say—"

"But Jesus is my God."

The guard shuffled his feet behind her. His shadow overtook hers on the floor as he moved closer.

"Are you certain you don't want to reconsider?" The magistrate smirked. "I'd hate to send such a beautiful woman to die."

She shook her head. "I won't change my mind."

He shrugged, then snapped his fingers. "Guard, take her to a holding cell in the arena. Tomorrow we'll see if she feels the same when she faces the lions."

Chapter Twenty-Four

Pelonia's guard led her down a dark corridor beneath the amphitheater. Bound and chained like the worst sort of criminal, she was trembling so hard she felt bruised from head to toe. The afternoon's games had yet to finish and the mob's roar dripped down to the holding pens like acid. Memories of the wolves ran rampant in her mind. She clung to her faith, praying incessantly to keep from going mad with fear.

The stench of urine and death gagged her. Weeping, angry tirades and insane ramblings escaped the condemned held in cells on each side of the narrow corridor.

The guard stopped abruptly and opened a cell to her right. Rodents shrieked and scurried to the shadows as torchlight invaded their subterranean nest.

"Welcome home, wench." The guard untied her hands and shoved her inside. Her ankles still shackled, she stumbled and slammed into the wall at the back of the tiny stall. "Don't worry," he said with a laugh, "you won't be here long. The mob will get their chance at you tomorrow. I hope your God appreciates you dying for Him."

"He did the same for me and you."

The guard grunted in reply. The door slammed behind him as he left, taking the light with him. Surrounded by darkness, she rubbed her arms to start the flow of blood after being bound and numb for hours. The chill of the place invaded her bones until her teeth began to chatter.

From across the hall, a tortured moan carried through the small, bar-covered opening in her door. Chains rattled and the cries for help from her fellow prisoners fell on deaf ears.

"Dear God, please help me," she whispered. "I need You like I've never needed You before. Please help me accept Your will. I offer You a sacrifice of praise, knowing that You alone are my Rock and my Salvation."

A sense of sweet peace settled over her and she recognized the influence of the Holy Spirit, her Comforter. In the months since her father's death, she'd known the Spirit was with her, but she hadn't *felt* His presence as she did now. A song of praise bubbled to her lips. Words of thanksgiving flowed from her mouth. The longer she focused on the Lord, the less she focused on her troubles or herself.

Caros left his horse with his Greek champion, Alexius, and pushed through the crowd leaving the amphitheatre. Charging down the steps that led to the behemoth's underbelly, he passed the waiting line and entered the editor's office.

"Get out," he ordered the client already in discussions with Spurius. Without hesitation, the man jumped to his feet, gathering an armful of half-rolled scrolls before he scuttled out the door.

Spurius leaned back in his chair, lacing his hands over the mountain of his belly. "Caros, you're here. I didn't expect you this quickly."

"I came as soon as I heard from you. Where is she?"

"She's in a holding cell like the magistrate ordered."

His gut clenched at the thought of Pelonia in one of the pits. "How much for her freedom?"

"What's she worth to you?"

Everything. Caros shrugged. "Fifteen hundred denarii is the usual price for a female slave."

Spurius chuckled and shuffled a few parchments on his desktop. "But this female is most *un*usual, is she not?

He studied his crafty former master with growing impatience. "Spurius, I have no time for games. Tell me her price so I can take her and leave."

"Her price is…*your* freedom."

Staggered by the unexpected blow, Caros willed himself to stay in control. "Explain."

"It's simple. You declare your loyalty to me—"

"You mean enslave myself again." The very thing he'd sworn never to do.

"Whatever you want to call it is up to you."

"I call it extortion."

"Perhaps." Spurius picked up a piece of parchment from his desk and began to roll it into a tube. "But if you want to see your woman returned to you unharmed, you'll meet my terms."

"Then she *is* unharmed?"

"For the time being, but that can change with the wind."

"You black-hearted worm! She's an innocent—"

"She's a commodity." Spurius stood up to put some distance between them. "While you and I are men of business. If you wish to buy my goods, let's strike a bargain. If not, I need to get back to those waiting in line outside my door."

Seething, Caros surged to his feet, his chair falling backward to crash against the concrete floor. "Then name your terms, old man, *all* of them and be warned, I know what a backstabbing cheat you are, so I'll have a few of my own."

"Your woman must have gold between her legs. What

else could inspire such ardor in the iron heart of Caros Viriathos?" The editor chuckled. "You haven't turned Christian, have you? Is that why you're concerned for her plight?"

"No," he answered, his voice cast in stone.

"Then you must be in love with the wench." Spurius's eyes took on a greedy light. "My terms are simple. Declare loyalty to me. Fight in the arena tomorrow for the amusement of the mob and your payment will be the girl. I'll take care of all legal ramifications if there are any, though I can't think there will be once I've paid off the magistrate."

On the surface, Spurius's terms were basic enough, but Caros saw through the loopholes immediately. "I'll agree to your terms—with some clarifications. First, I'll fight for you tomorrow afternoon for one contest and one contest only. Then I'll be a free man again. Second, I'll entertain the mob and make your riches for you. As my reward, Pelonia, my former slave—not just any girl—will be released and waiting for me alive, unharmed and well when I leave the arena. If I die, she'll be granted her freedom and returned unharmed to Senator Antonius Tacitus under the same terms she would have been given to me. Third, Pelonia will accompany me home tonight and return with me to the arena tomorrow. Fourth, this agreement will be put in writing and a copy delivered to my steward within the hour. Fifth, you will never darken my door or approach me to enter the arena again. If you do, you'll understand it's at your peril. And if you *ever* make another lewd suggestion concerning my woman, I'll make you wish you were dead. Am I clear?"

The editor swallowed hard and nodded. "Done, except for taking the girl home tonight. The magistrate's a stickler for body counts."

"Then release her to stay with her cousin at the senator's palace tonight and I'll take her place in the pit."

"Done!" The editor slapped his desk and did a little jig of glee. "Was that so difficult? Shall we have a drink to celebrate?"

Caros ignored the man and made for the door. He found Alexius waiting outside the editor's office. The corridor was less hectic, but a line remained to wait for Spurius.

"Who's he?" Alexius tipped his head toward a young man following them.

"Spurius's lackey. We're going to the holding cells. He's to speak with the jailer."

"Judging from your expression, the situation can't get worse."

"No," Caros admitted. "I've agreed to reenter the ring."

Alexius halted. "Impossible!"

"No. Spurius promised Pelonia's freedom if I fight one last time."

Alexius swore in Greek and hurried to catch up with Caros's quick steps. "So the dog's finally found your Achilles' heel. He's been after you for years to return to the games."

They both knew it was true. Only for Pelonia would he set aside his vow and become a slave again. Their rapid steps clipped along the concrete floor.

"I'm granting you your freedom," Caros said.

"I don't want it."

"As your master, I'm ordering you to take it."

Alexius frowned, but gave an ill-tempered nod of acceptance.

"While I'm in the arena, you'll be the *lanista* of the Ludus Maximus."

"You're mad!" Alexius's frown deepened.

"So everyone says. Now listen to me. We haven't much time. If I lose, Gaius will help you take control of the school. I've spoken with my steward in times past concerning this matter. He knows I intend for you to be my successor. I want you to train the men well. Pay special attention to the new man, Quintus. He has much to offer. Can I count on you?"

"How can I say no?" The Greek tried to smile. "You better *not* die…or I'll hunt you down in the afterlife and kill you myself."

"Ha! Even in death I'd best you." Grateful to have Alexius by his side, Caros thumped him on the back. "Don't worry, my friend, you won't have to be a free man for long. I expect to live and when the contest is over, I *will* want my school returned."

They stopped at the stairs leading down to the holding cells. Caros clapped his champion on the shoulder. "I'd like a few moments alone with Pelonia, but afterward you're to escort her to the senator's palace."

"This is madness. Why are you staying here when you have to fight tomorrow? You should be eating well and sleeping better in preparation. Just bring her home with us."

"No, it's part of the agreement."

"She's not going to let you take her place in the ring without a fight."

"She has no choice." Caros whipped the tail of his cloak over his forearm and started down the steep steps, the other two men following close on his heels.

At the holding level, the situation was explained and the jailer led him and Alexius through the complex maze of corridors to Pelonia's cell. Spurius's man returned to his master.

"Is that…singing I hear?" Alexius asked.

Caros listened to the faint song. "I believe so," he said with equal bewilderment.

"Obviously things have changed," the Greek said dryly. "There was nothing to sing about the last time I was here."

"Things haven't changed enough. It still smells like a sewer."

The melody grew louder. There was more than one voice and though the atmosphere was dank and cold, the usual moans and cries of the condemned were minimal.

"This way," the jailer said, leading them down a narrow hallway alive with singing voices. "You want to see the wench who started this racket. Before she got here, these Christians were resigned to their fate. Now they're praising their God like they've all lost their minds."

The key grated in the lock. Caros took the torch and sent the jailer on his way. To Alexius, he ordered, "Keep watch. I'll be a few moments, no more."

Caros pushed open the door and ducked to enter the cell without bumping his head. He placed the torch in the holder on the wall. His heart stopped when he saw Pelonia. Bathed in the fire's glow, she stood in the tiny cell, hands raised shoulder high, her eyes closed. Deep in meditation, she had yet to realize she wasn't alone.

She'd never looked more beautiful to him than she did in that moment. Surrounded by the moldy walls of her prison, he saw her for the indomitable spirit she was. He prided himself on strength, but next to her, he was a sapling compared to an oak.

Her sweet voice caressed his ears, stirring him to marvel at the greatness of her God, a God awesome enough to inspire worship even in the depths of a gaol.

Her song ended, though others down the corridor continued with their praise. Lowering her arms, Pelonia opened her eyes. A smile of such pure joy touched her face he was struck dumb by the splendor of it.

"Caros? What are you doing here?" She came to him, wrapping her arms around his waist to nestle close.

He closed his eyes and hugged her tight, dying a little inside when he realized that if the match didn't go his way tomorrow he'd never hold her again. He kissed the top of her head. "I came to rescue you. I thought you'd be terrified, but I see you've made yourself at home."

She laughed, but he felt the dampness of her tears through the linen of his tunic. "It's home now that you're here."

Startled by the admission, he lifted her chin and kissed her softly, his heart swelling with love until he thought his chest might burst with emotion. "Why didn't you lie this once and tell them—"

"Shhh…" She placed her fingertips over his lips. "You know why. I'd never deny my Lord."

He nodded, accepting her loyalty and belief in Jesus were part of what made her unique. "I know."

"But I *was* tempted."

"Of course you were," he said, doing his best to relieve the guilt in her eyes. "Who wouldn't want to cling to life when death is breathing down your neck?"

"No, I'm not afraid to die." She tried to smile. "I'm afraid of the pain beforehand, certainly, but not death itself. That's not why I was tempted."

"What other reason is there?"

Her eyes softened. "Until now I…I've had few regrets in life, Caros. I regret that my mother passed away at my birth and I never knew her. I regret not being able to tell my father how much I loved him one last time before he died. But in death tomorrow, I'll be reunited with them because they're waiting for me with the Lord."

"Then why—"

"Because my deepest regret," she continued, her bottom lip trembling, "is…is never having the chance to spend a lifetime with you."

His heart wrenched at her words. "I feel the same, love. Which is why I'm taking your place in the arena tomorrow."

The blood leeched from her face. "No! I won't allow it!"

He silenced her with a soft kiss. "You will, *mea carissima*. You have no choice in this. Alexius?"

Pelonia watched in horror as his champion entered the cell. "Caros? No!"

He nodded toward the Greek and Pelonia was swept from the cell. Her protests echoed through the pit's dark corridors. Her desperate sobs broke his heart, but for once in his life he was certain he'd done the right thing.

Caros couldn't sleep. Thoughts of tomorrow's contest crowded in on him like the cell's damp walls. Though not locked in, he'd promised to stay in the prison as part of the bargain. If he broke any part of the pact, experience had taught Spurius would use it against him. His cell door closed to keep the vermin at bay, he'd settled in for a miserable night of stones poking his back.

"*Lanista?* Where are you?"

"Quintus?" He rose to his feet, almost hitting his head on the ceiling. He pushed open the cell door. "I'm in here."

"Thank God." Quintus lifted the sack he held in each hand. "Pelonia sent bedding and food. I would have been here sooner, but I had to bribe the jailer."

Struck by her thoughtfulness, Caros nodded in understanding. "How is Pelonia?

"She's worried, of course, but clinging to her faith. She's peeved for having to leave you down here. She told me to tell you she and Annia will be in prayer all night, and to assure you she'll return tomorrow."

"I never doubted her. Pelonia's the most honorable woman I know."

"Then you two are a good match. You're an honorable man."

Taken aback by the Christian's unexpected praise, he muttered his thanks, then asked, "Have you heard anything about the contest tomorrow? Spurius always promotes his fights well, but this one is short notice."

"I think everyone in the city has heard. Criers have been all over town announcing your glorious return from retirement." Quintus handed him a sack. "There were placards posted near the amphitheater. Seems you're to fight a handful of men at once and a slew of wild beasts."

"Is that all?"

"From what I can tell." Quintus tilted his head in the direction of the other cells. "Have they been singing long?"

"Off and on."

"Are the Psalms bothersome to you?"

"No, I find them peaceful."

Quintus opened the second sack. "This is the food. There's meat, bread, fruit and skins filled with fresh water. Enough for tonight and tomorrow."

Seeing the bounty, Caros joked, "Enough for me *and* the rats."

"Your lady doesn't want you to starve."

"Apparently."

"She's concerned about you."

"She needn't be. I cut my teeth in the games."

"She's more concerned about your soul than your hide."

Caros dug into the food and pulled out a loaf of dark bread. He ripped off a piece and chewed it while he eyed his slave. He swallowed. "I'm convinced there's no hope for me."

Quintus stilled. "You think you'll lose tomorrow?"

He leaned against the doorframe, careful not to bump his head. "No, my body will be fine. It's my soul that's lost."

"Why are you so convinced you're irredeemable?"

He shook his head. "I've killed many Christians. How could your God forgive me when I've killed so many of His own?"

"Is *that* why you've had difficulty accepting the Way?"

His chest unbearably tight from guilt, Caros nodded.

"Whatever you've done makes no difference. Paul also murdered many believers before he came to the Lord. And yet the Lord used him mightily."

Stunned by the knowledge Pelonia's great teacher had committed the same sins as he, Caros was afraid to believe his ears.

Quintus grinned. "You've no reason to doubt Jesus loves you. He has His hand on your life. If you believe in Him, He'll be faithful to forgive you no matter what you've done."

Caros felt buoyed by the hope of forgiveness for the first time. "Thank you, Quintus."

Quintus clasped him on the shoulder as he turned to go. "Open your heart and accept the love of Jesus. Forgiveness is yours if you'll only believe."

Later, alone, warm and fed, Caros leaned against a stack of pillows contemplating his numerous talks with Pelonia and his latest discussion with Quintus. Except for the occasional rattle of chains and the constant drip of water somewhere beyond his cell, the pit was quiet.

Open your heart and accept the love of Jesus. Forgiveness is yours if you'll only believe.

Quintus's words went round and round in Caros's head. Since the first time Pelonia had told him about Christ's love, he'd wanted to believe in the possibility of forgiveness. But, having killed so many Christians, he'd been convinced there was no help to be found in their God.

After thinking for so long he was beyond salvation, the concept terrified him. What if he accepted, truly accepted Jesus as his God, only to find it was no more than a hoax?

He shook his head to ward off his doubts. Pelonia believed. Quintus believed. So had the many Christians he'd seen die in the ring.

Teetering on the edge between denial and what his heart told him was truth, he took a deep breath and prayed, "Jesus, if You'll have me, *I* believe in You."

Chapter Twenty-Five

Caros awoke the next morning, his mind and spirit at peace for the first time—like the shackles had been freed from his soul. Focusing on the contest before him, he accepted the years he'd spent as a gladiator were all part of God's plan for his life—all preparation for today's final battle.

To keep from being distracted, he allowed himself no more than a few moments to think of Pelonia. He looked forward to telling her about his newfound faith. He realized he'd told her everything about himself except how much he loved her. As soon as he saw her again he vowed to correct the matter and tell her every day for the rest of his life.

Hating the slave's garb Spurius sent, he dressed with grim resolve, unrepentant in the decision to break his vow if it meant rescuing Pelonia. Eager to see his mission accomplished, he stoked himself for victory until there was no room in his mind for failure.

Spurius collected him from the pit a short time later. Noticing the stack of pillows and discarded food cloths, the old man quirked an eyebrow. "I see if you lose today it can't be blamed on an uncomfortable night."

"I won't lose. I have unfinished business to attend to."

"Concerning your woman, no doubt. She arrived hours ago, in case you were wondering."

"I knew she'd come."

"Why? Because she'd be hunted down otherwise?"

"Because she's a woman like no other, Spurius. A woman of honor who lives by her word." The two men left the row of empty cells and ascended a flight of steps. "Where is she in the stands?" Caros asked.

"How should I know the exact spot?"

"Why do you sound suspicious, old man? Where is she?"

"The last I saw her, she was with her cousin," the editor grumbled.

"As long as she's safe."

"She is."

Unconvinced, Caros warned, "Don't forget our bargain. She's to be waiting for me alive and unharmed when I leave the arena."

"I've forgotten nothing. I'm hurt you don't trust me."

He motioned toward a bank of cages. "I trust you like I'd trust one of these predators at my back." Hearing the first muted cries of the mob, he grew impatient. "How many men do you intend for me to fight?"

"It wouldn't be a surprise if I told you." Spurius gave a crafty grin. "But I do have a finale to please every Roman's love of drama. You'll go back into retirement a god in their eyes."

"Don't do me any favors."

Spurius chuckled. "I'm not. I'm going to use your misery to lure the mob back into their seats tomorrow."

"You're a contemptible bit of slime, do you know that?"

"I've been called worse…just this morning, in fact."

Occasional snatches of sunlight began to cut through the

gloom. Slaves tended the cages filled with bears, panthers, tigers and other wildlife from all over the Empire.

He could feel the crowd's excitement pulse through his nerves. The roar of agitated lions mingled with the spectators' cry a level above them. The smell turned from one of moldy decay to the mixed stench of dung, overripe bodies and blood.

"The mob is frenzied today. All fifty thousand seats are filled and the balconies are overflowing." Pleased with himself, Spurius grinned. "It's all because of you. I told you there was a fortune to be made if you'd come back and fight."

"I don't expect you to understand, you filthy cur, but I wanted a peaceful life."

"And you chose to train gladiators?"

"What else was I fit for after you kept me enslaved all those years?"

Spurius shrugged. "Your livelihood wasn't my problem. I had my own mouth to feed."

They came to one of the platforms used to lift combatants directly into the arena. Sand sifted through the cracks in the floorboards. The impatient chant of the crowd shook the foundation.

Slaves waited nearby with the armor and sword of a Samnite. Caros strapped a leather greave to his left leg before lifting his large visored helmet over his head.

Accepting his shield with his left hand, he gripped a *gladius* in his right. His fingers caressed the leather hilt like the hand of a contentious, but oft relied upon friend.

"No wonder the crowds always loved you, you look like Mars himself." Spurius motioned for the slaves to lift Caros into the arena. The ropes creaked as one set of pulleys raised the platform, while another set parted the floorboards above his head. "Your woman is truly blessed by Fortuna," Spurius shouted up to him. "Who else but you could have saved her from death in the ring?"

Our God, Caros thought as he rode toward the cloudless blue sky. Tense with the anticipation of battle, he acknowledged Christ could have chosen to use a miracle to save her, but He'd chosen to honor him with the privilege instead.

As the top of his head crested with the floor, the announcer introduced him along with his long list of titles: *Lanista* of the Ludus Maximus, The Bone Grinder, The Undefeated Champion of Rome. The mob's fanatical cheer swept across the expanse like a whirlwind. The platform locked into place. He raised the *gladius* in a salute, drawing even more applause and stamping of feet.

Marveling at the sea of people, he left the platform and anchored his feet in the sand. Eyes focused on the main gate, he watched slaves wrestle it open.

An iron chariot thundered toward him, spewing a cloud of dust in its wake. Behind the driver, two archers flanked his first opponent. Flaming arrows streaked toward him. He blocked them with his shield, extinguishing them in the sand.

The chariot raced past him, so close he jumped back to avoid being hit. Dressed as a beast from the underworld in a horned helmet with snarling teeth, his opponent leaped from the back of the chariot. He swung his long blade with no mercy. Caros met the attack. Blood pumping, he gave himself over to the thrill of the sport.

Blade met blade over and over. Caros swiped the other man in the arm, drawing first blood. The crowd went wild. An arrow pierced the sand near his feet. Blocking his opponent's weapon with his own, he turned just in time to deflect a second arrow with his shield.

The chariot returned, dropping off another set of fighters. Aware he'd promised Spurius to entertain the crowd,

Caros fought all three men at once until a lioness was lifted into the arena.

Released from its binding, the cat launched herself into the fight. Grasping the wounded man from behind, she sank her teeth into his neck. The mob cheered for death and the man cried out in agony, but not for long.

Disgusted, but focused on his other two adversaries, Caros ignored the crack of bone as the lion tore into the dead man's flesh, and launched an offensive attack. Dividing the other two men, he wounded the first, weaker foe with a slice across the thigh and a blow to the chin. The gladiator staggered backward, falling to the sand.

The mob cried for murder. The sound of blood rushing in his ears, Caros ignored them. The sun beat down on him. His sweat flowed in rivulets. Raising the point of his sword, he went after the last man.

A giant from the untamed lands of Germania, Caros recognized the titan from previous contests. An expert with a trident and net, his opponent had only been defeated once, and that was by Alexius.

Eyes intent, he waited for the German to make the first move. The titan lifted the net. Swinging it in a circle above his head, he cast it toward Caros. Caros raised his shield and moved to avoid it, but the knotted rope ensnared him in its web.

Behind him, he heard the floor shift, another platform lift into place. Unable to turn in the jumble of cords and find his newest adversary, Caros expected the worst when the crowd stood and roared.

Slicing through the ropes that bound him, he threw off his helmet and worked free of the net just in time to avoid the trident piercing his chest. With a tactical swing of his *gladius,* he glanced over his shoulder. A rhino, its sharp horn glistening in the sun, barreled toward him. Reacting by instinct, he dropped his shield.

The mob gasped.

His free hand latched on to the post of the trident just below the prongs. He yanked with all his might and swung his massive foe toward the beast. The rhino's horn caught the German in the ribs. The momentum of the animal's pounding feet dragged the screaming man into the sand where he was trampled.

The mob chanted Caros's name with insane abandon. As he drank in air, he watched the rhino race toward the main gate where slaves angled it into a stall. He cast an eye toward the lioness. Lying in a circle of bloodstained sand, the cat continued to ravage its meal.

Trumpets blared, announcing a shift to the day's final entertainments. The lioness was caught and taken back to her cage. His interest keen, Caros watched a handful of slaves pull a covered wagon across the blood-spattered sands. At the same time, across the arena another hole opened in the floor.

The announcer began to weave a tale of a mighty gladiator whose prowess caught the eye of Venus. A hush fell over the crowd when they learned the warrior rejected the enamored goddess in favor of a human girl.

The crowd shrieked and clapped as the platform slowly lifted Pelonia into the arena. Dressed in a gossamer tunic, her black hair unbound and flowing in the breeze, she was tied to a stake, her hands trussed behind her back.

With dawning horror, Caros realized Spurius had cast him and Pelonia as actual leads in the drama. His feet heavy with fear, he ran toward her, listening keenly to what might unfold next.

The announcer's voice boomed across the theatre. "Furious, the goddess disguised herself as a predator and vowed to kill her rival."

All at once, the slaves tugged on the sheets covering the wagon. The billowing cloths fell away to reveal a large caged tiger. The cage door opened. The beast roared. Unlike the mob that was too far away, Caros saw the animal had been abused and frothed at the mouth.

The predator hissed and smacked at the slaves poking him with sharpened sticks. He leaped from his prison, landing between Caros and Pelonia. Straining every one of his sore and tired muscles, Caros picked up speed. The beast's golden eyes latched on Pelonia and bounded toward her. Terror kicked through Caros. He'd never get to her in time.

Terrified, Pelonia closed her eyes and gave herself up to prayer. At any moment, she expected the tiger's attack. Frozen, unable even to scream, she asked the Lord to protect Caros and see him safely from the arena. Animal footsteps galloped closer. She braced herself for pain.

Anger shot through her. How could she accept death like a coward? She forced her eyes open and… *"Cat?"*

The tiger leaped through the air, his roar sounding to her like a plaintive wail. He careened into her, driving the breath from her body in a groan of agony.

The spectators jumped to their feet, delighted by what at a distance must look like a fatal attack. As he usually did, Cat wallowed against her, rubbing his head and face across her chest.

Weak with relief, she tugged at her bonds, wanting to hug the dear animal. Seeing someone had abused him, her anger burned against the foul soul. *God help him if I ever find out who hurt my pet!*

Within the same heartbeat, Caros's shadow fell over her. He raised his *gladius,* intent on a deadly strike. The rage of battle still clouding his intense blue eyes, she could see he'd had no time to realize the animal was his own tiger.

"Caros, stop!" she cried. "It's Cat."

His facial muscles contorted with confusion, he managed to digest her warning and stop his weapon's mortal blow just before it sank between Cat's shoulders.

Seeing her love as a gladiator for the first time, she watched him grapple for control of the violence raging through him. Smeared with blood, his tunic torn, his fingers white from the tight grip on his weapon, he heaved in great breaths of air.

"Caros," she said for his ears only, casting away her fear. "Caros, we're all right."

Seemingly unaware of how close he came to death at the hand of his master, Cat bumped him with his nose.

Caros buried his fingers in the ruff of fur around Cat's neck. He opened his eyes and stared at her as though she'd just been raised from the grave. "You live?" he said in wonder. "I saw the tiger leap at you. I thought for certain you were dead."

The wild crowd forgotten, she gave him a gentle smile. "I'm well. We all owe thanks to you."

With tender care he cut her bonds and swept her into his arms. His quick steps took them to the sidelines, Cat trotting close behind them.

They crossed the threshold into the staging area. Caros buried his face in the curve of her neck. "Thank God you're safe."

Uncertain if she'd heard him correctly, she tipped her head to look intently into his eyes. "Which God do you thank?"

"Your God," he said, his low voice thick with conviction. "The true and living God whom I accepted last night as my own."

Overjoyed by the unexpected news, she squealed with delight. "How? Why? What happened to convince you?"

He carried her into a private alcove she guessed at one time served as an office. He set her on her feet and grabbed a towel from a peg on the wall. "Quintus visited me last night."

"I know," she said, stroking the top of Cat's head. "The Lord told me to send him."

He laughed, amazed by the God whose ways he had yet to fully comprehend. "Quintus explained that your teacher, Paul, was a killer the same as I before he came to believe."

"Well, yes," she said, her forehead puckered in her confusion. "Everyone knows… No, of course, you didn't know. How could you?"

He shrugged and used the cloth to wipe the sweat from his face, neck and chest. "I wish I had known. My guilt over killing so many in the past convinced me God would never want me."

"Oh, Caros! I'm sorry I didn't think to tell you." She wrapped her arms around his neck and buried her fingers in the damp curls at his nape. "Of course He wants you. He wants *everyone*."

"I believe it now." He held her tight, breathing in the joy radiating from the depths of her soul. "The question is, do *you* want me?"

She reared back, her smile soft and filled with love. "I—"

"Caros? Master, where are you?"

Caros groaned at the sound of Alexius's voice beyond the wall. He lifted his head. "Go on. Just ignore him."

"I—"

"There you are, Caros, Pelonia. By the gods, I've been looking for you everywhere."

"Go away, Alexius," Caros ordered.

"Is that all the thanks I get for switching out Cat?"

"Cat!" Pelonia shrieked. "My poor baby, I forgot all

about him." She dropped to her knees in the hay beside the tiger and began to examine the cuts on his face. The tiger recoiled and growled low from the pain, but he allowed her to fuss over his wounds. "Someone abused him. I'd like to know who did this. I'd make them sorry for certain."

"I believe it," Alexius said. "After last night I'll never doubt you're a firebrand."

Caros raised an eyebrow.

"What?" Alexius frowned. "She seems like such a mild little bird, but you should have seen her giving orders. If I weren't four times her size, I think she might have scared me witless. I'm warning you, my friend, she should have been a centurion."

"Who should have been a centurion?" Spurius asked, pushing his way around Alexius.

"Pelonia," the Greek answered. "She's got quite a temper."

"After today, she has quite a reputation. Do you hear the mob? They love her. They believe she really tamed the beast."

Alexius sent Caros a meaningful grin. "She has. Can't you tell?"

Caros wasn't amused. "Spurius, what was she doing out in the arena or *anywhere* near a tiger."

The editor paled. He hemmed and hawed, all the while backing away from Caros's angry glare.

"We had a bargain, you worm."

"Yes, we did. And here she is, safe and well just as we agreed. Now, if you'll excuse me I believe I'm needed elsewhere."

Alexius chuckled. "That's one way to get rid of fleas."

"What happened today?" Caros asked his champion, a tinge of the blinding fear he'd felt still with him.

The Greek leaned against the stone wall. "I arrived early this morning to see how you'd fared in the night. On my way to your cell, I overheard Spurius telling the day's plans to his slaves. I reckoned the situation wouldn't end if I escaped with the girl, so I simply changed out the tiger."

"You're a genius," Pelonia said. She stroked Cat's ear. "But do you know who cut him?"

"No, but if I find out you'll be the first to hear." Alexius tapped his thigh. "Let's go, boy. It's time to go home."

Cat lumbered past, giving Pelonia a gentle bump that sent her toppling into the hay. Caros lifted her to her feet.

"One last thing," Alexius said. "Gaius had a chariot delivered to convey you home."

As soon as they were alone, Caros pulled her back into his arms. "Before they interrupted, you were saying?"

"Hmm… Yes, what *was* I saying?"

He squeezed her, making her giggle. "I was saying, you dear, wonderful man, that I want you, too. I want you today and every day from here on out."

"That's good." His chest ached with tenderness. "Because I love you, Pelonia. I love you more than my own life."

"I love you, too," she said, her eyes soft with emotion. "I've known since the night we stargazed together. It's been torture thinking I could never have you."

"I want you to be my wife, *mea carissima,* to share the rest of my days."

Happiness brimmed and spilled over into every part of her being. She wrapped her arms around his lean waist and burrowed against him, offering her Heavenly Father a prayer of eternal gratitude. "I'll marry you, my love. I'd already decided I'd never wed anyone if I couldn't have you."

"I'll always be yours. I swore you'd admit I owned you, but from the first moment I saw you, you've owned my heart."

He dipped his head to savor her sweet lips with a kiss.

Joy overflowed from the depths of her soul and she gave

herself over to the happiness of being held by the one man she loved above anyone else.

"In case you ever doubt it, you *are* my life, Pelonia. Without you, I'd still be wandering in darkness, ignorant of the Lord's saving grace, lonely and hungry for peace. Why He chose to shower me with His favor is beyond my ken, but I vow to spend the rest of my days thanking Him for the gift of you."

She tried to hide her tears behind a smile. "I wasn't much of a gift. You did pay three thousand denarii for me."

"Money well spent for a woman beyond price. Knowing what I do now, I'd pay a thousand times that amount and consider myself blessed."

As Caros swept her into his arms and carried her into the warm afternoon, she glanced toward the sky, certain both her fathers smiled down on her from heaven. The sting of her slavery was gone, replaced by the freedom to love a man worthy of her trust and respect. She sighed with contentment.

He brushed her temple with his lips. "What are you thinking, *mea carissima?*"

Loving his deep blue eyes, she brushed a thick lock of hair behind his ear. "Only that I'm blessed and happy."

"Good." He set her on her feet in the chariot and kissed her softly. "That's exactly how I want you to be."

* * * * *

Dear Reader,

Thank you for reading my debut novel, *The Gladiator*. It is my sincerest hope that you enjoyed Caros and Pelonia's story of love and faith.

Since this is my first published novel, it's very near and dear to my heart. Especially since just before I began writing *The Gladiator*, I was at a low point and reconsidering the wisdom of "wasting" so much time writing if I might never be published. After a lot of prayer, I knew I had to give this novel a shot. As I began to outline the plot in my head, I just knew Romans 8:28 and God's never-ending ability to "work all things together for our good," had to be a major theme of the story.

I think for most of us it's natural to question God's will for our lives when we're slogging through difficult times. Like Pelonia, who suffered multiple tragedies, we feel God has abandoned us when we're in the midst of heartache. Sometimes, it's not until long after the fact that we can see how the Lord brought us through a trying situation and worked it to our benefit. I hope that if you're in a difficult time in your life, *The Gladiator* has encouraged your faith and helps you to wait on the blessings the Lord has in store for you.

I love to hear from my readers. Please visit my website, www.carlacapshaw.com, and/or write to me at carla@carlacapshaw.com. Join my newsletter to learn about upcoming releases and contests.

Be inspired,

Carla Capshaw

QUESTIONS FOR DISCUSSION

1. After her father is killed, Pelonia finds herself orphaned and feels abandoned by God. Have you ever found yourself in a situation where you felt abandoned? If so, did you question your faith or did you see the situation as a way to strengthen your relationship with the Lord?

2. When Pelonia is sold into slavery, she finds herself distanced from other Christians. Over time, she realizes how much she misses interaction with other believers. Do you work or interact in a situation where you are the only Christian? What can you do to keep your faith strong and active?

3. In the story, Pelonia's work in the garden is a metaphor for the seeds of faith she's planting and cultivating in Caros's life. What do you do to plant seeds of faith in the people around you?

4. Because of her jealousy, Lucia meant to hurt Pelonia. Have you ever been hurt by a friend or acquaintance? Were you able to forgive the person and continue the relationship?

5. Pelonia didn't realize that forgiving Lucia would be the catalyst for winning Caros to Christ. How have your actions (good or bad) affected your Christian witness to the people around you?

6. At first, Caros's friend, Adiona, seems unlikable, but Pelonia soon suspects there's more to the widow than

her outward demeanor. Do you know someone you disliked on first meeting, but who became a friend once you got to know them? What changed your opinion of the person? Did you learn something about their past that made you more compassionate? Or did you realize the change needed to be made in you before the friendship could grow?

7. During this time period in Rome, Christians faced extreme persecution. Christians still face persecution around the world today. Have you ever considered what you would do if you were persecuted for your faith?

8. After she returns from the arena, Pelonia is at her lowest ebb, but Christian friends are brought into her life that same day. Have you ever noticed that God brought just the right person into your life at the right time to encourage you when you needed help?

9. Because of years of violence and guilt, Caros had sworn never to fight again, but once he became a Christian, he realized God could use even the worst parts of his past for a greater good. Is there anything negative in your past that Christ was able to use for His purpose once you gave your life to Him?

10. Were you surprised Pelonia considered lying to the magistrate? Do you think her reasons were valid or not? In the same position, would you have acted the same or differently?

Here's a sneak peek at "Merry Mayhem"
by Margaret Daley,
one of the two riveting suspense stories in the
new collection CHRISTMAS PERIL,
available in December 2009
from Love Inspired Suspense.

"Run. Disappear… Don't trust anyone, especially the police."

Annie Coleman almost dropped the phone at her ex-boyfriend's words, but she couldn't. She had to keep it together for her daughter. Jayden played nearby, oblivious to the sheer terror Annie was feeling at hearing Bryan's gasped warning.

"Thought you could get away," a gruff voice she didn't recognize said between punches. "You haven't finished telling me what I need to know."

Annie panicked. What was going on? What was happening to Bryan on the other end? Confusion gripped her in a choke hold, her chest tightening with each inhalation.

"I don't want," Bryan's rattling gasp punctuated the brief silence, "any money. Just let me go. I'll forget everything."

"I'm not worried about you telling a soul." The menace in the assailant's tone underscored his deadly intent. "All I need to know is exactly where you hid it. If you tell me now, it will be a lot less painful."

"I can't—" Agony laced each word.

"What's that? A phone?" the man screamed.

The sounds of a struggle then a gunshot blasted her eardrum. Curses roared through the connection.

Fear paralyzed Annie in the middle of her kitchen. Was Bryan shot? Dead?

The voice on the phone returned. "Who's this? Who are you?"

The assailant's voice so clear on the phone panicked her. She slammed it down onto its cradle as though that action could sever the memories from her mind. But nothing would. Had she heard her daughter's father being killed? What information did Bryan have? Did that man know her name? Question after question bombarded her from all sides, but inertia held her still.

The ringing of the phone jarred her out of her trance. Her gaze zoomed in on the lighted panel on the receiver and saw the call was from Bryan's cell. The assailant had her home telephone number. He could discover where she lived. He knew what she'd heard.

"Mommy, what's wrong?"

Looking up at Jayden, Annie schooled her features into what she hoped was a calm expression while her stomach reeled. "You know, I've been thinking, honey, we need to take a vacation. It's time for us to have an adventure. Let's see how fast you can pack." Although she tried to make it sound like a game, her voice quavered, and Annie curled her trembling hands until her fingernails dug into her palms.

At the door, her daughter paused, cocking her head. "When will we be coming back?"

The question hung in the air, and Annie wondered if they'd ever be able to come back at all.

* * * * *

Follow Annie and Jayden as they flee to Christmas,
Oklahoma, and hide from a killer—with a little
help from a small-town police officer.

Look for CHRISTMAS PERIL
by Margaret Daley and Debby Giusti,
available December 2009
from Love Inspired Suspense.

REQUEST YOUR FREE BOOKS!

2 FREE INSPIRATIONAL NOVELS
PLUS 2
FREE
MYSTERY GIFTS

Love Inspired
HISTORICAL
INSPIRATIONAL HISTORICAL ROMANCE

YES! Please send me 2 FREE Love Inspired® Historical novels and my 2 FREE mystery gifts (gifts are worth about $10). After receiving them, if I don't wish to receive any more books, I can return the shipping statement marked "cancel". If I don't cancel, I will receive 4 brand-new novels every other month and be billed just $4.24 per book in the U.S. or $4.74 per book in Canada. That's a savings of over 20% off the cover price. It's quite a bargain! Shipping and handling is just 50¢ per book.* I understand that accepting the 2 free books and gifts places me under no obligation to buy anything. I can always return a shipment and cancel at any time. Even if I never buy another book, the two free books and gifts are mine to keep forever.

102 IDN EYPS 302 IDN EYP4

Name	(PLEASE PRINT)	
Address		Apt. #
City	State/Prov.	Zip/Postal Code

Signature (if under 18, a parent or guardian must sign)

Mail to Steeple Hill Reader Service:
IN U.S.A.: P.O. Box 1867, Buffalo, NY 14240-1867
IN CANADA: P.O. Box 609, Fort Erie, Ontario L2A 5X3

Not valid to current subscribers of Love Inspired Historical books.

Want to try two free books from another series?
Call 1-800-873-8635 or visit www.morefreebooks.com

* Terms and prices subject to change without notice. Prices do not include applicable taxes. Sales tax applicable in N.Y. Canadian residents will be charged applicable provincial taxes and GST. Offer not valid in Quebec. This offer is limited to one order per household. All orders subject to approval. Credit or debit balances in a customer's account(s) may be offset by any other outstanding balance owed by or to the customer. Please allow 4 to 6 weeks for delivery. Offer available while quantities last.

Your Privacy: Steeple Hill Books is committed to protecting your privacy. Our Privacy Policy is available online at www.SteepleHill.com or upon request from the Reader Service. From time to time we make our lists of customers available to reputable third parties who may have a product or service of interest to you. If you would prefer we not share your name and address, please check here. ☐

LIH09

Love Inspired
HISTORICAL

TITLES AVAILABLE NEXT MONTH

Available December 8, 2009

HER PATCHWORK FAMILY by Lyn Cote
The Gabriel Sisters
The Civil War may have ended, but Felicity Gabriel knows
there's still a battle to be fought. Despite the town's scorn,
she's determined to turn her inherited mansion into a home
for orphans. When a traumatized little girl takes refuge there,
Felicity discovers that helping her and the child's widowed
father may be the hardest challenge of all....

**MISTLETOE COURTSHIP by Janet Tronstad and
Sara Mitchell**
Two brand-new heartwarming Christmas stories in one
collection. In "Christmas Bells for Dry Creek," a motherless
little girl helps bring together the two adults bonded to
her. In "The Christmas Secret," a handsome doctor and a
bluestocking spinster get a second chance at love.